I0594259

Claws for Concern

A Maddie Sparks Mystery, Book Three

LESLEY A. DIEHL

CAMEL
PRESS

KENMORE, WA

PRESS

A Camel Press book published by Epicenter Press

Epicenter Press
6524 NE 181st St.
Suite 2
Kenmore, WA 98028

For more information go to:
www.Camelpress.com
www.Coffeetownpress.com
www.Epicenterpress.com
www.lesleyadiehl.com

All rights reserved. No part of this book may be reproduced or transmitted in any form or by any means, electronic or mechanical, including photocopying, recording, or any information storage and retrieval system, without permission in writing from the publisher.

This is a work of fiction. Names, characters, places, brands, media, and incidents are either the product of the author's imagination or are used fictitiously.

Cover design by Scott Book
Design by Melissa Vail Coffman

Claws for Concern
Copyright © 2025 by Lesley A. Diehl

Library of Congress Control Number: 2025942284

ISBN: 978-1-68492-270-3 (Trade Paper)
ISBN: 978-1-68492-271-0 (eBook)

To my neighbors: You make my life joyful.

CHAPTER 1

A BLAST OF SOUND RATTLED THE WINDOWS and shook the coffee table where my friend Jane and I sat having afternoon tea. "What was that? It sounded like an explosion coming from your driveway." I jumped off the couch and rushed to the side window. The noise enveloped the house, making Jane's tiny cottage tremble. I expected to see her single car garage demolished and engulfed in flames, but instead her driveway had filled with motorcycles, behemoth sized machines that roared and thundered. Leather clad, helmeted riders perched on each one.

"There's a gang of bikers in your drive, Jane. I'm calling 9-1-1."

Jane ran to the front door and opened it.

Before I could punch in the call, the lead biker cracked the throttle once more, then turned off the engine. The others did the same. The rider threw his leg over the machine, removed his helmet and waved. "Hey, Janie. It's me. I told you I'd be here this afternoon and here I am, darlin'. I hope you don't mind. I brought my mates."

His "mates" as he called them were also dressed in black jackets, jeans and boots. The fellow who had called out to Jane had tamed his gray beard by gathering it into a braid which moved up and down when he spoke. I couldn't take my eyes off it.

"Darren. C'mon in. I want you to meet someone." Jane stepped off her porch and hugged the biker named Darren of the braided chin hairs. "This my friend Maddie. We were having tea and you're all welcome."

All the riders followed Darren into the house, removing their boots inside the door.

Very polite of them, I thought. They each nodded and stood in line behind Darren to shake our hands.

The first held out his large bear-paw-sized hand and said, "Tommy"—short, white, long gray hair and full beard.

The next man shoved as large a hand out. "Adam."—short, white, long gray hair and beard.

The third one held out a hand that was missing a finger. "Tips"— short, white, long gray hair and beard. I smiled and nodded.

How would I ever tell them apart? Tips maybe, but if their hands were hidden? They looked as similar as triplets. All of them smiled and winked.

"Smithie." This biker was tall with broad shoulders and chest. His salt and pepper hair was cut so short, it left tiny corkscrew curls all over his head. While his lips were full like many Blacks, his beak of a nose was testament to perhaps some Native American ancestry.

The last one to reach out had stood behind the others. I was shocked to see this was no man, but a woman, long, dark hair with several white streaks through it, smaller than me—and I'm less than five feet two—and thin. I wondered how she could maneuver that giant motorcycle until she removed her leather jacket, and I saw her muscular arms.

"Lily." She smiled, showing one prominent gold incisor. "Pleased to meet both of you. Is it alright if I hang my jacket on your coat rack?"

"Sure or toss it on one of the dining room chairs," said Jane.

As Lily hung her leather coat on a hook, I noticed the logo on the back of it. It read "Upstate Riders."

"I hope we didn't upset your neighbors. Many don't feel the glorious thunder of a motorcycle engine is as heavenly as bikers do," Darren said.

"Please take a seat, everyone The tea will be ready in a jiffy. Maddie, could you help me?" Jane grabbed my arm and pulled me with her into the kitchen. "And Maddie, you should close your mouth. You look like a startled guppie."

"Oh, sorry, Jane. I've just never been this close to a gang of bikers before."

"I wouldn't call them a gang. They're just a group of riders who like to get together and hit the throttle. Or so Darren tells me." Jane turned on her electric kettle to heat up more water for tea, then pulled out a cannister of cookies from the cupboard above her sink.

"Uhm, how do you know Darren?"

"We went to high school together. I had a terrible crush on him." Jane held her hand over her mouth to suppress a giggle.

"It appears you still do."

"Maybe. I think I'm too old for a crush." Jane, with her bright blue eyes and curly white ringlets, had to be close to me in age— and I am over seventy. How much over, I'm not saying.

"Look at me, Jane. No one is too old for love." I had found the love of my life just this past summer, Zack Montgomery, retired county sheriff and a really fine man. He was handsome, slim and younger than me. Not by much, but I liked the idea of being in love with a younger man. We'd had our difficulties this fall when a woman he'd known in college came back into his life and threatened to come between us. She didn't.

Zack and my connection to each other has never been stronger. He was the inspiration for my romance novel about two lovers separated by family difficulties. Like Zack and me, my fictional lovers found each other again. Of course, there was the other part of our partnership—we solved crimes together.

"Darren was a bit of a renegade way back in high school too. He shoplifted from the corner gas station, a pack of cigarettes here and there, used a false ID to buy beer from the supermarket the next town over and . . ."

"Didn't he get caught?" I worried at the look of happiness on Jane's face. Did she think this youthful criminal behavior was hip?

"The store owners caught him a number of times, but Darren's manner was so disarming. That guy could talk his way out of shrink wrap." Jane stopped extracting cups from the cupboard and grinned. "And he talked his way into many young women's beds."

"Yours?" Jane and I had only known each other for a few months, but our friendship had quickly become close and honest. I knew I could ask her anything and she wouldn't be offended.

"Why Maddie Sharps." She put her fisted hands on her round hips, feigning being insulted. "I was a good girl. That came later when I came home at Thanksgiving my first year in college."

"He have a bike then?" I grinned at her.

"No, silly. It was in his dad's fifty-five Chevy, four-door with a nice wide back seat." She began to hum. "Grab that plate of cookies, would you?"

Before she reentered the living room, she turned. "I haven't seen him in years. I didn't even know he was around here. I ran into him a few days ago in the convenience store."

"Lifting some smokes and beer, was he?"

"He's changed, Maddie."

Had he? I wondered. He still exuded that bad boy charm. Even I found him kind of sexy. I remembered what a smooth talker my ex-husband Dan had been. I wasn't immune to macho charm, but I'd learned my lesson the hard way. I watched hubby bed a number of women before he left our marriage. I wish I could say I tossed him out, but no. He left me for a younger woman. Yet there was a positive aspect to my story. The new wife had finally wised up when he tried to pull the same philandering behavior on her, and she divorced him. He was now in prison for the role he played in killing someone. He was my walk on the wild side. I was glad I was rid of him.

Jane hummed a happy tune and grinned at me. "Oh, Darren's still a bad boy, I'll bet. And some down on his luck until he finds steady work. He doesn't have any place to store his bike this winter, so I offered my garage. I don't own a car, you know, so it's empty."

Jane and I had met this summer and since then, we'd become best friends. She'd been eager to help Zack and me in tracking down clues as we worked to identify murderers this summer and again in the fall. I guess she was as nosy a senior as I was. In all our discussions I'd never heard Jane mention a man in her life, so her interest in Darren was interesting, and given the kind of man I assumed him to be, it was also worrying.

Jane and I took the tray with teacups, pot and the platter of cookies into the living room and set it on the coffee table.

"Help yourselves, everyone. There are more cookies in the kitchen, so take as many as you like. Grab some chairs out of the dining room and bring them in here." Jane settled herself on the couch on one side of Darren. Lily sat on the other. I took the recliner across from them while Tips sat in the easy chair next to me. The others brought in dining room chairs.

No one spoke, the silence filled with the sound of tea sipping and cookie crunching. Finally Lily said, "You have a lovely house."

The boys looked up from their cups, nodded, smiled and then continued the chewing and swallowing.

"Yep, just lovely," said Darren, "except for that." He pointed to the corner of the room where a crack had formed in the ceiling.

"I know. I meant to get someone in to take care of it, but what with all our work," she shifted her gaze to me and grinned, "and my volunteering at the museum, I haven't had time to make the call. If I don't contact a repair person soon, it will be spring before anyone comes. It's hard to hire people around here. Not too many contractors want to take on small jobs. There's no money in it, I guess."

"Well, never mind. I can do it for you. No charge either. It shouldn't take more than a few hours to repair." Darren patted Jane's hand and gave her a look that could only be described as inviting.

It sounded as if Darren was getting quite a deal. Jane hadn't mentioned rent for the storing the bike in her garage. Half a day's work in exchange for six months of storage didn't sound like a fair exchange for Jane.

"Oh, would you?" Jane beamed at him.

I gave an internal sigh. Was everyone else as uncomfortable with the two doing googley eyes at each other? I looked around the room at Darren's friends. Yep. They stared at the ceiling, out the windows or into their teacups as if they were reading the leaves there, anyplace but at Darren and Jane who moved closer to each other. Lily gave them a sideways glance filled with a glint of annoyance. Was she Darren's girlfriend or biker babe or whatever was the designation for an older couple? Hmm. Zack and I were that couple. What did we call ourselves?

I got out of my chair. "Well, I've got to be going. Zack and I are closing down his travel trailer for the winter this weekend."

"I wondered when you would be doing that. It's kind of late into the season, isn't it?" Jane asked.

Zack had rented a campsite in the nearby state park for the fall, but the travel trailer he parked on the site couldn't remain there through the winter months when the park was closed. It had to be moved for the winter season. We'd put it off because the weather had remained unseasonably warm early this November and spending weekends in the park, especially sitting outside with a campfire keeping the chill off was our idea of heaven. Jane came into my house those weekends to feed my cat, Spike, and clean out his litter box. Although we might have wanted Spike along with us, I had heard many stories about cats sneaking out of trailers and getting lost. There were too many coyotes around the park to chance that.

I carried my cup into the kitchen, gave Jane a hug, said goodbye to everyone and started to leave.

"Say," said Darren, "I'm taking Jane for a ride on my bike, kind of a goodbye to the old gal, the bike, not Jane," Darren laughed and pursed his lips at Jane, "So maybe we could give you a ride home. You can ride on the back of anyone's bike."

Riding a motorcycle? That activity wasn't on my bucket list. "Uh, thanks anyway. It's not far to my place and I need the exercise. Nice meeting all of you." I scurried out the door before the invitation could be renewed.

Halfway home, I heard it. That bone-shattering racket. The motorcycles sped past me. I spied Jane on the back of Darren's bike, a black helmet on her head, her round body wrapped in her lined jeans jacket, a pair of wellies usually worn when she gardened on her feet. She waved to me, and the group roared on. Drops of rain hit my head and I pulled my coat collar up around my ears. The rain intensified and soon the roadway was wet. I increased my pace. At this time of the year, the rain was cold and who knew if it might turn to ice as temperatures dropped. I worried about Jane speeding down the highway on what I considered a two-wheeled death trap.

Chapter 2

When I arrived home, I tossed my bag on the chair inside the door and hung my coat on a wall hook over the chair. A shiver worked its way through my body. How did it get so cold so fast? If the temperature continued to drop, the rain could turn to sleet and make the road to the state park too treacherous to drive this evening.

A "meow" from the upstairs landing let me know Spike, my big, yellow cat, had been awaiting my return. He bounded down the stairs and into the kitchen area, stopping in front of his empty bowl.

"Alright, alright. I know I'm late. I'll feed you and then I'm jumping into the shower to warm up." I always talked to my cat and I'm certain he understood what I was saying. I poured crunchies into his bowl. He began to purr and eat at the same time. I patted his furry, round head and started for the stairs when the phone rang.

"I tried to reach you on your cellphone, but the call didn't go through. I think we should get going right now before the roads turn to ice." The voice was Zack's.

"No warm evening under the stars in front of the campfire tonight, huh? I got caught in the rain on the way home from Jane's and I'm soaked and cold. A quick shower and I'll be ready."

"I'll be right over." Zack ended the call with the sound of a kiss.

The hot water hitting my body felt heavenly. The last thing I wanted to do was go back out into the cold, but I'd promised Zack I'd help him close down the campsite and bring the trailer to the county fairground where there was storage space available for the winter months. Toward the end of September, Zack had replied to a listing in the local newspaper advertising a small travel trailer for sale. He and I discussed buying it and agreed it would be just the thing to use to travel this coming summer. The trailer needed little work as the previous owner had not used it much in the time he had it. It has been stored under cover in his barn. At only twenty-five feet in length, it was perfect for two people—a bathroom with shower, kitchen, couch, table and bedroom. It had an awning under which a small table and two chairs could be placed if it rained. We knew we only had a few weeks before it became too cold to use it at the park, but we sure enjoyed those weeks. Not only did we love sitting around the campfire, but I brought my laptop with us so I could write before or after dinner. Zack read while I wrote, or he prepared our food. The guy proved to be a competent cook, especially when it came to grilling steaks, chicken or fish over the charcoal grill outside.

When we talked about buying the trailer, Zack also brought up the possibility of visiting his daughter Amy who has just left a few weeks ago to return to Seattle.

"Maybe we could do a cross-country trip next summer. We could stop in to see Amy."

Amy had struggled with drug addiction and, when visiting her father this fall, had entered a local drug rehab program which had gotten her clean. She returned to Seattle where she had lived for several years previous to her visit to her father here. I knew Zack didn't want her to leave and he worried that returning to Seattle meant she would return to some of her friends there who were still using, but Amy insisted that was where she wanted to be.

"Some of my friends in Seattle don't use drugs, you know, and there's a chance I can return to my old job in the local newspaper." Amy convinced her father she was ready to return.

Zack reluctantly agreed. "There's not much around here for her."

Only her father, I thought, and he wanted her near him.

I turned my thoughts from Amy to quickly getting dressed for tonight. I jumped into a flannel shirt and pants and bounded down the stairs to the sound of a "beep, beep" from Zack's truck horn. On the way out, I grabbed my raincoat and put up the hood.

"Roads are getting slick," Zack said when I jumped into the front passenger's seat.

"I need to make a call to check on Jane. I'm worried about her."

"What's up?" Zack pulled the truck away from the curb and we headed north toward the park.

"She met an old flame, and he stopped by today with his friends. They're bikers!"

Zack shot me a look of curiosity. "So?"

"His past sounds sketchy."

"And? I think Jane can take care of herself. She's an adult."

I punched Jane's contact into my phone. It rang several times and then went to voice-mail.

"That's only part of my worry. She went off with the group on the back of his motorcycle. In this weather? And she's not answering her phone."

"Maybe she's busy." Zack grinned at me and winked.

"It's not funny. These aren't the kind of conditions for riding."

Zack pulled the truck to the side of the road. "What do you want to do, Maddie?"

"Well . . ."

"Okay." Zack backed the truck into the drive behind us, pulled out and headed the way we had come. "We'll check on Jane."

When we pulled up to Jane's house, only the front porch light was on. The rest of the house was dark. There were no motorcycles outside, so I knew Darren's biker buddies weren't around.

"Could you check the garage? Maybe his bike is there."

Zack jumped from the truck and ran to the garage, quickly opening the door and sticking his head in to look.

He closed the door and shook his head. "No motorcycle," he called to me.

Through the pounding rain I watched him go to Jane's front door and knock. No one responded.

Zack ran back to the truck and got in. "Nope. No one. She must be out for the evening."

"But how? Jane has no car. And you'd have to be an idiot to be out in this kind of weather on a bike. You'd think Darren and the others would have cut their ride short when it began to rain."

"Bikers have rain gear for bad weather."

"For this much rain? And the possibility of it turning to sleet or snow?"

My cell chirped at me. I looked at the contact. Jane.

"Hi, Maddie. I saw you called. I knew you were worried about me. Don't be. I'm home."

"Really?" There was enough sarcasm dripping from my tone to fill a swimming pool. "Because Zack and I are at your house right now."

"Oh. I guess I didn't hear anyone knock."

"Your house is dark, Jane. Where are you? Really?"

"I'll explain later." She disconnected.

I huffed in disgust. "Did you hear that? She won't tell me what's going on."

"Well, at least you know she's alive and safe." Zack pulled the truck back onto the road.

"Alive. Yes. But safe? I think she's somewhere with that Darren guy. Maybe at a motel."

"It's really none of your business, Maddie. Like I said before. She's an adult. We'd better move before the roads become too iffy to pull the trailer."

Zack was right, of course, about Jane being able to take care of herself, but I still worried. For Jane to have returned my call meant she was off the roads, maybe not at a motel, but perhaps at a restaurant having a meal, I told myself. If she was somewhere more intimate with Darren, well, as Zack said, she was an adult, one going kind of fast in this renewed relationship. I opened my mouth to say all of this to Zack, but I realized he had enough to worry about. The rain made visibility near zero. We crept along at less than thirty miles an hour. So far the rain hadn't turned to sleet, and despite the limited visibility, we easily climbed the steep hill to the park.

Zack stopped at the ranger station and went in to tell them we were here to move the trailer. I waited in the truck for him and thought, well, while I'm waiting why not call Jane again, just to say I was sorry I had intruded on her and whatever she was doing. The call went to voice-mail. I gave a huff of annoyance. Well, that was clear. She didn't want to talk to me.

At the campsite I went inside to tie down any items not secure for travel while Zack stowed the barbeque grill in the back of the pick-up. We never left anything around the site when we weren't there so the chairs and small table we used under the awning were already inside and Zack had rolled up the awning the last time we were at the park. While I double checked everything inside, Zack detached the sewer and water hoses. Backing up the truck to hitch the trailer to it was a job we did together. I usually directed Zack, and he maneuvered the truck into place, but tonight he told me to get into the truck because he couldn't see me give him directions through the pouring rain.

"How will you know where you are with the hitch?" I asked.

"I'll guess and hope for the best."

After several tries with me sitting in the passenger's seat biting my nails and hoping we didn't miss the hitch and back into the trailer, Zack eased his way back, then jumped out and attached the ball to the trailer hitch. We pulled out of the space and onto the campground road, honked as we passed the ranger station and turned onto the county road leading back into town.

"It's turning to sleet." Zack turned up the wind shield wipers to clear off the slushy rain and ice mix that gathered there, and we began our descent down the long hill we'd climbed less than an hour before. Halfway down, the trailer began to slide to the side behind the truck. Where I would have jammed on the brakes in panic, Zack gave the truck a bit more gas and straightened out the trailer, and we made it safely to the bottom. I let out the breath I had been holding as Zack reached over and patted my arm. "We're just fine, Maddie."

I smiled at him through the gloom of the dim lights on the instrument panel. "But," he said, "I sure could use a tot of brandy to take the edge off this trip when we get home. And a cuddle under a wool blanket in front of the fireplace."

Zack had moved into a B and B for a several weeks early this fall when our failure to communicate honestly with one another drove a wedge in our relationship. Zack had been living with me before that. After working out our issues and promising we would be candid with each other, we were now back together in my house.

We temporarily parked the trailer in my driveway because it was too late to enter the fairgrounds.

"I'll drive the trailer to the fairgrounds first thing tomorrow morning." Zack grabbed my arm, and we ran for the house. When we opened the door, Spike stood there, eyes squinty with anger that we'd been so foolish to be out in such awful weather. No, I wasn't guessing about how he felt. Just to let me know how perturbed he was, he then got up, turned his back and swished his tail back and forth on his way to his food bowl. Spike didn't need words to make his feelings known to humans.

Zack laughed. "It's as if you never feed that cat, Maddie. He's always hungry."

"Let's get out of our wet outerwear."

We hung up our coats, and Zack grabbed the newspaper, kindling and logs near the fireplace and began to build a fire. The fireplace threw little heat into the room, but the glow from the flames made it feel warmer.

I tossed a small amount of dry food in Spike's dish then walked over to the carved bar my grandfather had brought back from Hong Kong. I'd inherited it when he died, and it was a prized possession. I extracted the glass brandy decanter from one of the shelves, poured a healthy amount of the liquor into snifters and joined Zack on the couch. We nestled into each other, pulling a wool blanket around us. Soon the flames danced as the wood caught. Along with the brandy, the glow from the fire warmed us.

"This is almost as good as sitting around a campfire with stars above us." Zack set his brandy glass on the coffee table. "I'm still cold. How about you, Maddie? Should we get all of these damp clothes off?"

"What did you have in mind?" I turned into his body and his lips met mine. I wiggled my toes. Oh, boy. This was going to be a great night.

I WOKE UP THE NEXT MORNING SMELLING bacon and my mouth watered. Zack's side of the bed was empty. I jumped up and grabbed my robe.

"I'll be right there," I yelled down the stairway. I was starving and no wonder. We hadn't had any dinner last night because we had been too busy trying to warm up.

"Are you as hungry as I am?" Zack shoveled the fried bacon onto paper towels to drain and cracked eggs into the skillet.

"I'll do the toast." I kissed Zack's cheek as I slid past him to get the bread out of the cupboard. As I slipped the slices into the toaster, I glanced out the kitchen window.

"Huh. It must have warmed up instead of getting colder last night. There's no snow on the ground."

"It will come. According to the *Farmer's Almanac*, we're due for an unusually cold and snowy winter." Zack filled our plates while I pulled the golden toast out of the toaster and buttered it.

We took our plates to the kitchen table and began eating. Zack poured our coffee, and I took a sip. "Why does your coffee taste better than what I make?"

"It doesn't, really. Unless you count the secret ingredient I put in."

"Which is what?"

"Two teaspoons of love, not just one." He grinned at me.

"Silly man. Where's Spike? He's usually right here in the mornings wanting his food."

"I already fed him." Zack finished his breakfast and got up from the table to put his plate in the dishwasher. "I'm going to take the trailer to storage."

"Wait a minute and I'll come with you."

"Nope. You stay here and finish your coffee. This will only take a few minutes."

I carried my cup to the couch. Zack gave me a goodbye peck on my cheek and was out the door.

I leaned back into the couch and sighed. I had a few minutes before Zack returned so why not give Jane a ring.

The front door opened just as I was about to punch in Jane's connection.

Zack stuck his head in. "And don't call Jane. She'll contact you when she's ready to talk."

Caught in the act. "Oh, no. Of course not. I won't. She's working at the museum today. I don't bother people at work."

Zack gave me a grin of disbelief and closed the door.

I waited a minute until I heard the truck start up, then punched in Jane's number again.

At the end of the summer and into the fall I had volunteered at the nearby Meadowbrook Museum where my granddaughter Sara worked. She was now the acting director. I'd cut back on my hours there because of the March deadline to send my manuscript to my editor. Sara asked Jane if she'd like to volunteer, and Jane had eagerly stepped in. The museum's hours would be shortened at the end of December, opening only on weekends. For now, however, Jane was at the front desk every day with the exception of Wednesdays and Thursdays.

My call to Jane went directly to voice mail. Did that mean she was busy or was she reluctant to speak to me?

Maybe I should pop over to the museum later this afternoon, say hello and ask Jane if she wanted to have dinner at my house with Zack and me.

I got off the couch, started the dishwasher and went upstairs to get dressed. I heard Zack return from the fairgrounds as I finished brushing my teeth.

"What should we do today?" he called up the stairs.

"Lunch? Then I should get some writing done on my manuscript." I didn't share with Zack my idea to visit Jane at work. I'd spring that on him later.

"The Billinghouse Restaurant okay with you?" Zack had stopped at the gas station to pick up the newspaper. When I came back downstairs, he was on the couch reading it with a second cup of coffee.

The Billinghouse in the nearby town of Stone Creek was where Zack and I had our first date, and we returned there often. It was our favorite place to eat. The food was good and service great.

"I pulled the truck into your garage. I'm gonna give it a go-over before colder weather sets in."

"I'll be in my office writing when you finish."

The morning passed quickly. The words seemed to easily spill onto the computer screen. When I heard Zack come back into the house, I sat back and hit "Save." There. I was almost halfway into the manuscript, the point at which I usually stepped back for a week and then reread it. There was still a lot of work ahead, and the holidays were almost here, but I knew I could finish a rough draft by January, then polish it, print it out for a final review and then send it into my publisher. March seemed a long time away.

"Truck's all set for winter, although I would like to get a new set of tires for it." Zack had purchased the Ford pick-up late in the summer. It was over ten years old, but in decent shape and he liked to keep it that way doing as much work on it himself as he could.

"I finished my writing for the day and I'm ready for something to eat." I grabbed my coat off the hook near the door and we left for lunch.

Zack and I ordered a light lunch, chef salads, since we weren't that hungry after our bacon and egg breakfast. We both were careful about our diets. Zack looked as if he didn't need to worry about gaining weight. Although well into his sixties, he retained a lean, muscular body. I went to the local fitness center three times a week and walked whenever I had errands to run in my small town. What Zack did to remain fit I couldn't say, probably good genes and a high metabolism.

"Coffee?" asked our waitress.

Zack looked at me and I shook my head. "I'm still caffeinated from this morning."

When the waitress returned with the check, Zack raised one eyebrow and leaned into me. "So, a free afternoon. What will we do to fill it?"

"I was thinking we might go to the Meadowbrook Museum to see their new 'Our Neighbors' collection."

Zack leaned back and gave me a skeptical look. "You want to see Jane and grill her about what she was up to yesterday."

"No, really. It should be a wonderful showing." I batted my eyes at him in what I hoped was a look of innocence.

"Don't give me that look. I know that you're up to, Maddie Sparks. Manuscript coming along nicely, no volunteer hours, I wish there was a crime for you to pursue to keep your snoopy, lovely nose out of your friend's life."

I continued to gaze at Zack with feigned innocence. "I'm sure I don't know what you mean. We've solved two murders since we met. I'm sure that's about all this village can support. C'mon." I grabbed his hand and pulled him toward the truck. "We're going to do art, not murder."

CHAPTER 3

No, I was wrong about the issues of culture versus crime fighting. Murder has a nasty way of coming at you whether you're ready for it or not.

Chirp, chirp. On the way to the museum, my cell rang.

"Jane calling back?" asked Zack.

That was the problem with having someone close to you who could almost read your thoughts. Zack somehow knew I'd called Jane and left a message. I could keep nothing secret from him.

"How do you do that?"

"What?" he asked.

"Know what I do even when you aren't around?"

He grinned. "Easy. You're so transparent when it comes to concern for your friends and family."

I looked at the caller's name that came up on my phone. Not Jane, but my younger son, Richard.

"Hey, honey. Nice to hear your voice. What's up?"

I heard Richard clear his throat. "Uh, there's a problem, Mom. It's murder."

"That's your thing, isn't it? You're a defense attorney."

"I need help on a case."

"Zack's sitting right here beside me. Why didn't you call him instead of me? He's your primo detective."

Zack had worked as an investigator for Richard on a number of his cases, including one this fall. Recently, Richard told me a woman accused of killing her husband had contacted him about taking on her defense although she hadn't been charged with his murder yet but was worried she might be.

I wiggled my feet. Oh, goody. A crime. I could help.

"I'll put you on speaker so Zack can hear. I assume this is about that woman whom you talked to about the murder of her husband."

"Yeh, but here's the thing. Someone murdered *her* last night."

"So now you're defending the person accused of *her* murder?"

"Not unless I want to be my own lawyer."

The connection must have been bad. "What? Say that again."

"I'm the prime suspect. If I can't clear my name and find out who killed her, the sheriff will arrest me And soon. I'm at the sheriff's office right now waiting to be questioned."

"Oh, don't be silly. Sheriff Burroughs couldn't believe you're responsible."

"Anita. Uhm. Yes, well, Sheriff Anita Burroughs is doing her job, Mom. My soon-to-be client, Denise Werner, was found dead in her car. She'd been stabbed numerous times. I wanted you to know. Reporters have been sniffing around the crime scene and they saw me being put into a county deputy's car. I didn't want you to hear what was happening from anyone other than me. Gotta go, Mom. Here comes Anita to question me." Richard ended the call.

"Okay, let's go." Zack turned left on a road that would connect with the highway leading to the county office buildings including the sheriff's department.

"Why did Anita drag Richard in for questioning? The Werner woman was soon to be his client and assumed she would be arrested in the murder of her husband." What was Anita thinking?

Anita Burroughs was the county sheriff who had won election to the office several weeks ago. At one time she and Richard had been close, dating close, and I thought they had renewed that aspect of their relationship this past summer, but by fall and the most recent murder case Zack and I had helped on, it appeared their relationship was one of friends *without* benefits. That was probably smart considering they might be on opposite sides in any number of cases. I liked Anita and she was superb at her job. She's been appointed acting sheriff for several months before she won the election. Anita was tall, fit, blonde and a no-nonsense kind of public servant. Could she really believe Richard was capable of murder?

Zack reached over and patted my hand. "Everything will be fine, Maddie."

"I just can't believe this. Anita can't be thinking Richard is guilty."

"There will be evidence, We'll find out what it is."

When we walked into the sheriff's office, Anita was on her way down the hall to the interview room.

"Maddie. Zack. Richard must have called you. I haven't questioned him yet."

"You know this is nonsense, don't you?" There was anger in my voice, but it was really a cover for my worry.

Zack put his hand on my shoulder. "Let Sheriff Burroughs do her job, Maddie." He gave Anita a stern look. "We'll be here waiting."

Anita tucked her chin to her chest, turned and strode off.

An hour later, Richard and Anita emerged from the interview room.

"You know the drill, Mr. Sparks. Don't leave the area." Anita gave Richard a curt nod and walked past us to her office without a word to either Zack or me.

"I want to talk to her," I said and started after her as she closed her office door.

"Not now, Maddie." Zack grabbed my arm to stop me.

"Oh, you're right. That can wait." I turned to my son and threw my arms around him.

"I'm fine, Mom. Nothing to worry about. I'll tell you all about it if you give me a ride." His words were comforting, but his forehead was creased with worry lines.

"My truck is parked in the lot," said Zack.

"You're coming home with me." I slid into Zack's truck and patted the seat beside me for Richard. "I'll make us all a nice cup of tea."

Richard guffawed then erupted into laughter. "You think tea can make everything better, don't you, Mom?"

"Not unless it's accompanied by cookies, or muffins or scones or . . ."

"Or a shot of bourbon," said Zack.

"Will scotch do?" I asked.

Both men nodded.

"THERE HAVE TO BE A NUMBER of suspects in the stabbing murder of Denise Werner." I poured us all another shot of scotch. I sat on the couch next to Zack, and Richard perched on the easy chair across from us.

He'd leaned forward and sipped his drink. "I was just pulling together a case for Denise, uh, Ms. Werner and about to call you in to do some work for me, Zack. But now, this." Richard leaned back and ran his fingers through his hair. I'd never seen my son so tense. Something wasn't right. Why was he so concerned?

"Can you tell us what you know about Ms. Werner's murder and about the murder charge against her? They have to be linked somehow." Zack said.

Richard hesitated a moment, then said, "I think you're correct. Let me give you some background on Mr. Werner's murder. Denise, uh, Ms. Werner called 9-1-1 yesterday midafternoon, saying her husband had been shot, that he wasn't breathing. The authorities and an ambulance arrived at the Werner home ten minutes later. They found him in the backyard dead from a shotgun blast. The sheriff took Ms. Werner in for questioning and Denise called me. I arrived at the sheriff's department. The sheriff released her. The crime scene team continued to process the scene and to look for the weapon. Denise and I talked briefly outside the department and arranged to meet in my office this morning. Unfortunately, the sheriff's department found her dead this morning."

"Where?" I asked. "Or is that information we should not have access to?"

"The local newspaper was at the scene of the crime after her body was discovered, so that's public." Richard looked down at his feet and when his eyes met mine, I could see he was embarrassed.

"She was discovered in her car by the rural mail carrier. The car blocked him from the mailbox."

"What are you not telling us, Richard? You're chewing your lower lip, a habit from your childhood. You did that when you wanted to keep something from me, like skipping school or breaking something in the house."

Richard ran his fingers through his hair and raised his eyes to me. "This is hard for me, Mom. Her car was parked outside my house."

"What? How did it get there?" I was shocked.

"She dropped by the house last night around ten. She said she wanted to talk to me, but I sent her away. I told her we would meet this morning, that it would be unprofessional to see her outside of my office."

"No wonder the authorities see you as a suspect," said Zack.

"There's more. Somone stabbed her several times. With what looks like a kitchen knife, remarkably similar to my kitchen knives."

"How did someone get that knife?" I asked.

"I don't know, Mom. It was left in her car. The knife had been wiped clean of any prints."

Zack set his glass on the coffee table. "Now that's crazy. Why would you stab her in her car in front of your house with one of your kitchen knives, but wipe the knife clean of your prints? Anita must find that odd. Did they find one of your knives missing?"

Richard gave us a tiny smile. "I don't have a complete set of knives, and I don't know how many knives I have. Some have gone missing over the years, but the knife and the location of the car are compelling evidence. I'm sure I'll be arrested soon."

"Then you need to get yourself an attorney," I said.

Richard let out a bark of a laugh. "But I'm the best defense attorney around here. And I'm not so stupid as to try and defend myself."

"There are other good criminal attorneys, maybe not in this immediate area, but perhaps in Syracuse or Albany. Not as good as you, of course," I said.

"No, certainly not, but . . ." Richard sat back in his chair and thought for a moment. "There's my mentor from law school, Franklin Davies."

"Didn't I meet him when you graduated from law school?"

Richard nodded. "Yep."

"Good heavens, Richard. He looked like he was at least ninety years old then. He has to be what now?"

"He's still part time at the university, but I know he kept up his license." Richard reached for his phone.

"Part time. Hah. I'll bet he's senile and only uses his office to catch catnaps," I muttered under my breath.

"That's an ageist remark, my love, the kind of thing people say about us that you take offense at," Zack said.

"But we're not nearly that old. And we've got all our faculties."

"It was that full head of white hair, Mom. It made him look older than he was." Richard put his hand over the phone. "It's ringing." He waited for what seemed like minutes.

"Maybe he can't hear it. Perhaps he doesn't have his hearing aids in."

"Maddie! Just stop. If Richard thinks this man is right for the job, then he is."

I knew I was being pig-headed, but I wanted only the absolute best attorney for my son. Was Richard certain this man was the best to defend him?

"Franklin. This is Richard, Richard Sparks." Richard got out of his chair and put the phone against his chest to muffle the sound. "I'll take this outside." He stepped out onto my back deck.

"It's nearly time for dinner. And you made reservations for us tonight at the Billinghouse. Better call and cancel. I'll pull something out of the freezer to cook for us tonight."

"No. Let's take Richard with us. We all need food to think. I'll call and tell the restaurant to expect three of us instead of two."

The thought of Richard being accused of murder chased off any appetite I might have had, but Zack was right. We all needed to eat. I looked down at the khaki shirt and jeans I was wearing. "I'll go change." Despite my concern over Richard's situation, I wasn't about to sacrifice style to anxiety. Stiff upper lip, I told myself.

When I came back downstairs after washing my face and changing into a dress appropriate for dinner out, Richard had completed his phone conversation with the man he said he was going to hire as his attorney.

"Zack told me about your plans for dinner and invited me along, so if you don't think I'm interfering, I'll take you up on that. Would you mind if I asked Franklin to join us? We can get a table in a corner and talk about my situation, or if we can't find enough privacy at the restaurant, I'll have him drive me back home to my place, assuming the police are finished going through it."

"I know Maddie won't mind. It will give her a chance to question Franklin." Zack winked at me.

"You make it sound as if I'll be interrogating the man."

"Won't you be, Mom?"

"Well . . ."

"Oh, go on, Maddie. We're just kidding you. We both know you want to make certain Richard will be well represented if he's arrested. You're his mother. Of course, you're concerned."

I smiled. Zack was right. Last summer, my other son, Geoffrey had been arrested for murder also. I hoped this wasn't a family pattern. Who would be next? My daughter-in-law and Geoffrey's wife, Abigail? Or Sara my granddaughter. Or me? Was this the beginning of a Sharps family curse? I was being silly, I knew. But I hated that the charge of murder had come twice to this family.

SEATED AT A TABLE IN THE back of the restaurant away from the other diners, I played with my napkin while Zack and Richard talked about the weather. I rolled it up into a tube then smoothed it out and rolled it again in the other direction.

Zack touched my hand to still my fingers. "It's going to be fine, Maddie."

I looked up at him and saw the concern in his eyes. My gaze moved from him to the person who had approached our table.

Richard stood and smiled. "Franklin. So glad you could make it. Have a seat." Richard pulled out the chair next to him for Franklin Davies.

The man was as I remembered him from Richard's graduation from law school. Davies was short but trimly built. What distinguished him from other men his age was his full head of white hair. At first glance the hair made him look older than me, but on closer inspection, the probing nature of his gaze and his unlined face made him look less than sixty. Given that he was Richard's mentor in law school, however. Davies had to be closer to seventy.

"You remember my mother, Maddie Sparks?" Richard gestured to me. Before Franklin took his chair, he nodded to me, held out his hand and took mine in his, then he bent over it, not touching his lips to my fingers, but Poirot-like, tipped his head and almost clicked his heels together in greeting.

"Ms. Sparks, so pleased to see you again."

"Yes, but the circumstances are less than ideal."

"We'll change that surely," he replied, a small smile on his lips. "And you must be Zack Montgomery. I've heard about your past work as the sheriff and as an investigator. Richard is fortunate to have you working for him."

Zack and Davies shook hands, then Davies sat.

"Well, we seem to be tucked away here in the back, so we can talk freely I assume." Davies unfolded his napkin and slid it in his lap. "Let's eat and then to work, yes?"

We nodded, gave our selections for dinner to our waiter and then sat back.

"I understand you are an author, Ms. Sparks?"

"Call me Maddie, please"

"And I'm Franklin."

"I'm surprised you know of my work," I said.

"Your son talks about you a lot. He's enormously proud of his mother's achievements."

I wondered if Franklin was aware of my other line of work, amateur sleuthing, and what he would say about my playing any role in Richard's case. And, of course, I planned to play a role in the case. Yes, I did.

We all ordered coffee after dinner and got down to business. Or were about to when a man approached our table. From the reddish hue to his cheeks and the way he seemed to have difficulty standing without swaying, it was clear he was drunk. He was in his mid-forties , balding and paunchy.

"So they let you go, did they?" He pointed his finger at Richard as he leaned forward. I worried he was about to fall onto the table, but Zack stood and pulled him gently backwards with a hand on his shoulder.

"I think you need to sit down, fella," said Zack.

"Don't need your help, *fella.* I can take care of myself and this guy here. My sister trusted you and you killed her. First you took her to bed and then you killed her." The last sentence he shouted loud enough for everyone in the restaurant to hear. Heads turned in our direction.

Zack stepped in front of the man. "Maybe we should get some fresh air." The man raised his arm and took a swing at Zack. Zack sidestepped the blow, and the man fell forward. Had it not been for Zack's quick reflexes, the guy would have tumbled to the floor, but Zack caught him, and with an arm around his shoulders, walked him toward the front of the restaurant. The Billinghouse's manager met them at the door, and he helped steer the man outside. Zack and the manager came back inside and all eyes in the room focused on our table, zeroing in on Richard. Through the front window, I kept my gaze on the man, who straightened his jacket and turned to look back inside the restaurant, a smile on his face.

The silence that had fallen in the room was now broken by people whispering and continuing to stare at our table.

"Who was that man, Richard?" I asked.

"That was Denise Werner's brother. He ran into Ms. Werner and me when I talked with her outside the courthouse yesterday. I guess her husband and her brother were good friends, drinking buddies, she said. His name is Mannie Costa. He never liked me."

Zack slid back into his chair. "Why don't we go back to Maddie's house to resume our discussion."

I looked around the restaurant. Patrons continued to stare at us. "Good idea." I grabbed my sweater off the back of the chair, and we left.

"Franklin can just take me home, Mom."

"No, no. Come back to my place." If Franklin and Richard went to his house, I wouldn't have the chance to hear what was said.

Zack gave me that I-know-what-you're-up-to look.

"Besides, "I continued, "you'd just have to repeat everything to Zack."

"Well, Zack can come along with us," said Richard.

"I don't think that's what Maddie wants," said Zack. I don't know if Richard caught the implication in Zack's voice, but when I glanced at Franklin, he gave me a smile that said he knew I wanted to be in on the discussion.

"And you, too, Mom." Richard said.

"I have to go home and feed the cat. It's just simpler this way."

Franklin put his hand to his mouth and cleared his throat—to cover a laugh.

The man had my number. Would that prove an asset, or would he see me as interfering?

Chapter 4

"I'll put on a pot of decaf." Once home from the restaurant, I quickly headed for the kitchen and made fast work of getting the coffee ready. Although my kitchen and living room were open to each other, I didn't want to miss any of the discussion in case they spoke softly. "Everyone make themselves at home."

"Well, we now know one thing for sure in this case," said Franklin, settling into the easy chair across from the couch.

"And that is?" said Richard.

"Ms. Werner's brother isn't one of our suspects, otherwise he wouldn't have been so furious that he wanted to take a punch at you."

I sat on the arm of the couch. "I'm not so sure about that. He certainly made a public scene, but I watched through the front window after Zack and the manager led him outside. He straightened up quickly and looked back into the restaurant with a smile on his face. I think he staged that scene."

"Why would he do that?" asked Richard.

"For just the reason Franklin stated—to make it look as if he couldn't be guilty of her murder because he appeared infuriated that Richard had killed his sister."

"Perhaps," said Zack, "but he might have come to his senses

once he threw that punch, and we propelled him out of there with everyone staring at him."

Franklin looked thoughtful and didn't speak for a moment. "I think we all can agree that finding Ms. Werner's killer has to be related to who killed her husband. They may be the same person. Maddie may be right about her brother, Mannie Costa, so we'll keep him on our suspect list."

"Good idea, Franklin. Let's make a list of people who knew Ms. Werner, then Zack can talk with each of them." Richard patted his jacket pocket and looked lost for a moment. "The authorities wouldn't let me grab my briefcase this morning. Can you get me a pen and paper, Mom?"

"In the side table by the couch," I said.

"There may be others we don't know about. For example, why was Ms. Werner getting a divorce? Clearly because they had marital difficulties. Could it be that those difficulties included marital infidelity on the part of one or both of them?" Zack said.

Richard looked up from the notes he had been taking. "I don't know who was handling the divorce and I don't live in this community. There could have been talk around the village."

"I haven't heard anything, but I've been concentrating on my writing, so I haven't spent much time talking with friends here or gone to the historical society's meeting or to work out at my physical fitness place."

Richard looked at me. "I guess you know this village better than any of us."

"Yes, I do. I'll see what I can find out." Oh, boy. I tried to keep the pure joy of being included in the case off my face by turning back to the kitchen.

"Just a minute, Maddie," said Zack. "I'm not comfortable with your getting too involved in all of this. There have been two murders. You could be poking your nose into dangerous places."

"I have lived in this village most of my adult life. People know me well. And, besides, you can't control my taking up my past interests and attending meetings or going to the diner, or the post office and talking with people."

Zack gave a deep sigh. "I know. I know. You'll just do it anyway, won't you?"

"I'll be listening to what people say, Zack, not interrogating them."

He gave me a dubious look.

"I can be subtle."

"Can you?" asked Richard.

"You're my son and I want to help in the only way I can help—by being who I am."

Franklin reached over and patted my hand. "Maddie, I think everyone wants you to be safe."

"Just being Mom means she's going to be in the middle of this case. I think we need to face that. We can't confine her to her house." A tiny smile crossed Richard's lips. "But if I hear about anything happening to you, then . . ."

"Then you can lock me in my room."

"As if that would work. You'd sneak out."

"Like you did when you were a kid."

Richard looked surprised.

"What? You weren't aware I knew you climbed out your bedroom window to go smoke with your friends?"

Franklin let out a guffaw. "I hate to say it, Maddie, but I think you're just the woman for this job."

I was about to get our coffee when there was a knock on the door.

"I'll get it, Mom." Richard opened the door to Sheriff Burroughs.

"Come to arrest me, have you?"

"Not yet. I know I shouldn't be talking to you, but what I have to say will become public soon enough." Anita stepped in and looked around the room. "I guess I'm interrupting work."

"We were about to have coffee. Join us." Richard offered to take Anita's coat.

"I'm not staying."

"Do you know Franklin? He's my attorney."

Anita and Franklin shook hands.

"It's nice to meet the other side," said Franklin with a smile.

Anita did not return the smile. "I'm not 'the other side.' I'm the law. I just talked to the DA, and he's satisfied that Denise Werner murdered her husband. Our crime scene teams scoured the nearby woods and found a shot gun identified as being Mrs. Werner's with her prints on it, recently fired. That pretty much wraps up his murder."

Zack stepped forward. "Maybe the DA could get a conviction against Ms. Werner if he brought the case to court, but you and I know it could be any 20-gauge shotgun that fired the buck shot. Unlike a rifle, there's no way to determine what gun fired that shot—no shell, no rifling marks to determine which weapon."

Anita met Zack's gaze. "You're right, but the evidence of her gun found in the woods behind the Werner's back yard is strong evidence. I buy it." She then turned her attention to Richard. "You would have been defending Mr. Werner's killer if his wife wasn't killed also. If you knew that, it might have been a case you would have lost."

"So you think I killed her to get out of being her lawyer?" Richard's face showed both shock and anger. "I'm not stupid, Anita. You know that."

"Maybe you're not responsible for Ms. Werner's murder, but you should consider yourself lucky the case against her husband is not going to court." Anita looked around the room and saw the disgust on all our faces.

"You're saying Richard was at best 'lucky' Ms. Werner is dead?"

"I think I'd better leave. I was only trying to be helpful." Anita clapped her hat on her head and opened the door.

Before she walked out, I said, "You and the DA may think you now have only one murder to solve, but we know better. We'll be doing twice the work. You can thank us later." After she walked out, I slammed the door after her.

I took a minute to shake off my anger, then turned back and smiled at everyone. "Coffee?"

When everyone had their coffee, Richard crossed his legs and sat back in his chair. "I didn't have the chance to talk with Ms. Werner for any length of time. I was taken by surprise when she showed up last night at my house."

"Why do you think she did that?" asked Franklin.

"She seemed both desperate and scared. She told me that when she heard the shot, she saw someone run off into the woods. When I asked her if she could identify the person, she hesitated and said, 'I'm not sure.' She also said she thought someone was following her and had been for a few days," Richard said.

"So she came to you for help. Did she say she'd told anyone else, a friend, perhaps? And who are her friends?" I asked. "Did she have a job, a career?"

Richard shook his head. "We have a lot of ground to cover, and we lack personnel to investigate. You can't do everything, Zack. And, no, Mom, you are not doing anything on this case other than keeping your eyes and ears open in the village. You are not to begin investigating. If you hear anything important to the case, you bring it to Franklin's or Zack's attention. No following up on leads." Richard's tone was stern.

I tried to meet his gaze with an expression of compliance and honesty. I apparently failed.

"Mom! Do you hear me?"

"Yes, dear."

"Maybe you can talk sense into her, Zack." Richard's voice softened. "Look, Mom. We can't keep an eye on you to make certain you're staying out of trouble."

"I know. I'll behave. I just want to help. You're my son. I love you."

Richard got out of his chair, came over to me and hugged me.

Franklin cleared his throat. "We don't know much about Ms. Werner or about her husband. We have two murders to investigate. We'd better get started on developing a plan."

I leaned back and did what the others expected me to do. I ruminated over what we knew while they laid out their approach to the murders.

"What was Mr. Werner doing at their house? Hadn't he moved out when they filed for divorce?"

Richard looked perturbed at my interruption. "Denise said he was raking leaves. The sheriff's office confirmed that. There were piles of leaves at the curb ready to be picked up by the village town crew and a rake at his side."

"From what I heard the divorce was pretty contentious, arguments in public, shouting heard by neighbors. Don't you think it odd he would be raking leaves for her?"

Zack cocked an eyebrow at me and looked puzzled, but Richard shrugged and said, "Maybe he wanted to keep the yard looking manicured so they would sell the house quickly and for a good price to settle the divorce."

That sounded possible, but a husband raking leaves for a wife who hated him and whom he hated still didn't work for me.

We spent the remainder of the evening laying out an approach to clear Richard's name and discover who was responsible for the Werners' murders. We had limited resources in terms of numbers, but we had the best people on the case. Along with Zack, Richard could work in his own defense, unless he was arrested. Then the responsibility for identifying the murder fell to Zack, Franklin and of course, me.

"And, Mom," Richard said to me as he was about to leave for the night, "do not under any circumstances bring your snoopy friend, Jane, in on this case."

Oh, boy. Richard had read my mind.

"Oh, no, of course I won't." Like a silly child I crossed my fingers behind my back as I made this promise.

As ZACK AND I TALKED OVER coffee the next morning, the spitting rain had turned to wet snow, not yet sticking, but the sky was gray with heavy clouds.

Zack and I stood at the kitchen window and looked out over the stream that ran through my backyard.

"It's the kind of day for reading a book in front of the fire," said Zack.

"Then maybe chicken soup for supper," I suggested.

Sundays were quiet days in the village. Nothing was open except for the gas station on the corner.

"Or," Zack said, "we could put our heads together and begin to tackle the list of items we need to address to find information on our two murder victims."

I was thrilled Zack wanted to begin working on the case and he wanted me to join him.

"I mean," he said with a twinkle in his eye, "what harm can come to a snoopy gal detective if she's sitting in front of her own computer in her own office?'

"That's it, then, is it?" I said. "I do grunt work on the computer while you have all the fun chasing the bad guys I've identified for you."

"We'll do the grunt work. I can use my laptop at the kitchen table while you work in your office but first let's see what leads we need to follow. We have little information on Ms. Werner or her husband. We'll toss a coin to see which one of us does a search on whom."

I don't know if I won the toss or lost it, but I began exploring Ms. Werner's husband, William Werner, and discovered he and his wife had lived here in the village for the ten years of their marriage. He worked as a reporter for the newspaper in Stone Side during that time. How exciting, I thought. I had a contact there. Well, to be honest, the last time I saw reporter Agnes Danderfield was at a funeral and we parted on not so friendly terms. That would probably not stop me from contacting her. My ex-husband had also worked for our local newspaper until it folded several decades ago, less of a useful lead since his time on the newspaper and that of Mr. Werner at the larger paper in Stone Side didn't overlap. I had no idea if my ex stayed connected with any newspaper folks in the area after the paper closed up, but I wasn't eager to contact him anyway. He was serving a term in state prison. I'd never visited him there and I didn't intend to start now . . . unless it was necessary to help Richard's case. Hmmm. I wondered if either of my sons had visited their father in prison. I'd ask them.

My computer search revealed nothing about Mr. Werner farther back than a few decades. It was as if he didn't exist before that time.

"Zack, honey. Could you come here a minute?"

There was no reply, so I left my office to see if Zack was still at the table. He wasn't. Instead, he had moved his laptop to the coffee table, lay down on the couch and was fast asleep. I could hear his breathing and an occasional soft snort, the beginning of a snore.

"Zack." I gently shook him.

He opened his eyes. "Oh, hi, Maddie."

"Boring stuff, huh?"

"Yeah. I'd rather be out talking to people."

"So would I, but somehow you think assigning me the boring stuff will make me think I'm part of the case. Tomorrow you'll be out there chasing down clues, doing the really important work."

"This is important."

"Boring and . . . safe."

"I could continue my nap upstairs and you could join me."

"Don't think you can make up to me by suggesting a bounce on the mattress. I do have an idea, however."

His face lit up.

"I don't mean any kissy face stuff. That new coffeehouse in town is open on Sundays. Let's go for a midmorning coffee."

Zack looked skeptical. "What are you up to?"

"There's sure to be a crowd of people there today and all of them will be talking about the murder, or the murders."

"You do know when we enter, everyone there will be paying attention to the mother of the lawyer questioned in the murder.?"

"That simply means they'll be eager to talk to me. Let's go."

When we stepped outside to get into the truck, large white flakes drifted from the sky.

"It's gotten colder," Zack said. "I think we're in for an early snow." He cleared the slush off the truck's windshield, and we headed for the coffee shop.

THE COFFEEHOUSE WAS AS BUSY AS I expected it to be on a Sunday morning, and Zack was right. Most heads turned as we entered the shop.

The coffeehouse was a new addition to our village. As well as offering a line of coffees and teas, it also sold other items—ceramic cups, small linens, candies, cookies and other snacks. The chairs and tables in the main area were the kind often found in ice cream shops, wrought iron chairs and matching small tables. In another room, there were overstuffed chairs and a comfy couch. It had become a favorite gathering place for folks wanting their morning coffee or an afternoon latte or cup of tea. The owners hoped it would become a meeting place for village residents, and it looked as if their dreams were being realized. The several times I had frequented the place it was filled with people.

"How's Richard doing after, well, you know?" A woman around Richard's age posed the question in a sympathetic voice.

I recognized her from when she and Richard was in high school. She had maintained her youthful appearance, still slender with blonde hair cut short and round eyes the color of caramel. "Ellen Hawkins, isn't it?"

She nodded. I introduced her and Zack.

"Richard's fine. The authorities had to question him because he, uh, had information about the murders." I told her the truth, just not all of it.

Ellen raised one eyebrow. "Oh, I wondered why he was brought in for questioning so soon after her body was found."

Another woman—this one I recognized as having been in

the same class as Richard during high school—overheard the conversation.

"Ellen," she said to the first woman, "Ms. Werner's body was found in her car which was parked outside Richard's house." She sounded less sympathetic in her comments and more excited that she knew some unsavory details about the case, but she quickly directed her next comment to me. "So sorry, Maddie, but . . ."

She certainly didn't sound sorry. Rather, she looked at me expectantly as if she wanted me to both confirm her knowledge about the case and to add to it.

"You're Sandy Longworth, aren't you? You were a friend of Richard's back in high school."

"I was a classmate, but I really wasn't a friend."

I remembered Sandy as one of the popular girls in high school, a cheerleader and member of the student council. Like Ellen, she was also blonde, but her hair was lighter than I remembered when she was young, and she wore it long. She wore makeup, her eyes made to look larger by the expert application of dark mascara and eyeshadow.

She sounded as if she wanted to distance herself from Richard just in case, I suspected, he was the murderer.

"The two of you dated in your junior year," said Ellen.

"Uhm," said Sandy, "I think my coffee order is ready." She spun on her heel and headed for the counter to pick up her drink.

"I think she still feels the sting of Richard breaking up with her in high school, but she did refuse his invitation to go to the prom and then accepted one from the captain of the football team who subsequently dropped her for the head cheerleader. Poor Sandy tried to get back with Richard, but your son was too smart for that." The way she said "poor Sandy" alerted me that she felt Sandy got what she deserved from Richard.

"That was so long ago, over twenty years," I said.

"But the past never really leaves us does it?" Ellen stared across the room as if she had been transported back in time.

I wondered what memories from back then still haunted her. Ellen's glance swept through the crowd of people, some of whom still focused on my presence. "Let's take our drinks into the other room. It's quieter there. Join me."

CHAPTER 5

Z ACK AND I PUT IN OUR orders, waited for our coffees and then took them into the second room where Ellen was seated in the overstuffed chair across from the sofa. No one else was in the room. Voices from the main room of the coffeehouse formed a muffled backdrop. Zack and I took seats on the couch.

"Sandy and Richard were an item back in high school, weren't they?" I gazed at her over the rim of my cup.

"They dated for a time, but I think she was more into athletes than the smart boys like Richard." Ellen set her cup on the coffee table between us and looked into the other room as if she didn't want anyone there to overhear her. "Actually, Sandy liked to collect boys. Richard was one of the many fellas she had in her stable of admirers. Gosh, I guess that's kind of mean of me to say about her." She looked a bit contrite but didn't withdraw the comment.

I smiled at her. "You had a crush on my son, didn't you?"

She giggled at little. "Yep, but I was only a freshman when he was a junior, so I was out of his league."

"Are you married?" I asked.

Zack, attuned to where I was going with this question, grabbed my hand under the table and squeezed it as if to remind me we were here to get information about our murder victims and not to find Richard a woman to date.

"Divorced," she replied.

"Sorry, I'm so nosy."

"Yes, she is," said Zack.

"Oh, it's fine. The divorce is long over. It was a mutual break-up." She looked down at her coffee, then up at me. "I wasn't the only girl in high school that had a crush on your son."

"Richard was and still is a handsome and intelligent man. Of course, as his mother, I'm biased."

"You have a right to be. He's great."

Her tone of voice told me she still had interest in Richard.

Zack kicked me under the table. I ignored him.

"Have you . . ."I began, but Zack interrupted me.

"Some special girl you're referring to?" asked Zack.

"There were a few girls circling around Richard, but . . ."

She was stopped from saying more by the sudden appearance of Sandy.

"Do you think your son is guilty?" asked Sandy.

"That's a pretty insensitive thing to ask." Ellen gave Sandy an annoyed look.

"I'm only asking because he had history with Denise. You might want to check into that. I'm sure the sheriff already knows about Richard and Denise."

Ellen was right when she said some memories stuck with us for a long time. Despite Richard only being part of her collection of boys, Sandy sounded as if the sting of his rejection of her in high school remained.

"History?" I said.

Sandy smirked. "I've said too much, haven't I?"

I was about to encourage her to continue, when she turned at the sound of her name being called from the other room.

"Got to run. That's my husband calling me. We have guests coming for dinner tonight." Sandy smiled again in her not-so-friendly manner and left.

"History?" I looked at Ellen. "Did Ms. Werner also attend high school with Richard, you and Sandy. I don't remember him mentioning her."

"Well, yes, but . . ."

"You're keeping something from me, aren't you?"

"I'm sure it's nothing. Just gossip from back in the day. You know how teenagers are."

"Tell me."

Ellen stood. "I'm not Sandy, so I'm not about to pass on rumors that probably aren't true. I think you should ask Richard. I'm so sorry Richard got mixed up in all this. Tell him I said hello." Without another word she left.

"What was that all about?" I asked Zack.

"Probably just what Ellen said. Some kind of gossip going around among high schoolers." Zack tried to reassure me with his words, but his brow wrinkled with worry.

"I know what you're thinking. This gossip is something we need to explore."

"I'll look into it."

I reached out and touched his arm. "No, you won't. I will. Ellen is right. I'll ask Richard."

Zack let out a guffaw. "That's my Maddie. No sneaking behind anyone's back. Go right to the source."

"I'm his mother. It's my right to know."

I'd heard about a number of crushes girls had on Richard in high school and of Richard's own short romances, nothing serious, not like my other son, Geoffrey who started dating his wife of twenty plus years in high school. Geoffrey and Abigail had gone steady all through high school, went to the same college and married when they graduated. Geoffrey and Richard were polar opposites in many ways. Where Richard was charming, smart and athletic, Geoffrey was also bright but spent time out of class in math club and chess club. Richard preferred drama club and was the lead in the senior class play. As for Richard's girlfriends during high school years and into college, I could only remember one that I thought he was serious about and that was Sheriff Anita Burroughs, but although they dated for several years, she married another man after college graduation. The marriage hadn't lasted for long, and I thought she and Richard were still interested in each other, but nothing had come of that recent interest. I assume it was a mutual decision perhaps because they worried about conflict of interest in their roles as sheriff and defense attorney. What if it was something else? Had Richard's past come back to haunt him, and Anita found out something about it that made her decide not to pursue a relationship with him? Well, if I had to, I'd ask both of them to get at the truth.

"I assume you'll want to talk to Richard before you have a chat with Anita. Am I right?" Zack gathered our cups together and held out his hand to help me from the couch.

"How do you do that? I asked, irritated that he had read my mind again.

"I know you, Maddie."

"Aren't you going to talk me out of it?" I grabbed my coat and followed Zack. He tossed our paper cups into the trash and helped me into my coat.

In the time we had been in the coffeehouse, the snow had increased, and the street was covered in white.

"I was right. We're in for some snow." Zack pulled up the collar of his coat and settled his hat more firmly on his head as a gust of wind came up. "Let's get home and make that chicken soup. This is no day to be out driving around."

"I'M NOT GOING TO CALL RICHARD." I said as Zack built a fire in the fireplace when we got home.

"No, of course not. You'll want to talk to him in person, see the expression on his face."

"I want to see the expression on his face."

Zack turned from his work placing logs and looked at me. "That's what I just said."

"Sorry. I'm off in my own thoughts."

"Maddie, I know you'd like us to see Richard, but it's snowing hard outside. This is no time to be out in this mess. The roads haven't been cleared yet and won't be until morning in preparation for the school buses."

"You're right. We'd be stupid to go out in this."

Zack settled back on his heels. "I'm not giving in to pressure, my love. We're not going out in this and that's final."

I sighed. "I'll go start the soup. Meantime do you want some lunch?"

He clapped his hands together to get the wood chips off them. "I could go for a bite of something, maybe just some crackers and cheese. And another nap, the two of us." He winked at me.

"You're trying to take my mind off Richard."

"Is it working?"

"The soup can wait. And so can cheese and crackers."

Zack took my hand and started to lead me upstairs.

"You just started the fire. It would be a shame to waste the ambience."

"What do you suggest?" he asked.

I went to the closet in my office and grabbed an old comforter I sometimes used in the winter when the office got too cold. I wrapped it around myself while I worked at my keyboard.

Zack and I shoved the coffee table back against the sofa to make space in front of the fire, then spread the comforter on the floor.

"We can snuggle." I sat and reached up to Zack.

"Do you think our old bones can manage the hard floor?"

"I said 'snuggle,' and that's all. Otherwise we're both going to need chiropractic intervention tomorrow."

We snuggled for over an hour, happy being so close to each other, while the snow fell outside and the wind blew, but we were snug and warm. We both got up before our backs were sore from the floor and together we made the chicken soup, chopping vegetables and chatting while we worked. Zack put more wood on the fire and, when the soup was ready, we took our bowls to the couch and ate.

"How about a little brandy?" Zack said.

"How about some more snuggling instead?" I shifted my glance to the stairway and held out my hand to lead Zack upstairs.

"We'll probably have to kick Spike off the bed."

"No need." I went to the kitchen and poured some crunchies into Spike's bowl.

"Here he comes," said Zack.

A blur of yellow fur dashed down the stairs and into the kitchen area, plunging his head into the bowl of food and gobbling madly.

"Now." Zack smiled invitingly at me, but before we could mount the stairs, the lights went off.

"What happened?" I grabbed Zack's hand.

"I suspect the snow was heavy enough that it downed some power lines, or the wind could have taken them out. Tell me where you keep your candles, and I'll get them. You stay put."

I felt something brush against my leg. The fireplace gave enough light for me to see Spike who mewed seeking some comfort from contact with me.

"Candles are under the sink."

I saw Zack's shadow in the kitchen. He returned with several candles which he lit using the fireplace matches. I reached over and picked up Spike to cuddle him and assure him everything would be fine.

"This couldn't be more romantic, fire in the fireplace, candles flickering and our cozy spot in front of . . ."

". . . the only source of heat we have until the power comes back on and it doesn't throw much heat." I wrapped my arms around myself.

"We can keep each other warm with body heat." Zack sounded delighted with the situation. I wasn't. Winter storms always put me on edge. No electricity was one thing, but the wind had picked up and I worried it might blow a branch from one of my large maple trees onto the roof. I shivered at the thought of cold penetrating the house.

"You're really frightened, aren't you Maddie?"

I didn't reply but glanced around the room. "I think I left my cellphone in your truck. With no power, the landline will be dead. I want to call the boys to make sure they're okay. And Sara, too." Sara was Geoffrey and Abigail's daughter, my only grandchild. She had her own apartment in the village.

"I'm sure they're all fine. Sara probably has her fiancé, Leon, with her." Zack looked into my eyes. "Okay. We'll just use my cell to make the calls if it will make you feel better."

Zack grabbed his phone from where he had left it on the coffee table. "Oh, no. I forgot to charge it. It's dead."

I picked up the landline, just in case. "Nope. Dead."

"Do you want me to go out to the truck for your phone?"

I wasn't about to send Zack out in the storm even though the truck was only out front. "I'm being silly. Everyone will be fine."

"They're probably doing what we're doing if they've lost electricity too."

We wrapped ourselves in one another's arms and I tried to ignore the sound of the wind howling outside. I heard a few branches hit the roof and jerked in fear. Zack grabbed me tighter. Spike curled up at our feet. I relaxed and began to drop off to sleep when a loud bang awoke me.

Zack touched my arm. "Someone is at the door. Who is crazy enough to be out in this storm?"

He went to the door and opened it enough to let two people in out of the swirling snow. Despite the snow covering them, I recognized Geoffrey and Abigail.

"Geoffrey, Abigail! What are you doing here? What's wrong?" I sprung up from the comforter and ran across the room.

"We were worried about you. I tried your phone here at the

house, but the line is obviously down. And your cell rang and rang and then went to voice mail. The same thing happened with Zack's. We thought we'd check to make certain everything was all right."

"How did you drive in this mess? The roads can't be passable."

"We walked." Geoffrey said. "It's only across town."

He and Abigail looked frozen.

"Take off those wet coats and come in here by the fire. I assumed your electricity has gone out also. I'll get some more blankets from upstairs."

"You stay put, Maddie. I'll get the blankets." Zack dashed up the stairs and returned with several wool blankets from the spare bedroom.

We moved the sofa and chairs closer to the fire and all bundled up in blankets as close as we dared to get to the heat.

"Fireplaces don't throw much heat, but better than nothing," said Abigail. "We thought about installing a gas burning stove, but we never got around to it. Usually power outages around here don't last long."

She and Geoffrey had settled themselves on the floor in front of the sofa while Zack and I sat on the couch.

Geoffrey held his hands out to the fire. "My fingers are stiff with the cold."

"How about a brandy?" asked Zack.

"Sure," we said in chorus.

"Have you been in touch with Sara?" I asked.

"Yes. She had a gas-fueled stove at her apartment. She and Leon are there now." Geoffrey leaned closer to the fire.

"So we could all go over there and keep warm," I said.

"I think we should stay put here. We're warm, dry and safe. Besides, I don't think Sara and Leon need our company." Zack shot me a meaningful look.

"Did you think of contacting Richard?" I asked Abigail and Geoffrey.

Abigail snuggled closer to Geoffrey. "We did and he didn't answer his phone."

"Although it's Sunday, I suppose he could be working at his office. Try his number there," I said.

Geoffrey punched in the contact for Richard. "It's ringing. Nope. It went to voice mail."

Suddenly the lights came back on, and I heard the furnace kick in.

"I think we all could use a snack. I'll make some sandwiches and heat up the soup we had for dinner tonight. The two of you," I glanced at Abigail and Geoffrey, "still look frozen. Food will warm you up. Try Richard again at his office, on his landline there as well as his cellphone."

As the house began to warm up, Geoffrey continued to try to contact Richard but had no success.

I served up grilled cheese sandwiches and the heated-up soup. "Go ahead and dig in. I want to make a call of my own." Since my landline was now working. I punched in Jane's number, but only got her voice mail. "Where can she be? I'll call Sara and ask who gave Jane a ride home from the museum this afternoon."

I heard a number of rings and thought the connection would go to voice mail, but she picked up, sounding a little breathless.

"Gram. Is everything okay?"

"Yes, of course. Your parents couldn't contact me, so they walked over here in this storm. Can you believe that? We're just having a midnight snack. Zack will drive them home as soon as the snowplows clear the streets." I heard a rumbling outside. "There goes a plow now."

"You know I have a gas-fired stove. The electricity was off here too, but we're warm and . . ." I heard her giggle through the connection, "we managed."

"Have you heard from your uncle? Or tried to call him?"

"No, but he may be in the office working. I know he's worried about the suspicion that fell on him from his client's murder."

"We tried his office. No luck. When the roads are in better shape, Zack will take your parents home and then we can drive to Richard's house and check on him."

"Why so worried, Gramm?"

I thought about the threats made against Richard by the client's brother. "No reason other than motherly concern."

Before I ended the call I asked Sara if Jane worked at the museum this afternoon.

"She did. I gave her a ride home."

I disconnected and joined everyone at the table although I had no appetite.

"I heard what you told Sara on the phone, Maddie. We'll give the plows and sanders a chance to do their job, then we'll see how the roads are." Zack left his chair and peered through the front window. "The snow is slackening."

Zack knew how much I hated winter driving, so if I was willing to get into his truck on these roads, he knew I was concerned about Richard. He came back to the table and leaned over and whispered in my ear. "I doubt Ms. Werner's brother would go out in this weather to confront Richard." He patted my shoulder.

"Probably not. I'm such a worrier when it comes to my boys."

Geoffrey overheard me "Men, Mom. We're men, not boys."

"I know you are, but I think of you still as my boys."

I made a pot of tea to have with our food and we sat around the table and talked for an hour after we finished eating. I fidgeted, picking at my nails and constantly checking the windows to determine if the snow had stopped. The amber lights from passing snowplows and sanders assured us the road crews were busy clearing the roads. The village depended on the crews because we were situated in a valley and the only roads out led up long winding hills.

Zack bundled up and went out to clear off the truck, His vehicle was a four-door so there was plenty of room for Georffrey and Abigail in the back seat.

Snow clearing equipment continued to work the village streets as the snow lessened. We dropped Geoffrey and Abigail at their house and headed out of the village. The road leading to Richard's house in the next town over had been plowed and partially sanded, but Zack dropped the truck in four-wheel drive and took it slow up the hill that lead out of town toward Richard's house.

"It certainly dropped a lot of snow in such a short time," said Zack.

Halfway to the top of the long grade, we saw flashing lights and heard sirens behind us.

Zack grimaced as he checked the rearview mirror. "It's a fire truck, but he can't get by me on this hill, and I have no place to pull over because of the snow piled on the edge of the road. This could be dicey."

The driver of the firetruck seemed to understand the issue and held back. Before the final uphill climb, a snowplow rounded the curve coming down the hill toward us. Zack and the firetruck behind us moved as far to the right as possible to let the snowplow pass. I gripped the door handle and held on as the bright flashing lights of the plow appeared to come right at us. The plow passed to the side of both of us with little room to spare. I let out the breath I was holding and tried to relax.

"Tight," Zack said.

As soon as the road leveled out and there were no vehicles approaching from the other direction, Zack slowed, and the fire-truck passed us.

"That was scary. It was lucky the driver knew not to pass on the hill and that curve," I said.

Zack reached out and patted my hand. "Everything is fine, Maddie."

"I know. You're a good driver and I'm glad you're at the wheel and not me. I hate driving in the winter."

"It's not quite winter yet, you know. This is only November."

I tried to settle back in my seat and relax the remainder of the drive, but patches of snow on the road made me uneasy.

"I wonder where that fire truck was going," I said. The truck's lights were no longer visible ahead of us.

"You know how it is, Maddie. The electricity goes out and people decide to heat their house by turning on the stoves they use for cooking. It's not safe. We're almost at the turn for Richard's house."

Zack signaled and turned left, and that was when we saw it.

Richard's house was in flames.

CHAPTER 6

I BURIED MY FACE IN MY HANDS, sobbing and yelling, "No, no!" I reached for the door handle, but Zack restrained me.

"Stay in the truck, Maddie."

A fire officer stopped us a half block down the road from the house.

The officer signaled to Zack to roll down his window. "Sorry, sir, but you can't get any closer. Please turn around and leave the area."

I pulled myself together and leaned toward the driver's side window. "We don't want to get in the way, but that house is owned by my son. Is anyone inside, do you know?" My voice was so shaky I could hardly speak.

"Here comes another fire truck. Please back up and turn down the street behind you. You're blocking access."

Zack did as requested, and we parked a block away on a side street that had been plowed. I jumped out of the truck as soon as Zack put it in park.

"Maddie! Come back here."

I ignored his call and rushed down the street, slipping and skidding on the ice and snow still present on the street. When I once more approached the official who had directed us away from the scene, I tried to push past him.

He reached out and prevented me from going around him. "Sorry, ma'am. I can't let you go closer."

"You don't understand. My son lives in that house. He could still be in there."

Zack caught up with me. "Is there someone to whom we can talk? There may be a person inside."

With a thunderous crash, the roof of the house collapsed, showering burning debris only feet from us.

"Clear this area," called another fire official.

Zack tapped me on the shoulder. "You stay here, Maddie. That's the fire chief from this town. He knows me. I'll see if I can talk to him." Zack caught the attention of the chief who beckoned him to approach and the two of them began talking. I shook with fear, so overwhelmed by the thought of Richard in that burning house that my body shuddered with each breath.

Zack ended his conversation with the fire chief and returned to me. "Maddie, you're shaking from the cold. Let's get you back in the truck."

"I'm not cold. I'm terrified that Richard is in that house."

"We don't know that. Let's not leap to conclusions. The fire chief said we won't get any answers until tomorrow at the earliest. Richard could have been spending the night elsewhere."

"He didn't answer his cell or the phone in his office when we tried to call. Maybe he couldn't answer because . . ." I stared at the burning house.

Zack walked me back to the truck. We got in and he started the engine and turned up the heat. The warmth reduced my trembling.

"I know you're not going to want to do this, but we need to go home."

"I want to wait here." I crossed my arms over my chest and shot him my stubbornest look.

He shook his head, his glance at me more stubborn. I knew he was right, but I felt as if I was abandoning my son.

"There is nothing we can do here. I gave the fire chief my cell number and he said he'd call me when he had news."

"I know you're right, but . . ." I began to cry. Zack put his arms around me and let me sob until I had no more tears in me.

Zack shifted into drive, and we headed back home. We said nothing to each other on the drive.

Once inside the house, Zack built up the fire again then went to the kitchen and put water in my electric kettle.

"What are you doing?" I asked.

"You can use some heavily sugared tea and then you should get some sleep."

"You know I won't sleep."

"The tea will warm you. Relax on the couch and I'll bring it to you."

Zack's concern for me made me want to cry again. I sniffled and tried to hold back my tears, but I couldn't. Zack enveloped me in his arms and rocked me until the tea kettle whistled.

After I drank a cup of tea and had warmed myself in front of the fire, Zack helped me up the stairs and tucked me into bed. Spike jumped onto the bed and curled in a ball at my feet.

"I'm not tired."

"I know but try to rest a little."

I lay down for a minute then sat back up. "I should call Georffrey and Abigail . . . and Sara."

"I'll take care of making those calls," Zack said. "Then I'll come back up here and see how you're doing."

The adrenaline that coursed through my body must have exhausted me. The next thing I knew Zack stood over me with a cup of coffee in his hand.

"How about some toast?"

I jumped out of bed. The sun had risen, and the air was clear.

"Did anyone call?"

He shook his head. "It's still too early."

"I want to go back up there. Now."

Zack sighed. "Okay, but first eat a piece of toast. It could be a long day for you."

I sat at the kitchen table and picked at my toast. "Did you call Abigail and Geoffrey and Sara?"

"Yes. I told them what we knew, and of course they were shocked. They'll . . ."

A knock at the door interrupted Zack.

He opened the door to Abigail and Sara who hurried across the room and hugged me.

"Where is Geoffrey?" I asked.

"He dropped us here and then went to Richard's house to determine if there was any news yet," said Abigail.

"Aren't you supposed to be at the museum, Sara?"

"I called and told Francis I would be in late, if in at all. She understood after I told her what happened."

Always the voice of reason, Zack said, "We don't yet know the whole story."

"Then where is Richard? He should have contacted us by now." My voice broke and I began trembling again as if a fierce cold had penetrated my body. Uncontrolled tears ran down my face. A sense of loss overwhelmed me. How could I bear it if Richard was gone?

Sara pulled me into her arms. "Uncle Richard is okay. I know it. I just know it. C'mon, Gram. Sit down and finish your breakfast."

There was another knock at the door.

Zack opened the door to Geoffrey.

I jumped out of my chair, ran to him and grabbed him by the front of his coat. "What did you find out?"

He gently pulled my fists away and hugged me to him.

"Let's all sit, and I'll tell you what I know. I could use a cup of coffee. That wind out there is cold."

"Of course, hon. We have a fresh pot." I poured him a cup. "Anybody want a refill or are we all caffeinated enough?"

Everyone shook their heads at my offer, and we took seats in front of the fireplace. Zack loaded more logs on the grate and built up the flame. Geoffrey held his hands out to the warmth.

"There's not much known yet about the fire except it looks suspicious. The fire marshal was at the scene and told me he might have a report on the origin of the blaze this afternoon."

"That's it? Nothing more."

Geoffrey's gaze met mine. "I'm afraid there is more and it's not good."

Zack put his arm around me. "Tell us."

"Richard's car was in his garage." Geoffrey said.

Sara put her hand over her mouth and said what I couldn't say out loud. "Oh, no. That means he was home."

"No, it doesn't. It only means his car was in the garage. He could have gone out with someone. We need to remain optimistic about this." Zack gently massaged my shoulder.

I swiped at the tears on my face and lifted my chin in an attempt at defiance. "You're right, Zack. That's all we know for now."

No one dared say what we all must have been thinking: if they found a body in the house, it was likely Richard's.

Where was Richard? If he hadn't been in the house at the time of the fire, and I prayed that was the case, then where was he? And why wasn't he answering his cell?

"I'm going to call Richard's office. Maybe his secretary knows something." I punched in his contact. The phone rang several times, then went to a recording: "Our office hours are nine to five Monday through Friday. Leave a message with your contact information and we will return your call."

I looked at my watch. Today was Monday, and it was past ten o'clock. Richard's secretary should be in the office by now.

"C'mon, Maddie. Get your coat. We're going to Richard's office." Zack grabbed his coat and hat.

"No one is there. What's the point?" I asked.

"There might be a sign on the door explaining why the office isn't open yet."

I don't know if Zack actually believed that might be the case, but he knew sitting around the house only made me think of the worst. Taking some kind of action could get us information we didn't have. I hoped what we found out would be positive.

"Meantime, you're all welcome to stay here or come with us," said Zack.

I shrugged into my coat and put on a knit cap to keep my ears warm. "Sara, honey, you should go on in to work. We'll keep in touch by phone and call if we find out anything."

Sara nodded. "Call us even if there's no new information."

Spike came to the top of the stairs and glared at me, then let out a loud howl while he descended the stairs. "Oops. I forgot to feed him this morning." Poor fella. With the fire and our concern for Richard, we'd completely ignored Spike.

I dashed to the fridge and got out his can of food, spooned half into his dish and put the remainder back into the fridge. He plunged his head into the bowl, gobbled the food and made his usual eating sounds halfway between purring and growling.

"I guess Abigail and I should get home. We need to open our office." Geoffrey and his wife ran a successful real estate and land management business.

"Maybe you should take turns working today. One naps while the other runs the office. I doubt you got much sleep last night," I said.

"I don't think either of us can sleep until we know more about Richard. Grab your coat, Sara. We'll drop you at your apartment," said Abigail.

I knew how they felt. I'd slept, but it wasn't a restful sleep. It was the sleep that came as the result of emotional exhaustion. I knew there was no chance I'd get any real rest until I knew Richard was safe. I hoped visiting his office would give us more information. If not, we'd have to wait for the fire marshal and fire investigator to tell us more.

By the time we arrived at Richard's office, the lights inside were on and the door open.

I greeted Marsha, Richard's secretary. By the expression on her face, she had heard about the fire.

"Terrible, isn't it? I'm sure Richard must be horrified. I don't expect him in this morning. He'll have a lot on his hands, conferring with the fire investigation team, contacting the insurance company . . . How is he doing?"

"You haven't heard from him?"

"No. I assumed he was at your place, getting a few hours of sleep."

Zack put his arm around me. "We don't know where he is. We do know his car was parked in the garage. It wasn't touched by the fire."

Marsha dropped into her chair. "You mean he's . . .?"

"We don't know anything, and we won't until the fire authorities have gone through what's left of the structure. They can't do that until the fire is completely out and everything has cooled," Zack said.

I slumped against him. My legs could no longer hold me up. Zack helped me to the couch across from Marsha's desk.

Marsha stood and wrung her hands. "Can I get you a glass of water, Ms. Sharp?"

"No, dear. What I want is my son back unharmed."

MARSHA CLOSED THE OFFICE AND LEFT a note on the door saying it was closed for the day. Zack and I accompanied her to her car.

"Let me know if you hear anything," she said. "I'm sure Richard is safe somewhere."

Everyone wanted to reassure me of Richard's safety, and I wanted to believe them, but my mind wouldn't stop spinning worse case scenarios fueled by the adrenalin and worry that flooded my brain.

"I'm taking you home, Maddie, where I'm making us something to eat. I know you won't sleep, but I want you to eat something and then go upstairs and at least lie down."

Zack sat me down on the couch when we got home, stoked the fire again and wrapped one of the wool blankets around me, then he went to the kitchen. I heard him enter the back storage room.

"What are you up to?" I asked.

"Making you some comfort food. You just stay there and rest."

Comfort food. I smiled to myself. Zack knew the only thing I might eat under these circumstances was the food I seemed to favor when I wasn't feeling well physically or those times when I encountered something in my life that upset me, times like now.

I began to drift off at the sound of water being run into a pan and Zack turning on my stove. The sound of a metal utensil against the side of a pot brought me back to the present.

"Here you go, love," Zack held a plate with something white glistening with melted butter. "Mashed potatoes."

I took the plate holding it up to my nose and breathed in the smell of warm potatoes and hot melting butter. "That was a lot of trouble on your part, but you know me so well. Did you salt them?"

"Probably not enough." He held out the saltshaker. "I also made tea."

He went back to the kitchen area and returned with a cup. "Sugared."

I couldn't have asked for a better partner. I usually drank my tea without sugar but when I wanted to indulge myself, I added at least two teaspoons of sugar. It was the way my grandparents drank their tea, and I had grown up on it. It brought back memories of home and family. Hot, sweet, sweet tea and smooth, silky mashed potatoes.

"Zack, you are so wonderful." I took a forkful of the potatoes and savored their creaminess and the tang of the butter, followed by the hot tea. I continued to eat until I could no longer take in another mouthful. "I can't eat all this." I handed my plate to Zack.

He took the plate into the kitchen and then helped me up the stairs to the bedroom.

"Stay here," Zack said. I heard the water run in the bathroom. "Take off your clothes."

I raised one eyebrow in surprise.

"Don't be silly, Maddie, I'm running you a hot bath."

"None of this will get me to sleep, but I'm grateful."

I sank into the hot water to which Zack had added scented bath salts. I began to feel my muscles relax.

"Don't let the water get cold," said Zack from the bedroom. He opened the door to the bathroom and placed a towel on the edge of the tub. "I warmed it for you in the dryer."

What a good, considerate man he was. I was a lucky woman. I stepped out of the tub, dried myself with the toasty towel and slipped into my nightgown.

"Bed awaits you," he said when I entered the bedroom.

"You've gone to so much trouble which I appreciate, but I know I can't sleep, not until I've heard from Richard."

Zack leaned over me once I got comfy in bed. "I know but try." He turned to leave the room.

"Stay here with me. We can talk."

"Not about Richard."

"No. Tell me about growing up. I know so little about your past life."

As it turned out, I wasn't going to learn much about his childhood, because the next thing I knew, the sun was going down. I had slept though the late morning and into afternoon. I grabbed my robe and went downstairs.

Zack looked up from where he was seated on the couch. "Good. You got some sleep." His voice sounded like he was happy for me, but the look in his eyes said there was something he wanted to tell me.

"What have you heard?"

"The fire was set. The fire investigator found accelerant near the front door."

I sat on the couch. "Did they find anything else?"

"You mean . . ."

"Yes. Did they find a body?"

CHAPTER 7

"NO BODY, MADDIE."

I leaned into him, and he put his arm around me and pulled me closer. Richard was alive, somewhere.

"Where is he?" I asked.

"I was thinking about that and wondered if he went home with Franklin for some reason, so I called Franklin's home phone. There was no answer."

"I can't stand not knowing. Two murders and Richard missing. There has to be some connection."

I heard a car pull up in front of the house. I ran to the front door and flung it open. "Richard?"

"No, Maddie. It's me."

"Jane."

She threw her arms around me. "I'm so sorry I've not been in touch, but I only just heard about the fire."

Behind her stood another figure, Darren, her biker friend.

I hesitated a moment, then said, "Come in," although I was less than happy to see Darren still with Jane.

"I didn't know you had a car, Darren."

"You can't ride a bike in this weather. I borrowed Lily's car."

I introduced Zack and Darren. "I'll be right back. I need to get dressed." I started for the stairs.

"I guess we came at an inconvenient time. We can come back tomorrow," Jane said.

"Don't be silly. I was worried about you when I couldn't get in touch. I'll be just a minute. Zack can make some coffee."

I ran up the stairs and jumped into the clothes I'd worn yesterday, ran a comb through my hair and took a quick glance at myself in the mirror. My hair lay flat to my head where I'd slept on it. Oh, well. It was my good friend Jane, not someone I needed to impress. I gave Spike a pat on his head. "You can come down and join us, you know." He blinked twice and closed his eyes. Spike understood what I said, of that I was certain, but only the promise of food would disturb a good cat's nap.

"Oh, look what you've done." Spike loved to knead soft materials like sweaters, blankets, wool coats, and knit scarves. This time he'd chosen the blanket on my bed and pulled threads out of it. Sometimes when his claws got too long, they would get caught in the materials he kneaded, and he found it difficult to free himself. "I need to clip your claws, don't I?" But not now, I told myself. I'd do it soon, maybe tomorrow. "I'm sorry I haven't had time for you recently," I gave him a pet on his head. He purred at my touch then his purrs turned into a soft snore, and he returned to his cat dreams of food, no doubt. I tiptoed out of the room and went downstairs.

"Coffee, Maddie?" Zack held the pot up after he'd poured cups for Jane and Darren.

"I think I could use a jolt of caffeine."

"Hungry?" he asked. "I can whip up some eggs or a sandwich."

I shook my head.

Jane took a sip of her coffee then set the cup on the side table next to her chair. "Do you know how the fire started?" she asked.

"It was arson," said Zack.

Both Jane and Darren expressed shock at the news.

"Richard wasn't hurt, was he?" Jane asked.

"We can't find Richard anywhere. We know he wasn't in the house, but his car is still in the garage."

Jane reached out her hand to me. "Oh, Maddie, you must be worried sick. I'm so sorry."

At Jane's expression of sympathy, I broke down in tears again. She rose from her chair, came over to me and hugged me.

"Is there anything I can do?"

"No, but it's so good to have you here."

"We won't stay long. I just wanted to find out if you were okay, well, if Richard was okay. Who would want to set Richard's house on fire?" Jane asked.

"I don't know but I wonder if it was the person who killed Ms. Werner, the woman who Richard was to represent for her husband's murder. Richard is under suspicion for her murder."

Jane's hand flew to her mouth in shock. "That's ridiculous."

"Yes, I know."

There was a knock on the door. Zack opened the door to Sheriff Burroughs.

"Anita. Come in." I said.

"I'm looking for Richard. Is he here?" she asked, standing just inside the doorway.

"No. We have no idea where he is," Zack said. "C'mon in and have a seat. Can I get you coffee?"

"No." Anita didn't move farther into the room, and she shuffled her feet back and forth as if she was uncomfortable. "I know about the fire and that it was set. I'll be working to find out who did that, I assure you, but I've still got a murder on my hands, well, two murders although I'm convinced Ms. Werner killed her husband."

I crossed my arms over my chest and frowned. "You still think Richard is your primary suspect in her murder, don't you?"

"What I think isn't important. I do want to question him about the fire, and I have a few more questions about Ms. Werner's murder, so if you hear from him, let me know. His disappearance is suspicious." Anita nodded, then turned and left.

The sheriff's appearance only upset me more. Did she think Richard was hiding out from the authorities? She knew him better than that, didn't she?

Jane and Darren prepared to leave. "Stay in touch, Maddie. I'm sure there's a reasonable explanation for Richard's absence."

"Sounds like the sheriff thinks he might be the guilty party in that woman's murder," said Darren.

"Yes, thank you, Darren, for your so astute observation." I put as much sarcasm in my voice as I could manage.

Jane gave Darren an angry look and pushed him out the door, turning back to mouth, "I'm sorry."

"Jane's got herself quite a catch there, hasn't he?" Zack's tone of voice told me he wasn't impressed with the man. "Real sensitive sort."

"I'm worried about her."

"Maddie, you have enough to worry about. Jane's a grown woman. She'll come to her senses."

"Will she? Love at our age is hard to find . . . and powerful when you think you've found it. She had a crush on Darren in high school."

"She thinks she's got what we have, Maddie. Can you blame her for hanging on to see what happens between them?"

Zack was right, but I had a bad feeling about Darren.

"Let's keep trying Richard's cell, and we can call Franklin again." Zack punched in the contacts on his cell. "No answer. Voice mail for both the numbers."

"We've been calling Franklin's home phone. I don't know if he has a cell, but he does have an office at the university. Let's try there."

The main university number connected me to Franklin's office. It rang several times, and I was about to disconnect when a female voice answered. "You've reached Franklin Davies office. This is Stacie Mendosa, his research assistant."

"Ms. Mendosa. Is Dr. Davies around?"

"No, he's not here."

I identified myself and explained why I was looking for Dr. Davies. "Do you know if he came in today?"

"He's usually in early every morning. I wasn't in , so I don't know whether he was or not, but I'm surprised he's not here now, unless he went to his cabin in the Adirondacks this weekend and got stuck in the snow there. They had a lot more snow than we had."

"He has a cabin up there?"

"Yes. He usually closes it down the end of October, but it's been a warm fall. He may have gone there for a final weekend and got trapped. The cabin is at least a mile off the main highway on a road that's seasonally maintained."

"Does he have a phone at the cabin?"

"Just a minute. I'll see if I can find that number."

After several minutes, Stacie returned to the phone and recited the number to me. "I can't guarantee the number will work. He probably had it disconnected for the season."

"Where is this cabin?" I asked.

"I don't have an exact address, but I think it's somewhere north of Tupper Lake. I've never been there, but I may know someone who has. I can check and see if I can get you a location."

I gave her both my numbers, landline and cell, as well as Zack's cell. "If you get an address for the cabin, call me, and if Dr. Davies comes in, have him call me, immediately."

I told Zack what I had learned. "Maybe Richard is with him at the cabin," said Zack. "They may have gotten snowed in and couldn't call us because there were no cell towers nearby and the landline was out."

Zack's analysis sounded reasonable, and I felt buoyed up by the possibility that I might hear from someone soon.

"Do you think if they're at the cabin that they're safe? I mean, if they're snowed in and it's a remote location on a road that's probably not going to be plowed . . ."

"I'll make some calls to my buddies up north. They may know more." Zack busied himself making contacts with state troopers and others he knew from his years as a county sheriff. I sat on the couch staring into the flames in the fireplace and thought of all the horrible things that could have happened to Richard.

"Enough with the worrying, Maddie. I've put out feelers all over the Tupper Lake area. Someone will know of the cabin."

Spike came downstairs for food, of course.

"I'm not hungry, but I'll bet you could eat something." I went to the fridge to get Spike's food and took a look at what leftovers might be there. I scooped Spike's food into his dish. That was one hungry mouth in the house fed, but what about Zack?

"Not much in the way of leftovers, is there? I looked earlier." Zack opened the fridge door and put the remainder of the can of cat food back in. Zack looked at his watch. "I'll bet the market on Main Street still has some of their rotisserie chicken left. I'll run up there and get one along with some sides. Steak fries and slaw okay with you, Maddie?"

I shrugged. "Get what you might like to eat. I have no appetite."

"Be right back." He kissed me, grabbed his coat and left.

I returned to the couch and curled up in front of the fire. Spike joined me and put out a loud purr. Was he happy or trying to comfort me? I'd heard cats sometimes purred to make themselves feel better. Did Spike think I needed some comforting purrs?

I must have nodded off for a few minutes because the next thing I remembered was the front door opening.

"That was quick, Zack."

"It's not Zack. It's me, Mom."

"Richard!" I sprang from the couch, rushed over to him and gave him a huge hug.

"Hey, Mom. Let up. You're squeezing me to death."

I let go and pushed him back so I could get a better look at him. He looked tired and it was clear he hadn't shaved for several days. "Where were you?"

Richard shrugged out of his coat. "It's a long story."

Zack burst through the door. "That's Richard's car out there. What's going on?"

"I was about to tell Mom. Hey, that smells good. I'm starved."

I smiled. "Suddenly I could eat a bite, too. Let's get some food into us and then you can tell us what happened. We were so worried."

"I knew you would be, so I had Franklin drive me back to my house to get my car. Imagine my surprise when I found I no longer had a house. I knew you'd be worried when the house burned and you couldn't locate me, so I talked briefly with the fire engineers still there, then jumped in my car and came right here."

Zack thumped Richard on the back and began to set out the food on the table. "I told Maddie there was a reasonable explanation for your absence."

We sat at the table and ate. It appeared we were all hungry as no one spoke until we'd finished most of the food.

I made a pot of decaf, and we took our cups into the living room to sip in front of the fire.

"Brandy?" offered Zack.

"That would be great," said Richard.

"Maddie?"

"Sure. Why not."

Richard sat back into his chair with a sigh and began his account of what happened. "You know I rode with Franklin back to my house, but when I got there, the place was crawling with television, newspaper and radio personnel. Your favorite newspaper reporter was there, Mom."

I snorted. "You mean Agnes Danderfield, not really my pal."

"No one recognized Franklin's car, so I told him to drive past. I was in no mood to talk to the press. 'Can I stay with you, at least until I feel more able to handle the publicity?' Franklin had a better idea. He has a cabin in the Adirondacks."

"We were so worried when no one heard from you that we called Dr. Davies' office. His assistant told us about the cabin," I said.

"I'm sorry I couldn't get word to you, Mom. You know I would have if it was possible."

"We know," said Zack.

"Franklin suggested we go to the cabin, and I could help him close it for the winter. A bit of physical labor sounded good. We stopped by his house and then headed for the cabin. We had no idea snow was coming in. Although the skies looked gray when we awakened Sunday morning, we thought we could beat the snow out and continued to work on the place until the afternoon, not really paying attention to the weather. When the snow started we had only about an hour's work left, so we forged ahead. Before we knew it, there was a blizzard outside, and the wind was driving the snow sideways. 'Best to hunker down, Franklin said.'"

"Why didn't you call us?" I asked.

"Franklin has no cell, the landline at the cabin had been disconnected for the winter and my cell was useless. You know how few towers there are up in those mountains. The electricity went out Sunday night and stayed out. By Monday, the snow had piled halfway up the door. 'What now, I asked Franklin.' 'We wait,' he said. If they plow this road, and that's a big if, because I'm the only cabin on it, they'll clear it after they're hit all the other roads.' I looked outside. It was still snowing heavily. Franklin didn't seem worried. 'It's an early snow. It'll warm up and melt soon. Then we'll get out.' We spent Sunday and most of today trapped there. We had firewood for the woodburning stove, and the supplies Franklin kept in the cabin, so we were comfortable and fed. This afternoon, a snowplow followed by a state trooper made their way down the road. The trooper said he was a friend of yours, Zack, and that you had called to inquire about Franklin's cabin." Richard's gaze settled on me. "I don't suppose you got much sleep, did you?"

"I'll catch up tonight. Stay with us for the night. You can have the spare bedroom."

"I can't do that. I need to go to the office and catch up on my work." He stood to go.

"Tonight? you've been through a lot. Just where do you think you'll sleep?

"I've got a comfortable couch in my office."

"We know you've got a lot to do—check with your house insurance, replace the clothing that was burned and talk with the fire investigators and the police . . ." Zack said.

"The fire investigators told me the fire was purposely set. I'll meet with them for further discussions tomorrow."

"Franklin knows about the fire being arson then?" said Zack. "And what did he say?"

"He told me to get some sleep, and we'd talk tomorrow."

"He was worried, wasn't he?" I asked.

Richard gave a curt nod. He grabbed his coat off the hook by the door and then came back to me. "Mom, I'll be fine."

"Will you? Someone has framed you for murder, the brother of the dead woman threatened you, and then someone set your house on fire."

"Your mother is right, Richard. There's the matter of your safety. Someone out there wants you dead or, at the very least, in jail for a murder you didn't commit. I'm following you back to your house where you'll drop off your car and I'll drive you to your office. You can work for a few hours, then I'll bring you back here so you can get the sleep you need."

Richard started to argue, but Zack held up his hand. "I insist. Meantime, Maddie, keep the door locked and don't open it to anyone but family or me. We'll be back tonight."

"Late." Richard added as they left.

Zack and Richard returned sometime after three in the morning. I had fallen asleep on the couch with Spike at my feet.

"Mom," Richard said, "if you believe I shouldn't sleep on my office couch, what makes you think you're any better sleeping on your couch especially when you have a comfy bed upstairs?"

Zack, looking as bone weary as I felt, laughed. "You didn't really think she'd do the sensible thing and go to bed while we were gone, did you? We all need rest. Let's get some sleep and we'll talk in the morning. The fire complicated the plans we made at dinner. Richard was on the phone tonight with Franklin and we made some decisions about what we need to do going forward. Richard didn't like some of what Franklin and I said . . ."

"Like what?" I asked.

"We think Richard should consider hiring a bodyguard."

"A bodyguard!"

Richard shook his head. "There's no need."

"Yes, there is." Zack's tone of voice said there was no sense arguing with him.

"I assume I figure in these decisions, and I say you need a bodyguard," I said. They knew better than to leave me out. I hadn't gotten the reputation for being "Snoopy Maddie" for no reason. "Now that we've settled that, I'm going to bed."

"Of course." Zack spoke in a reassuring tone of voice, but as I turned to go upstairs I caught him wink at Richard out of the corner of my eye.

I turned and faced both of them. "I will not be relegated to taking notes. I can be helpful."

"Of course," said Zack and winked at Richard.

"I saw that. Again." I gave Zack a playful punch in the arm.

"Ouch."

"You could be charged with assault, Mom."

"I'm not worried. I know a good defense lawyer."

Chapter 8

RICHARD LEFT EARLY THE NEXT MORNING to take care of everything needed to settle the insurance, talk with the authorities and meet Franklin at his law office.

"You're sure he's safe alone?" I asked Zack.

"He's not alone. He'll be with the insurance people and the police and then Franklin at his office. But I intend to move quickly to find him a bodyguard."

"Do you have someone in mind?"

"I do, a person who's somewhat unconventional, but competent."

"Unconventional?"

"Yes, I put in a call early this morning and the individual will meet me at Richard's office later today."

"Can I come with you? I'd like to meet this *unconventional* bodyguard."

Zack hesitated a moment and I could almost hear the arguments against my accompanying him whirling around in his head.

"I won't make trouble, I'll keep quiet and not ask embarrassing questions and I'll leave the final decision to you and Richard."

"You know I don't believe a word of that, but if I leave you here, you'll simply get in your car and drive yourself to Richard's office anyway."

I stood on tiptoe and gave him a peck on the cheek. "Thanks. I'll be ready in a minute."

At Richard's office, his secretary greeted us. "Everyone is so relieved your son is safe."

"Whoever set that fire thought he was home because his car was in the garage," said Zack.

"Richard was lucky," she said. "Go on into his conference room. Everyone is there already."

Richard and Dr. Davies were joined by another individual, a person I recognized, but never expected to see again, Lily, the female biker, part of Darren's group of biker friends.

Richard rose and stepped forward. "You already know Zack, but I don't think you've met my mother."

I nodded to Lily. "We've met. Actually, it was at Jane's house."

"Ms. Sparks," said Lily.

Zack looked surprised.

"At Jane's house? When was that, Maddie?"

"I told you that a group of bikers came by, one of whom was Darren, Jane's current, uh, friend. Lily was one of the others, but I don't understand why she's here now." Then it hit me. "You can't mean she's going to be Richard's bodyguard?"

"She's eminently suited for the job, Mom. Zack tells me Lily is retired from law enforcement, so she has the experience to protect me."

"Oh," was all I could say. If Zack knew her and had cleared her for the position, then who was I to object?

"I assure you, Ms. Sparks, I'm ready to do whatever is necessary to protect your son." Lily had traded in her biker leathers for a dark blue pantsuit. Her hair was pulled back in a fashionable knot low on her neck. She swept her suit jacket to one side, and I noticed the gun at her waist.

I cleared my throat and smiled at her. "Well, then, welcome to the team. However, you don't look like a scary bodyguard."

"She's not supposed to. I'm telling everyone she's my assistant."

Richard looked pleased at having Lily on the team.

"Let's review our list of suspects." Richard gestured to the empty chairs at his conference table. "I assume you'll be staying for this discussion, Mom."

"You bet. I wouldn't miss this for anything."

If Lily was surprised I was being treated as part of the investigative team, she hid it well, but I wanted to make certain she understood my vital role in finding out who has killed Richard's client and who had set fire to his house.

"I have my pulse on the local goings on in the village." I looked directly at her, and she nodded in understanding.

"Invaluable," she said.

"So far we only have one lead, the brother of Denise Werner, Mannie Costa, who threatened Richard at dinner the other night. At first we thought it was only drunken threats, but I checked on his past and he has a record of assault," said Zack.

"We'll want to determine if there's anyone around here with a record of arson," said Davies.

"What about Denise's background? You knew her in high school, didn't you, Richard?"

"She was a classmate." Richard cleared this throat, and his gaze wouldn't meet mine.

"I understand there was more to your relationship than that," I said.

"I may have dated her."

"When Zack and I stopped by the coffeehouse in town on Sunday, we ran into Ellen Hawkins and Sandy Longworth, also friends of yours from high school. Sandy seemed to suggest that you and Denise were an item."

Franklin gave Richard a stern look. "If that's so, the DA's office will find that interesting. We should get ahead of this."

Richard deflected Franklin's comment by saying, "We all were in high school together, although Ellen was two years younger. She, Sandy and Denise always hung out together. Best friends I guess."

I thought back to my high school days and the girls I was friends with. Like Ellen, Denise and Sandy, there were three of us. When two of the girls had an argument, the third girl was forced to take sides. I assumed that was true of these girls too.

"I'll talk to Ellen and Sandy again," I said.

Richard cleared his throat and shook his head. "I can tell you all you want to know, Mom."

"Good. With the addition of your input, I'll get all of the background needed then."

"Did Denise have family other than her brother?" Zack asked Richard.

"I don't know. Parents, of course, but I don't think they're still living," said Richard.

"I don't suppose the lawyer Denise hired for her divorce would give us any information about why she was seeking a divorce, but it's worth trying. If you have his name, Richard, I can make a run at him."

Richard tapped on his keyboard. "Got it. Hmm. It's not someone local, but from Syracuse. A woman."

"Do you know her?" asked Davies.

"Only by reputation. She often defends women who have suffered domestic violence, not that we should assume it was the case with Denise Werner unless there are rumors around town." Zack looked at me when he said this.

"If her husband was hitting her, that may be motive for her killing her husband, but what does that have to do with Denise's death?" Unless . . .," I began, but stopped.

"Unless what, Maddie?" asked Zack.

"Maybe there was another woman who thought Denise was responsible for the husband's death. Perhaps that woman was in a relationship with Mr. Werner, and she killed Denise out of anger or grief, setting it up to look as if Richard was the guilty one."

"That is truly convoluted, Mom, although possible I guess." Richard seemed relieved the focus was no longer on his relationship with Denise.

"We need more information. Let's get busy and do some field work, talk with the leads we have now, and find out more about the Werners and their marriage." Zack stood and held out his hand to me.

"So what are we doing when we talk to people? Are we trying to find out who killed Denise or who killed her husband or both?" I asked.

"The sheriff thinks the evidence points to Ms. Werner as her husband's killer, so the authorities think that's a closed case, but I think the crimes have to be related." Davies tapped his pencil on the table and closed his notebook. "That means more work for our team."

Davies and Zack started to leave, but, I hung back. "I'll be with you in a minute. I need to talk to Richard." I gave Lily a pointed look. She followed Davies out of the conference room.

Zack frowned at me and told Davies good-bye as if he thought he would stay while I talked to Richard.

"Family matters, Zack. I'll tell you later."

Zack cocked one eyebrow at me but left the conference room closing the door behind him.

"So, Richard. You're forcing my hand here. What's the story between you and Denise?" I returned to my chair prepared to hear the truth about the relationship if it took planting myself in his conference room the rest of the day.

"Like I told you. We dated for a while. Sandy misinformed you if she said it was more than that."

"Oh I believe you. In high school it might have been dating, but what about after that? What about the summer before you went to college? Do you think Sandy's remarks didn't jog a memory for me? You think I don't remember how secretive you were that summer?"

Richard opened his mouth to stop me talking.

"You also took to sneaking out of the house late at night that summer."

"There were a few girls I was interested in that summer." Richard leaned back in his chair with a grin on his face. "You know how it is; leaving home to begin a new adventure, saying goodbye to the past to begin a new chapter in life."

"A 'few girls.' That must have made Denise feel so special," I said sarcastically.

"I don't like saying anything bad about her. She was a good kid, but she was wild. When I found out she was running around with a fast crowd, I decided she wasn't for me."

"So am I to understand that dating other girls was fine for you, but Denise wasn't supposed to have other boys in her life?" I was so disappointed my son would have held a double standard of behavior for males and females.

"You misunderstood what I meant, Mom. It wasn't the other boys that bothered me. We were never exclusive. The crowd she ran with and wanted me to join with her were into shoplifting, drinking and generally tearing around town engaging in vandalism of graves and private property, keying cars for example. I don't think she ever got caught, but some did, like her brother, Manny, who was part of that group. He eventually graduated to assault and battery and did time in prison."

"Sorry, Richard. I should know you wouldn't go for those kinds of friends."

"To tell you the truth, I don't think Denise's heart was in it. I talked to her about what she was doing at the time and told her she could get into serious trouble. She told me she knew, but she implied that her brother encouraged her. He was a few years older than her, and she wanted to prove she could keep up with him and his fast crowd. I think his arrest scared her enough that she rethought what she was doing."

"Did you know her husband?"

"No." Richard looked down and I knew he was keeping something from me. Finally, he looked into my eyes and sighed. "I kind of kept tabs on her over the years."

"You were in touch with her then?"

"I was worried about her, so, yeah, I kept in touch." Richard cleared his throat and looked away again.

"How recent was your contact with her? She didn't come to you to represent you in the murder of her husband unexpectedly, did she? You know more about what was happening in that divorce than you've let on."

Richard rose from his chair. "Look, Mom, I can't say any more about the situation. She told me things she would only tell an attorney. I still feel ethically bound to keep her confidence."

"Both she and her husband are dead. Murdered. And you're the primary suspect in her death. What you know, confidential or not, could clear you of any charges. This is your freedom as well as your career. Do you at least mean to talk with Franklin about Denise?"

He ran his fingers through his hair. "I need time to think about all of this. It's more complicated than what I've told you."

"Is there a chance anyone else knows about your contact with Denise and your knowledge, whatever that is, about the relationship between her and her husband?"

"I don't know. Maybe."

"You need to protect yourself, Richard. At least talk this over with Franklin. If they charge you with Denise's murder, he needs to know everything pertinent to this case in order to defend you."

"I know that, Mom." Richard stepped up to me and put his arms around me. "Please don't tell Zack about our conversation, at least until I decide what to do."

"Of course, dear." It was a promise I didn't want to make, but for the time being, I owed it to Richard to wait until he determined his path. My problem now was what I could tell Zack about why I wanted to talk with Richard alone.

When I left Richard's law office, Zack was waiting for me in his truck. Standing outside near the entrance to the building was Lily.

"A word, Ms. Sparks?"

I waved to Zack to let him know I'd just be a minute.

"You and your son are very close, aren't you?" said Lily.

"I'm close to both my sons and my daughter-in-law and my granddaughter. We're family and we look out for one another."

"I never had that. I had a brother who was off to college when I was born. I guess I was what you'd call a late in life accident. My parents were killed in a car crash when I was five and I went to live with an aunt. She was kind to me, but we were never close."

"What about your brother?" I asked.

"There were too many years separating us. I only saw him on rare occasions. When I was older, we exchanged a few birthday cards and called sometimes. I don't even know where he is now."

"I'm sorry to hear that, but . . ."

"I wanted to assure you that I may not have experienced family, but I can see how important Rihard is to you and how much he loves you. I will protect him."

I looked into her eyes and could see she was sincere. "Thank you, my dear." I reached out, touched her arm and turned to go.

"There's something else. You may think you know your son well, but he's keeping something from all of us."

I hesitated and stepped back toward her. "I know that."

"You need to find out what it is." Her words irritated me.

"You think I don't know that?"

"You may find out things you don't want to hear, things which his defense team needs to know to save him from a murder charge. You might find you want to hold back on what you discover thinking it will protect him, but it won't." She seemed so certain about what she was telling me. Who was this woman, and did she know something about Richard? But how could she? She had never met Richard before today.

"What do you know?" My tone was sharper than I intended, almost accusatory, and not likely to encourage her to confide in me.

"I don't know anything concrete, but I'm like you, Ms. Sparks. I read people well. You do it instinctively. I do it because I was trained to. Your instinct has served you well. It can do the same in this case if you're open to it." She gave me a half smile of encouragement. My earlier sense that she was baiting me with some knowledge about Richard only she knew was altered slightly. Maybe she did, because she never had someone she was close to, understand by default what family meant.

"I also have a question for you, one I suspect you can answer. What do you know about Darren, your motorcycle riding buddy?"

Her expression changed and although the tiny smile lingered, her eyes were shuttered. "I can't say much about him, but if I were your friend Jane, I wouldn't waste my time. I'd be careful with him. He leaves his mark on women."

I wanted to ask her what she meant, but she turned and walked back into the building. My friendship with Jane was new, but it felt as if we had been friends forever. I loved her like family and wanted to protect her. Was my initial impression of the man, my instincts, as Lily had suggested, telling me there was something dangerous about him? What a dilemma. There was nothing concrete I could tell Jane about Darren. If I pushed too hard about their relationship, Jane, just like a rebellious teen, would be more inclined to pursue him.

I walked over to the truck where Zack waited for me and got in.

"Do you want to tell me about your conversation?"

"The one with Richard or the one with Lily?"

"Either," he said.

"Lily and Darren may ride together but I don't think she particularly likes him or trusts him."

"That both confirms your opinion of the man and adds to your worry about Jane."

He said no more but waited in case I wanted to add to his analysis. I didn't.

"Where do you suggest we begin today?"

He started the truck. "If you can tolerate visiting Richard's house or what's left of it, I'd like to take a look around. I'm sure the fire investigators as well as the police combed through everything quite thoroughly, but in case they missed anything . . ."

"You like to do your own investigating, don't you? I'm not keen on seeing the remains of the house, but two sets of eyes are better than one, so I'll come with you."

We drove in silence to Richard's. I made a promise to Richard I wouldn't discuss his past with Ms. Werner until he talked with Franklin, but I also felt guilty keeping our conversation from Zack.

When we pulled up in front of the burned house, Zack glanced at me. "I also suspect Richard and Ms. Werner were closer than he's letting on."

"They were," I admitted, "but I don't know the details."

"Lily thinks so, too, doesn't she?"

I simply nodded and got out of the truck. I wasn't prepared for the scene before me. I'd seen the house burning, but the blackened timbers and scorched ground looked like a scene from a war zone.

"It's all gone." Tears came to my eyes.

"We don't have to do this, Maddie. I can take you home."

I shuddered and took a deep breath. "No. I wanted to be part of this investigation and that's what I'm going to do. Where do we begin?"

Chapter 9

Most of the snow near the house was gone, melted from the heat of the fire, but small, black encrusted piles remained at the periphery of the property. Zack and I walked the edges, Zack kicking the dirty patches with his boot.

"What do you expect to find that the authorities didn't spot?" I asked.

"I don't know, just being thorough."

On the far side of the garage where the building had protected the snow from the heat of the fire, Zack continued scaping the ground with his boots. Near the tree line where crusty snow had piled up against the trunk of one tree, his boot hit something. He bent over and dug the object from the snow and held it up to show me.

"What is it?"

"A piece of plastic. I knew our arsonist had to have some mode of transportation to get here. It looks like the vehicle hit the tree and a piece of it broke off."

"From a car? How could it get here in all that snow?"

"Not a car, Maddie. A snowmobile."

We both turned from our inspection of the plastic when we heard a car pull into Richard's drive.

"It's Sheriff Burroughs," I said.

Anita walked over to us. "Find anything?"

"Maybe." Zack handed Anita the plastic. "I think it's a broken piece of plastic from a snowmobile."

Anita examined it closely. "It could have been here for months."

"I don't think so. See the scrape on the tree? That's relatively new. And I pulled the plastic out of the snowbank, so it was here after it began snowing and before it stopped."

"I'll get it to our crime evidence people and see what they say." Anita started to go back to her car without saying anything else, so I decided I would.

"I assume you've talked with Richard," I said.

"Richard disappearing like that for several days made the DA suspicious. I believed Richard's story about being trapped in the snowstorm in his defense attorney's cabin, but I warned him to stay available for further questioning." Anita started to leave again but stopped and turned back to us. "I understand you've added to Richard's defense team."

I opened my mouth to explain about Richard's assistant, but Anita held up a hand to stop me.

"Look. I understand why the team took those steps assuming he's innocent of Ms. Werner's murder. Together with the arson at his house, I'd be concerned too."

Zack and I watched her walk back to her car, get in and drive off.

"Does that mean she thinks Richard is innocent?" I asked Zack.

"Probably. Let's get going. I think I've seen what I need to here. Should I drop you at home, Maddie?"

"Thanks. I'd like to pick up my car. I think I'll drop by the museum and chat with Jane."

"A chat about what?"

"Nothing special. I'd like to see how her friendship with Darren is going."

"You think she'll tell you about it?"

"Oh, she'll tell me, that's certain. If it's off, she'll want to cry about it if he dumped her or tell me what a bum he is if she decided to call it off. If the relationship is going well, there will be nothing else she'd rather talk about than romance."

THE ROADS TO THE MUSEUM WERE clear; the ice and snow had melted as the weather turned unseasonably warm after the snowstorm of the weekend. My stomach growled as I pulled into the museum visitors' parking lot. I looked at my watch and realized it was after one in the afternoon. Maybe I could talk Jane into a late lunch.

As I entered the museum, Jane was sitting at the entrance desk, a position I had only recently vacated when I decided I needed to spend more time on my writing . . . and with Zack.

"Maddie!" she said in a cheerful voice, alerting me that all had to be going well with Darren.

"Can you get someone to sit here for you while we go have lunch?"

"Oh, sure. One of our young volunteers can take my place, but only for a short lunch."

"While you arrange that, I'll grab a couple of sandwiches from the snack shop here and meet you in the dining area next to the sandwich counter." The museum offered a small selection of items such as salads and sandwiches, coffee and tea available for sale. Next to the counter where the food was sold was an area with a few tables. In warmer weather, it was possible to sit outside on a brick patio but today was too windy for outdoors dining. Five minutes later, Jane came to join me at my table.

"You didn't say what you'd like, so I ordered us chicken salad on croissants and tea."

Jane pulled the chair out across the table and dropped into it with a whump. "You came by just in time. I needed a break and something to eat."

"You look exhausted, Jane. What's up?"

She unwrapped the sandwich, bit into it and chewed. "Everything good, really. Darren keeps me busy," she gave me a coquettish look, "and I love having him around. It's nice to cook for someone and look after them, you know, like you do for Zack."

"Yes, but I wouldn't say he takes a great deal of looking after."

"Well, you know what I mean." She quickly added, "He's repairing that crack in my ceiling and doing some painting in the kitchen."

"Things are going pretty quickly for you two, aren't they?"

I could tell she didn't like my comment. She squinted her eyes at me and stopped eating. "And you don't approve? It seems you and Zack moved ahead with your relationship at warp speed. Don't forget. I've known Darren since high school."

I was about to mention that high school was a long time ago and she had missed seeing him for many years between then and now, but I thought better of it and for once kept my thoughts to myself.

"That's true."

Her mouth curved upward again in a smile. "He's been living with two of the guys he rides with and sleeping on their couch, so I told him he could move into my spare room."

"Uh, huh." The danger signals went off in my head. It sounded like Darren had no job and no permanent place to live.

"I'm not rushing into things, you know. It's not like we've been spending every moment together. I have my work here at the museum . . ."

"And where does Darren work?" I asked.

She glanced away for a moment as if my question made her nervous. "Uh, he mentioned that motorcycle repair place outside town."

"So had he moved into your place by Sunday?"

"Sunday, uh . . ."

"The night of the storm."

"Oh, of course." Her gaze wouldn't meet mine.

"So one of his roommates gave him a ride to your place."

"Yup."

"What time was that? Before or after the snow began?"

"Maddie. I feel as if you're cross-examining me. I know you have reservations about Darren what with his background and all, but isn't that my decision?"

Jane was right. As Zack had cautioned me, Jane was an adult. She had to make up her own mind whether or not I agreed with her. I wasn't about to end a friendship with someone I genuinely loved.

I reached across the table and patted her hand. "Sorry, Jane. I'm being a busybody and a snoop. I just want to be certain Darren treats you well because you deserve a good man in your life. I mean if that's what you want."

"Oh, Maddie, you know what you think is important to me. Having Darren around feels good to me, but I am trying to take this slow. He's in my spare room, not in my bedroom."

Her words reassured me about her and Darren, but why wouldn't she answer my question about Sunday night, the night someone torched Richard's house? When listing our suspects for the murders and the fire, Darren's name hadn't come up. Why would it? My concern for Jane's love life was making me paranoid.

"I assume you're busy helping Zack with Richard's case."

I crumpled up my napkin and put it on my plate, sat back and sipped my tea. "It's a very complicated situation as you can surmise: the murder of Ms. Werner's husband, her murder and then Richard's house being torched."

"I guess you assume they're all connected, even the arson?"

"Of course, especially since Ms. Werner's brother threatened Richard the other night when we were out to dinner."

"Oh, you mean Manny Costa. Now, he's a piece of work."

"What do you know about him?"

"The man has always been in trouble from the time he was in high school into adulthood when he was convicted of assaulting one of his sister's boyfriends. In fact, I think the boyfriend became her husband, the one she's accused of killing." Jane leaned forward and said in a whisper, "If I were you, I'd take a close look at Manny for the husband's death."

"Well, confidentially, he is on our list of suspects even though everyone thinks she killed her husband. I understand they fought all the time, and they were getting a divorce."

"Maybe not." Jane sat back with a self-satisfied smile on her face.

"Okay, give. What do you know?"

"One of my friends told me she saw them hiking in the state park holding hands just a few days before he was murdered."

"I need to talk to your friend."

"Meet me here after work today and we'll talk with her together." Jane's face lit up with delight.

I hesitated to say yes because I wasn't certain it was a good idea to bring Jane into this investigation. "I don't know if . . ."

She slid back in her chair and crossed her arms over her chest, a stubborn look on her face. "If you don't let me help, then I'm not telling the name of my friend."

"You know if you don't, I'll tell Richard's lawyer, and you could be charged with impeding an investigation." I was being just plain mean, but my concern for Richard made me intolerant of anyone standing in the way of the investigation into the murder of Ms. Werner.

"Maddie! Why would you do that to me when you know how important I've been to your investigations in the past."

"I remember you drove my car without a license, and I took the blame for your driving the car into a neighbor's garbage cans and across some rose bushes." To her credit, Jane had drawn attention away from my search of a suspect's house, and she could be counted on to keep secrets I told her to herself even if confronted by my very persuasive boyfriend or law enforcement. Richard was my son, but Jane was my best friend. I was torn.

I let out a deep sigh. My primary responsibility was helping Richard, and Jane knew as many folks in the village as I did. She could be valuable to the case, or so I told myself. I'd have to keep my eye on her to make sure she followed my lead and didn't go off on her own. It was also true that Zack wouldn't be pleased with one more amateur snoop meddling in the investigation. He was concerned enough about my role in the case.

I gave in, eager to find out what Jane's friend knew.

"Oh, all right. When are you done here? I hope it's early enough that I can be home by dinnertime or Zack will get suspicious. I don't think he'd like you working on this case. He'd be worried about you too."

"Now who would think anything of two old ladies having coffee with a friend?"

"I've got a reputation in the village as a snoop, and everyone knows I've helped Zack on two past cases."

"All the more reason to have me on the case. I can pry information out of people who might not trust you." Jane looked absolutely delighted at being included as one of the team. I wondered if I'd made a mistake.

I left Jane at the desk to continue her work there but stopped by my granddaughter's office. The museum board had appointed Sara as the interim museum director. She wouldn't be graduating with her museum studies degree until this coming May when she'd be eligible to apply for the position on a permanent basis. Everyone was convinced she was certain to be chosen for the position, but Sara had expressed her reservations about the directorship, saying she was torn between remaining in the area or applying for something in a larger museum. Since she had been dating a young man enrolled in the business program at the local university, and they were clearly devoted to each other, her commitment to their relationship made her decision more difficult.

I rapped on her office door and stuck my head in. "Hi, honey."

"Oh, Gram. Come on in. I have something to tell you." She got up from her desk and held out her arms to me.

One look at her face told me her news had to be something

good. She brimmed over with happiness, smiling, dancing across the room and then grabbing me and twirling me around.

"My goodness. You're bubbling with joy."

"Yes. I haven't told anyone else my news. You'll be the first to know. Oh, sorry. How rude of me to keep you standing. Sit down, Gram."

"Is the news earth shattering enough to knock me off my feet?" Her smile got wider.

"Leon has asked me to marry him and we're planning on a June wedding right after my graduation. Isn't it exciting?"

"Oh, how wonderful. I'm so happy for you. He's a wonderful young man." Leon Powles was the son of a local Native American leader who had been accused of murder this past autumn. Albert Powles had reluctantly hired Richard as his defense attorney, a choice that led to the charges being dropped against him. Not trusting white people's justice, Mr. Powles proved a somewhat difficult man to defend, but Richard triumphed and earned the respect of Powles and his family's members. I had gotten to know Powles' wife and we had begun a friendship that both of us hoped would grow in the months ahead. My entire family liked Leon, and the Powles family felt the same about Sara.

"I guess this means you'll be staying in this area, taking the position here at the museum."

Sara's smile faltered. "That's not resolved yet, Gram. Leon has another year for his MBA at the university. I may defer making a decision. I could apply for the directorship here, but . . ."

"You need to be certain that's what you really want." I reached out and patted her hand. "You have some time before you have to decide. The search for the permanent director hasn't yet begun, has it?"

"Not yet. The announcement for it comes out in the statewide museum journal in January, with the deadline for application in March." Sara put her finger over her mouth. "Keep the wedding plans under your hat, Gram. Leon and I haven't told our families yet."

Suddenly the joy on her face faded.

"What's wrong, honey?"

"I'm worried how Leon's father will react. The family has strong traditions and Native American roots that go back centuries. And I'm, well, I'm white."

I understood her concerns. Mr. Powles wasn't trusting of white people, but I rushed to reassure her. "I'm sure that won't be an issue."

"I'm just being silly, aren't I?"

"You shouldn't worry about something before you have all the facts. You and Leon need to tell his family. You shouldn't keep this a secret, but I won't say anything until you tell me to."

I left her realizing that wrestling with the decision about the museum position and what Leon's father would say when he heard might dim her joy about the upcoming marriage, but Sara was a level-headed young woman and her relationship with Leon was solid. I knew they'd work out what was best. Like Sara's parents, I wanted her near me. I didn't tell her that. My saying it now would only increase pressure on her. She knew I loved her and I would support whatever she and Leon decided no matter how sad her leaving here might make me.

I stopped on my way out of the museum to tell Jane I'd pick her up after I ran a few errands nearby. She waved as I left. "Don't be late. I'm eager to get things rolling."

I drove to a nearby farmer's market to pick up bread, milk and farm fresh eggs as well as some of their goat milk cheese which I knew Zack loved to eat on his bagels.

As I entered the store, I caught sight of Darren at the meat counter. I almost left the store to avoid having to speak to him. He was in an intense conversation with a woman, her back to me, so I couldn't see who she was. They spoke so softly I couldn't make out the words. I knew I didn't want them to spot me, so I stepped to my right into an aisle out of their sight.

I peeked around the corner and saw her lean toward him. I could see her face was suffused with anger and she whispered something in his ear, then suddenly she stepped back and yelled at him "You're useless." As she turned to leave, I saw him reach for her arm.

"Don't touch me!" She jerked her hand away and stalked off.

A lovers' spat? As she strode past me, I recognized her. The woman was Sandy Longworth, and her face was almost purple with rage.

Now what were Darren and Sandy Longworth arguing about? I was surprised they knew each other. I wasn't surprised Darren had another woman in his life—it was the kind of betrayal I thought Darren capable of—but the age gap between them had to be at least thirty years. A delayed midlife crisis for Darren, I wondered, a younger woman to bolster his ego?

CHAPTER 10

I LET DARREN CASH OUT AND LEAVE the store, but Sandy returned to the meat counter, so I decided I couldn't hide in the aisle any longer.

"Hey, Sandy," I said, coming up behind her. "You shop here for meats? They're more expensive than at the supermarkets, but the quality is excellent."

She turned and the expression on her face was at first startled, then displeased followed by a phony smile she quickly pasted on her face.

"Ms. Sparks. How nice to see you."

What a liar. She was anything but pleased to run into me. Was she worried I might have seen her talking to Darren?

"Isn't this a bit out of the way for you to shop?"

"I could say the same for you," she shot back.

"I was in the area. I'm giving my friend Jane a ride. Do you know Jane?" I thought it was worth bringing up Jane's name to see if she reacted.

"Jane? Oh, yes, I know her." Sandy looked around the store, worry lines wrinkling her forehead. "She's not with you, is she?"

"No. I'm on my way to pick her up from the museum. She volunteers there."

"Oh." Sandy looked relieved. "Well, I should be going. Good to run into you."

"You, too." I could lie well, too.

I GRABBED MY GROCERIES AND JUMPED INTO my car. On the road back to the museum I mulled over what I had seen at the store. What had I seen? Darren and Sandy talking, then arguing. What was wrong with that? Should I tell Jane? Tell her what? I was still undecided when I pulled up in front of the museum just before closing time. I left my car idling to run in and get Jane. She wasn't at the desk, but I caught Sara as she came out of her office.

"Where's Jane? I was supposed to give her a ride."

"Oh. You missed her by minutes."

"Gone? But how? Did she get a ride with someone here?"

"No, a man picked her up. She introduced him as Darren, but I don't remember his last name. She asked me to tell you she'd be in touch soon. She was positively beaming with happiness when she left. It must be love."

Oh, it was love alright—on Jane's part.

"I'll catch up to her at home. Thanks, Sara."

"Oh, and, Gram, Leon and I will be talking to his parents tonight."

"Good. I assume you'll be letting your parents know this evening also."

On the drive back to my house, I mulled over the dilemma that I faced. Should I tell Jane what I saw or not? But exactly what could I tell her? I'd seen Sandy and Darren talking and arguing. That was what I observed, but my gut told me there was something else going on. If I told Jane, would she believe what I suspected or dismiss my concerns as an attempt to infer with her life? She knew I didn't care much for Darren. If I didn't warn her, he could hurt her. The quandary was solved when I pulled into my drive and saw two people sitting in a car parked in front of the house.

The passenger rolled down her window. "Hi, Maddie. Sorry I didn't wait for you, but Darren came by and offered me a ride. How could I refuse him?" She grinned, turned her head toward him and gave him a peck on the cheek. "He assured me you'd understand, but I asked him to stop by here so I could tell you we're off to the coffeehouse. Want to come along?"

I looked at the car they were in. It was old with rust on the fenders. "Another car borrowed from one of your friends, Darren?"

"Nope. I bought her. She looks a little rough, but the price was right, and she runs real good."

I was about to ask him if the price was right because another "friend" floated him a loan, but I decided against being so snarky. My words would only hurt Jane and undermine our friendship.

"Zack should be back soon, so I'll have to say no to your invitation."

"Leave him a note and tell him where you are and to join us," said Jane.

Before I could stop myself, I said, "You could come in and we can have coffee here." Why did I say that? It meant I would have to tolerate Darren's company, and in my own home.

"Great idea." Darren popped out of the car, opened the passenger's door for Jane and they followed me up the walk to the house.

I had even more of a dilemma. Zack might not come home for hours if he was pursuing leads in Richard's case. Now I'd done it, trapped with my least favorite person, the man who was the two-timing lover of my best friend. As if I needed more proof that Darren wasn't the man for Jane, Spike sat at the top of the stairs twitching his tail back and forth and letting out low growls. I tried to tempt him down with a bowl of his favorite treat, cooked chicken breast, but he was having none of that. He finally turned his back on us and left. I found Spike to be a wonderful judge of character, and he obviously found Darren had none.

"What's with Spike?" asked Jane.

I shrugged. "It must be the weather."

I made a small pot of tea and found some cookies, probably

stale, in my cupboard. Perhaps if my offerings were not the best, Jane and Darren would leave and head for the coffee shop after all.

I didn't offer to make another pot of tea after the first ran out.

Darren bit into one of my cookies and then yelled, "Ouch."

"What's wrong, honey?" asked Jane.

"I think I broke a tooth on the cookie." Darren held his hand to the side of his face and moved his tongue around in his mouth.

"They are kind of hard." Jane gave me an accusing look.

"I apologize. I haven't had time to shop what with Richard's situation and all."

"Your son's got himself in a pickle, hasn't he," said Darren, continuing moving his tongue around in his mouth.

"No, he has not. He's not guilty and everyone knows that." I stood and glared at Darren.

"Of course, he isn't," said Jane, "But Darren doesn't know him like we do, Maddie."

I couldn't believe Jane would defend Darren's comment. "That may be true, but he is my son, and I won't have people coming into my house and making accusatory comments about him. I think you should leave. Besides," I bent over and lifted the teapot, "we're out of tea."

Jane stood, her lips drawn in a thin line, "And out of stale cookies, too, I guess." She handed me the empty cookie plate and the two of them headed toward the door.

I felt bad I had insulted Jane. I had tried so hard not to let her know how I felt about Darren and now it looked as if I might have ruined our friendship.

Before they reached the door, it opened, and Zack entered. "Oh, having tea, are you? I could use a cup."

"We were just leaving." Jane brushed by him, and she and Darren left without a word of goodbye.

"Something wrong, Maddie?" Zack asked.

I nodded my head and then broke into sobs. "I think I just lost my best friend."

Zack put his arms around me, and I sobbed into his shoulder.

"And it's my fault," I said through my tears. I then told Zack what had happened.

"You were trying to defend Richard. I'm sure Jane saw that."

"No, she didn't. She's so into that man, that creep, that . . ."

"She'll come around. Let it go for now and then in a day or so, the two of you can talk."

I sank into the couch. "You don't know the whole story." I told Zack about seeing Darren and Sandy in the market this afternoon. "I need to warn Jane somehow. He could break her heart."

"I think you need to leave it alone for now and see what happens tomorrow or the next day. I mean, what exactly did you see or hear?"

I thought back on what had transpired between Sandy and Darren. Probably nothing that would convince Jane to stop seeing Darren, but my gut told me something wasn't right. I would leave it for a day or so, or I could talk to someone else about the incident. What I was contemplating was interrupted by Zack saying, "How about dinner out tonight? And then, I have an idea for tomorrow."

"Some research you want me to do?"

Zack caught the boredom in my voice.

"Oh, no. Something much more exciting than that."

WE DINED AT THE BILLINGHOUSE RESTAURANT, our favorite place where we had our first date. The next morning we grabbed toast and coffee and were on our way early. Zack wouldn't tell me where we were going, but as long as we were together and I wasn't consigned to a computer but out in the field with Zack, I didn't care.

The snow had all melted from our recent storm, but the weight of it was heavy enough to flatten all remaining vegetation and pull the last leaves from the trees. The fields devoid of their corn stalks looked ready for winter to begin despite the warm temperatures that followed the snow. Puddles formed at the sides of the road and filled with mud.

"Ugh. I almost wish it would snow again. Look at this." I swept my hand toward the view outside the truck. "Brown, gray, everything's dead."

"We'll get another storm soon enough, and, remember, you hate the cold weather and driving in the snow."

"I'm glad I surrendered my job at the museum to Jane. I hated the commute on icy roads. I can spend the winter editing my manuscript and beginning work on my next one."

"I would have driven you to work."

"You don't know what work may come up for you or, for that matter, how much time you'll be spending on Richard's case."

Zack smiled at me and patted my hand. "Be honest, my dear. You also hate being a passenger when the roads are bad."

Zack slowed the truck, and we turned onto a side road. "It's just up ahead."

"Whose house it this?" I asked.

"Manny Costa's."

"Ah ha."

Zack and I jumped out of the truck and headed up the sidewalk toward the front door of the house.

Zack knocked and waited, then knocked again. He gave me a grin. "No one's home."

"Too bad. He's probably at work."

"That's what I'm thinking."

"Why are you looking so pleased about that? It means you'll have to make another trip to talk with him."

"Right, but we can take a quick look around." Zack stepped off the porch and headed back down the sidewalk but turned at the corner of the house. A rickety shed stood at the rear of the property. Beside it a tarp covered an object about three feet wide and ten feet long.

Zack grabbed the end of the tarp and pulled. "Well, isn't that too bad. The wind blew the cover off."

Under the tarp rested a snowmobile. Zack walked around it,

examining it carefully, even bending down to look under the housing. As he stooped to gaze at the front fender, a voice came from behind us.

"Looking for something?"

"Oh. Sheriff Burroughs. We, uh, wanted to talk with Mr. Costa, but he's not home," I said.

"I'd like a word with him also. I could have saved you the trip." Anita did not look pleased to see us in Manny's yard.

"We were just leaving when I saw the wind had blown the cover off Manny's snowmobile. You know how avid snowmobilers feel about their machinery. I was replacing it for him." Zack was quick on his feet, for sure. He dusted his hands together and greeted Anita. "Cover's filthy. I don't think anyone has ridden this since last winter."

Anita walked over to Zack, and she also scrutinized the machine. "Kind of beaten up, but I don't think that piece of plastic you found at Richard's house came from this one."

"I agree."

"Any other machines you think are worthy of your examination?"

"Not that I can connect to the fire. Most people around here have a snowmobile."

Anita nodded. "Well, I'm sure Mr. Costa would be pleased to know you covered his machine, but I recommend you don't try to help others." Anita tipped her hat to us and walked past the house to the road where she had parked her cruiser.

"Wind's let up some," Zack called to her, "so I don't imagine I'll need to replace other covers. At least not today."

She waved, got into her car and sped off. A car coming from the other direction turned into the drive and a woman got out. She looked to be in her late forties, plump. Her brown hair was streaked with gray, and exhaustion lined her face. When she spotted us on the property, she shook her fist and yelled, "Hey what are you doing? Who are you? This is private property."

Zack stepped forward and held out his hand. "You must be

Mrs. Costa. I'm Zack Montgomery, an investigator hired to look into Denise Werner's murder. This is my, ah, assistant."

The suspicious expression on Mrs. Costa's face didn't waver. "I thought my sister-in-law's murder had been solved. That lawyer did it, didn't he?"

"That's not certain," said Zack. "There are some issues that need clarifying. I wanted to talk with Mr. Costa."

"He's at work, and I just got home from my job as head cook at the local school. I go to work at five each morning and I need a nap." She brushed by us and reached for the front door, unlocked it and swung it open.

"Could I just have a minute of your time?" asked Zack.

"I'll give you a minute then off you go." She stood on the step with her back to the front door.

"What do you know about the Werner's marriage?"

"Not a lot. Manny wouldn't like me saying this, but his sister had real uppity ways, thought she was better than us. Didn't much care for her husband either. He was always sticking his nose in our business, telling us how to raise our kids. I know our kids got into a lot of trouble but who was he to tell us how to be parents."

"How many children do you have, Mrs. Costa?" I asked.

"Six boys. They're all grown now, thank goodness. They gave me nothing but trouble also. Now, if that's all you need, I've got to get off my feet. If you want to talk to Manny, he's working. He won't be home until late." She entered the house, slamming the door. We heard the lock click.

"Not a pleasant woman," said Zack.

"It sounds like she's had a difficult life, raising six unruly boys alone while Manny did prison time. Her job at the school can't be easy. Everybody hates cafeteria food and the lunch ladies that serve it."

We got back into the truck.

"Did you really want to talk to Manny, or did you expect him to be gone so you could snoop around his property?" I asked.

"What do you think?" Zack smiled.

"Now what?" I buckled my seat belt and settled back.

"I'm going to Richard's office. I'll drop you off at home."

"I'll come along."

"I don't know how long I'll be."

"I'll sit in a corner quiet as a mouse until you need me."

Zack raised his eyebrows at me. "You don't think I believe that for one minute, do you?"

"I brought my laptop with me." I held up my bag. "I can work on my manuscript or something."

"I might as well give in. I'd just have to repeat what we talked about if I don't let you come along."

I tried to hide my smile of satisfaction, but realized I failed.

"Don't look so smug."

LILY SAT IN RICHARD'S OUTER OFFICE.

"On the job, I see," I said.

She nodded. "Yes, Ms. Sparks."

"What about at night?"

Richard appeared in the doorway of his office. "She stays in the spare bedroom at the condo I rented. Anything else you'd like to know, Mom? What we had for dinner last night? Or what time we got up this morning?"

"I'm sure your mother is simply expressing her concern for your safety, not trying to pry," Lily said.

I gave her a quick glance. Was she being sarcastic? Everyone knew I like to know what was going on whether it was my business or not. I couldn't read her face.

"C'mon in, Zack. And I suppose you better come in also, Mom."

"I'll be there in a minute. I need to ask Lily something."

Richard gave me a suspicious look.

"It's about a friend we have in common."

Zack groaned, knowing I wanted to pump Lily for information about Darren since they rode bikes together.

After Richard closed the door to his office to confer with Zack, I took a seat on the couch across from Lilly.

"You know Darren has been seeing my friend Jane."

"Yep, I do."

"How well do you know him?"

I wasn't certain Lily would answer my question, but she settled back in her chair and began talking.

"Darren and I along with the other fellas you met at Jane's house a while back have ridden together for many years, but Darren and I go back long before that. You know he went to prison?"

I nodded but said nothing eager not to interrupt her story.

"Anyway, I served as his parole officer when he got out. Then after he was released from parole, we ran into each other one day at a coffee shop and got to talking about bikes. I was looking for a group to ride with and he suggested I join him and his mates."

"How long ago was that?"

"Couple of years or so."

Lily appeared to be through talking about her and Darren's association.

"You told me the other day that Darren used women or was bad for them. What did you mean?"

Lily chuckled. "You might not think so but underneath that grizzled exterior, he's a suave one, but he can't seem to commit to one woman at a time."

"You and Darren must be close then, if you know about his exploits."

"Correction. We were close at one time." She refused to meet my gaze. She had something more to tell me, so I decided to wait her out.

"I was in love with him. I probably still am."

Oh, ick.

CHAPTER 11

LILY LIFTED HER GAZE AND LOOKED at me with a steady regard. "I'm not proud of what I did, although having a relationship with him wasn't technically wrong because I was no longer a parole officer, but it wasn't very professional or smart of me. Looking back on it, I made a mistake."

"You're not even fifty yet, are you? Darren is over seventy."

"He likes younger women."

I thought about Sandy and Darren in the market yesterday. Sandy had to be around forty. "How much younger?" I asked.

Lily let out a bark of a laugh. "Probably there are no limits for him. That's why I'm a bit surprised at his relationship with your friend. She's probably the most age-appropriate woman he's dated."

"How does Darren feel about married women?"

"I don't think he cares about a woman's marital status. Why are you asking?"

"I saw him with a younger woman whom I know to be married. They didn't see me. At first they seemed friendly but then they seemed to have some kind of a disagreement."

"Who was she?"

"She was one of Richard's classmates in high school. I'd rather not give her name until I find out more about what was going on."

"Well, if you change your mind, I could talk with her."

"For now I don't want her to know what I saw. I think I'll keep this to myself. The information might come in handy in the future."

Zack stuck his head out of the door of Richard's office. "Maddie, could you come in? We have something we want to ask you."

I smiled at Lily and went into the office.

"Since I moved out of the village, I've lost track of most of my classmates from high school, Denise included," said Richard. "Do you know anything about her husband?"

"You mean anything like town gossip?" I asked.

"Exactly," said Zack. "You did a computer search on him and found no record of anything, not even a parking ticket. Was he from around here?"

I thought back on what I might have heard from my "sources"— the library, historical society, the convenience store, the places I frequented where I had run into villagers who liked to chat . . . or gossip.

"I think they both worked in Stone Side. He was a maintenance supervisor for a metal roofing manufacturer, and she was a teacher, although they owned a house here. No kids that I know of, but Jane passed on some information from one of her friends that the divorce pending between them was off."

"Can you track down the person who told Jane that?" asked Richard.

"Well, uh, Jane was going to hook me up with the person who told her, but we, that is, she, I mean, both of us got sidetracked."

"Maybe you should try to talk with Jane, soon." Zack said.

"But you told me to let it rest for a while."

"This may be important. Is she working this afternoon at the museum?"

"Yes."

"Then I'll drive you there and both of us will talk to her. I'll convince her information is more important that the anger and hurt you caused by what you said yesterday."

"Me? What about her stupid infatuation with that bum?"

"Fine. She's at fault too for having bad taste in men, but I suggest you walk away from that for now. This might be important for Richard's case."

"But I know some things about Darren, some unsavory things."

Zack took my arm and started to walk me out of Richard's office. "I'm sure with my help, Jane will forgive you for what you said."

"But I don't need to be forgiven. I did nothing wrong."

He shook his finger at me. "Look, Maddie, you have to decide whether you want to work with us on this case or spend your time trying to run Jane's life."

"I'm good at multitasking. I can do both."

Zack stopped and turned me to face him. "Let's try it this way. Let's say you're Jane and you've found a man you like but your best friend tries to interfere in the relationship. How would you react?"

"I'd ask her what she knew about the guy."

"No, you wouldn't, Maddie. You'd tell her to butt out."

Okay, so he was right, but I continued to stew about the situation all the way to the museum.

"OH, IT'S YOU." JANE LOOKED UP from her station at the entry desk with a less than welcoming smile.

"She's here to apologize."

"Now why would Maddie Sparks apologize for being who she is?"

"I know I'm a busy body, but I'm just trying to protect you."

"Look," Zack intervened before Jane and I escalated our jabs at each other, "Let's just say that both of you only want what's best for each other, but that being interfering is part of your DNA. You're good friends. Why let a man ruin that?"

Jane and I continued to stare at each other.

Finally, I leaned forward on the counter and touched Jane's hand. "I am sorry, Jane. Zack is right. We are so like each other that our snoopiness is bound to overflow into overprotectiveness."

"All I ask is that you treat me like I'm a mature adult, capable of making up my own mind about whether Darren is right for me or not."

I couldn't help myself. "Even if he's seeing other women?"

Zack groaned. Jane slid back in her chair, and I thought we were off again on exchanging barbs, but her expression softened. "I know there are other women in his life. I don't care as long as he treats me well and with respect."

I opened my mouth, but Jane spoke before I could. "And don't ask me about bedroom stuff. That really is none of anyone's business, including yours."

For once I held my tongue and we smiled at each other.

Zack stepped forward. "Now that peace had been restored, I understand you know someone who saw Denise Werner and her husband together after they filed for divorce. We'd like to talk with that individual. It's been assumed that the motive for Denise killing her husband was because they didn't get along, they argued and hated each other. If the divorce was off, then they changed their minds, meaning she didn't have reason to kill him."

"I really wish my source had come forth before. I urged her to talk with the authorities, but she seemed unwilling to get involved."

"It's really important for Richard's case," said Zack.

"Okay. It was Ellen Hawkins."

I was surprised. "I didn't know you knew Ellen. She's close to Richard's age."

"I met her through the arts and craft center in town. There was an artisans event there a few weeks ago. She was one of the artists displaying her pottery work. She is extraordinarily talented. I love the glazes she uses. She's also a member of the gardening club. It's a mix of men and women of all ages. It wouldn't hurt you to become a member, Maddie, not that you need gardening advice," she added quickly knowing that the only plants I grew well were weeds, "but it's a wonderful source of village information."

"Village gossip, you mean."

"Indeed."

"When's the next meeting?"

"We have one coming up. We'll be discussing how to help your plants winter over."

"I'd like to come. I'll drive you."

Jane hesitated.

"Unless you already have a ride."

"Uhm, no. Seven next Thursday night. Will you and Zack talk to Ellen before then?"

"We'll stop by her house after we leave here. I want to move quickly on piecing together Denise's relationship with her husband."

RIDING BACK TO THE VILLAGE, ZACK turned to me. "See. Was that so hard? Jane seems to be very levelheaded about Darren."

"I wonder. Did you know Lily was his parole officer? And that she and Darren had an intimate relationship?'

Zack glanced at me. "Yes to the former. No to the other."

"Does that concern you?"

"I assume that's in the past."

"Maybe. I'm not so sure." I didn't tell Zack that Lily told me she still loved the guy.

When we pulled up in front of Ellen's house, a car was in the driveway.

"I assume the car is hers and means she's at home," I said, unbuckling my seat belt.

"You can do the talking." I gave Zack one of my ingenuous smiles.

"Ms. Sparks. How nice to see you." Ellen welcomed us into her home.

"This is my friend, Zack Montgomery. He's the private investigator for my son's case."

"Oh." Now her friendly smile seemed less open, and her eyes held a wary look.

"We think you have some information that might prove important to Richard's case, " Zack began.

"You talked to Jane."

"Yes. She and I are good friends, and she knew what you told her was significant in the murder of Denise Werner's husband. Can you tell us what you saw?"

"I was struggling with what I had seen and wanted to tell the authorities. Jane told me I should, but I kept silent. Anyway, I know I'll feel better if I tell you. I was taking a hike in the state park about two weeks ago. I think it was several days before Mr. Werner's murder. I heard laughter coming ahead of me on the path and saw a couple holding hands and hiking the trail. They stopped and kissed, a passionate kiss, so I didn't want to interrupt them. I hid behind a tree and kept watch until they continued on up the hill. It was the Werners."

"We thought she was divorcing him. Our understanding is that she suspected him of having an affair and that was the reason behind the divorce. You're sure it was them?"

Ellen hesitated before answering. "Yes."

"Please call the sheriff's office and tell them what you saw. They need to know. It sounds as if they had reconciled. Someone else was likely responsible for Mr. Werner's death."

"Of course." Ellen walked us to the door.

"You didn't talk to anyone other than Jane about this, did you?"

"No," she said, but her gaze didn't meet ours.

"SHE'S LYING," I SAID. "NOT ABOUT what she saw, but she did tell someone else."

"I wonder who," said Zack.

"This case gets more and more complicated."

Zack shot me a worried look. "The authorities thought Denise killed her husband, but if she didn't, then the real killer has lost a layer of protection."

"And Jane and Ellen may have jeopardized themselves," Zack added.

"That all depends on who Ellen told besides Jane."

If there was to be no divorce because the couple had worked through their problems, it could mean that either or both of them had broken off their affairs . . . if they were having affairs.

"Maybe we're dealing with a mistress who thought she had a chance at being Werner's wife if he divorced."

"But if he changed his mind," I said, "and there was to be no divorce, someone would feel betrayed."

"I'd like to talk with Sheriff Burroughs about Mr. Werner's murder." Zack headed the truck toward the county seat.

"Do you think she'd be willing to discuss the details with you?" Zack shrugged. "It's worth a try."

Sheriff Burroughs was in her office and invited us to take a seat across from her.

"I wanted to discuss some of the details of Mr. Werner's murder if you're willing to talk with me."

"The papers covered most of the crime scene and we're certain Mrs. Werner killed him. Now that she's dead, the case appears wrapped up. Most of it you already know."

Sheriff Burroughs sat back in her chair and reviewed the case.

"I don't understand why Mr. Werner was raking leaves in their yard when they hated each other so much," I said.

Anita tapped her pencil against the desktop. "Mrs. Werner told me they had resolved their differences and were getting back together, but that seemed unlikely given the number of people who had seen them arguing in public. In fact, they had been in the coffee shop a few weeks earlier. He had come into the shop first, then Mrs. Werner came in. A heated discussion occurred, and she stormed out yelling that she 'would kill him.' The evidence at the scene said she did, despite what she told us. Richard stepped in as her lawyer and then you know how that turned out."

"Actually we don't know. I don't think you believe Richard killed her. What reason would he have?"

"What I believe and what the evidence we have say are two different things."

"Back to Mr. Werner's murder," said Zack. "Isn't it possible that the two of them had reconciled?"

"If so, their months of public arguments would have to have been resolved within the past few weeks."

"Has Ellen Hawkins contacted you? Asked Zack.

"No. Why?"

"She told us she saw them the day before Mr. Werner's murder holding hands in the state park and that corroborates what Ms. Werner told you."

Anita leaned forward in her chair, her eyes sharp with interest.

"You know we found her shotgun, the shell casing in the woods and her fingerprints on the weapon. We've been through all this before." Anita sounded frustrated.

"Why would she shoot him, run into the house and call 9-1-1, leaving the shotgun behind? She had to know you'd find it. The woman wasn't stupid," I said.

"She wasn't thinking clearly. She'd just killed her husband. Or she thought she'd come back later and remove the evidence."

I flapped my hand in the air dismissively.

Anita's eyes widened in anger. "It was her shotgun."

"Everyone around this country village owns a gun of some sort, many of them are shotguns. You know you can't trace that shotgun shell and the gun to the murder." Zack met Anita's determined gaze with one of his own.

Anita stood abruptly and looked as if she was about to throw us out of her office. I leaned forward and opened my mouth to continue the argument. Zack laid a restraining hand on my shoulder. "Maybe we should go."

Someone knocked at the office door. One of Anita's officers swung it open. "There's a Ms. Hawkins on the phone. She says she needs to see you. She said it's important."

Anita stepped to the door. "Tell her to come into the department now. I'll see her as soon as she arrives."

Zack and I got up to leave. "Thanks for talking with us."

Anita escorted us out of her office and seemed to have gathered her composure "I'll be interested to hear what Ms. Hawkins has to say. I'm pleased you told her to get in touch."

"So I'm right then?" I said, not able to hide my glee that Anita sounded interested in what Ellen had to say.

"Oh, Maddie, you're usually right about these things, aren't you?" Anita didn't sound as happy to make that concession as I would have wanted her to be.

"We've made some progress in the case, haven't we?" I said as Zack and I headed back to the house.

"If we're right about the Werners' reconciling, we know that Mrs. Werner would have no reason to kill him."

"And we know Richard didn't kill Denise Werner. And I think the person responsible for setting Richard's house ablaze thought he was inside. I also think that person killed the Werners and worried Mrs. Werner told Richard something about her husband's murder, something that would clear her and would implicate someone else."

Ahead of us, blue lights flashed, and we heard sirens blaring.

"An ambulance. There's been an accident,"

A state trooper held up his hand to stop us. "You'll have to wait until the road is cleared."

I rolled down my window and stuck out my head to see what was happening. A car was off the road down the hill. The ambulance crew was carrying someone on a stretcher from the car. I could see the woman's face. "That looks like Ellen Hawkins."

CHAPTER 12

THE AMBULANCE RACED AWAY, LIGHTS AND sirens on full. Half an hour later, the road cleared, we headed toward the hospital.

"This is probably a useless trip. The hospital won't let us see her or give us any information," Zack said.

"I know a few people who work there. Maybe I can wheedle some information out of one of them."

There was no need for me to locate any of my sources because Anita's car was parked in the emergency room drive and she was inside talking with one of the emergency nurses. Zack and I held back until she finished.

"How is she?" I asked.

"Unconscious," said Anita. "I won't be able to talk with her now, but I'll wait until the doctor is available to see what he says."

"Ellen's car was off the side of the road down an embankment. It looked as if she swerved to miss something, maybe another car in her lane?" asked Zack.

"It's too early to tell until I get a report from the state police who are checking out the scene, but from what I saw, I'd say you're correct."

"She was on her way to talk with you."

"I assume so." Anita began to pace back and forth.

"But you know what she told us and Jane about the Werners."

"I need to hear it from her." Anita's voice was filled with frustration.

A man in a white medical coat approached Anita and drew her to one side. After a few minutes' conversation, Anita nodded then walked back to us.

"She's in no condition to talk now. The doctor told me to come back tomorrow."

"Do you think she's in any danger?" I asked.

Anita looked at me in surprise. "What are you saying?"

"What she saw means it was unlikely the Werners were divorcing and thus that Mrs. Werner had no reason to kill her husband. Maybe someone wanted to keep Ellen from telling what she saw between them." I gave Anita a few moments to let what I was suggesting sink in.

"So maybe someone intentionally ran her off the road." Anita clapped her hat on her head and started for the exit. "I need to find out exactly what happened in that accident. You may be right and if so, she may indeed be in danger."

I gave Zack a small smile. "If Denise didn't kill her husband, then who did?"

"You tell me, Maddie. You're the one with all the contacts in the village. Didn't you say something about a rumor that one or both of the Werners was having an affair?"

I grabbed Zack's arm and pulled him toward the door. "I think we need to get afternoon coffee, don't you?"

"Let's split up the work. I'll drop you at the coffee house. Your contacts might be more willing to chat with you if I'm not around."

I settled back in my seat. "You're probably right. I'm like them, a hound for gossip. You, on the other hand, are a private detective, looking for information. There's a difference. You make them nervous."

Zack laughed.

"What are you going to do while I embrace the rumor mill?"

"Richard said Manny Costa, Denise Werner's brother, beat him up before they were married, so there has to be some history on him although your search didn't turn up anything. I'm going to check the high school yearbooks and the newspaper archives in Stone Creek. The man has to have had some kind of background. If I have time, I'll check with the Werners' neighbors to see what they know about the couple. Maybe someone saw another car near the Werner's house the day he was killed."

"Haven't the authorities already done that?" I asked.

"It never hurts to cover old ground."

THE COFFEE HOUSE WAS STILL CROWDED although they were closing in a half hour. I grabbed a cup of tea, said hello to some folks I knew, circulated for a few minutes, then spied Sandy Longworth sitting at a table alone. She had a troubled look on her face.

"Mind if I join you?" I slid into the chair opposite hers before she could object.

She looked up at me and I could tell from her expression that she didn't really want me to join her. "Uh, sure."

"You look upset."

"Haven't you heard?"

"You mean about Ellen? Yes, I have, but I'm surprised you know already. Word certainly gets around fast in this village, doesn't it? How did you hear about her accident?"

Sandy nodded in the direction of a man wearing khaki pants and a blue knit shirt with an insignia on his sleeve.

"Matt Evans. He's on the ambulance squad. He was one of the EMTs at the scene. He just got off duty and came in for a quick coffee. He's had a difficult couple of weeks, you know."

I didn't, but I was interested to hear what Sandy clearly wanted to report. "Oh?"

The bleak look on her face disappeared. She licked her lips and leaned forward. I could smell coffee on her breath.

"Well, it's rumored that he and Denise Werner were 'close,' if you know what I mean."

I leaned in to encourage her to continue.

"I heard he and Denise were the reason the Werners separated in the first place."

"Oh, I heard it was because Mr. Werner was having an affair."

Sandy jerked back into her chair. "Well, I suppose he needed someone after Denise kicked him out."

"You don't happen to know who that someone was, do you?"

"Well, I suppose it doesn't hurt now to talk about it, but I think it was Ellen."

"Ellen confided in you?"

"Of course. We're good friends, have been since high school."

"But I heard Matt and Ellen were an item. You're telling me Ellen was in a relationship with both Matt Evans and Denise's husband."

Sandy giggled. "Not at the same time."

"So what was the time frame then?"

"Let's see now." Sandy raised her glance as if she was reviewing what she knew. "I don't really know, to be honest."

I wasn't certain Sandy was honest about anything. From what I knew about Ellen, it seemed out of character for her to be in a relationship with a married man. I raised my eyebrows at Sandy in a skeptical look.

She let forth a huff of disgust and prepared to leave the table "If you don't believe me, check."

"Sit down, Sandy. I didn't mean to insult you, but I find it hard to believe Ellen and Mr. Werner had a "thing." That seems like an unlikely pairing."

Sandy sat back down and the irritation on her face disappeared. "I know. I tried to tell her she was being foolish. She broke up with Matt to see Werner. Frankly, I can't see what either Denise or Ellen saw in the man."

"I didn't know him, so I can't say what the attraction might have been."

Sandy's lips curled in repugnance. "Maybe he was a daddy figure."

"Did she need a daddy figure? Was her relationship with her own father troubled?" I asked.

Sandy shrugged her shoulders.

"Well, you just never can tell what draws people to each other, can you?" I thought about what I had seen between Sandy and Darren, a man I also couldn't fathom as a catch for any woman regardless of her age. Maybe she saw Darren as a "daddy" figure.

"Ready to go?" A man approached our table.

Sandy stuffed her napkins into her coffee cup and leaned down to grab her purse. "My husband, Jonathan. Do you know Ms. Sparks?"

Jonathan, a tall man with wavy brown hair and a warm smile was, on the other hand, a real catch.

I reached out my hand and we shook.

"Everybody in this village knows Ms. Sparks," he said pleasantly. "She's a local author who writes mysteries and solves crimes in real life."

"You're manager of the local bank, aren't you?" I said. "Please, if you're not in a hurry, have a cup with us."

He pulled out a chair. Sandy gave him a sharp look as if she didn't want to remain. "I thought we should get home."

"Stay and keep me company while I finish my tea," I said.

Sandy tried to suppress a sigh, but I caught the outrush of breath.

"Speaking of rumors," I said, "I heard something about the bank wanting to close our branch. I hope that's not true."

Jonathan shifted around in his chair, and I knew I'd put him on the spot, but it was what I do and do well.

"I can't confirm that."

"Well, I hope it's not true. We don't need an empty building on our main street. Besides, the bank has served this community for over one hundred years. We depend on you." I sipped my coffee and then looked Jonathan in the eye. "Would you lose your job, or would they relocate you?"

Jonathan met my gaze with concern which he quickly turned into a quick laugh. "Now I understand why you help the authorities with their investigations. You're quite the interrogator, aren't you?"

"Curious, is the word I'd prefer."

Sandy stood and nodded to Jonathan. "My husband is a valued employee at the bank and has been for years. If this branch closes, rest assured that he'll be in for a promotion at another branch. C'mon, dear. We really should go now." She stalked off.

Jonathan stood to follow her, but before he did, the pleasant expression on his face was replaced by a grim one. "I understand your curiosity has put you in some dangerous situations, Ms. Sparks. I'd spend my time focusing on fiction if I were you." He again tried a smile, but it failed, and his lips settled into a tight line.

My, my, my, and he seemed like such a congenial man the times I ran into him at the bank and even at the beginning of our encounter today. Ah, well, if the bank were to close perhaps his hope for a better position wasn't assured. That would put him and Sandy on edge. Maybe I should look into the bank issue more closely, I thought, then reminded myself that I had more important lines of inquiry to pursue. I waved to Matt Evans, the EMT, who still stood on the other side of the coffee house and signaled him to join me.

"Ms. Sparks." Matt sank into the chair Sandy had vacated.

"The coffeehouse is so crowded that I thought you might like to sit down, especially after the afternoon you've had. Zack, my partner and I were right behind the ambulance after it left the accident. I understand you and Ellen were close friends."

His brown eyes were saddened and filled with unshed tears. "Yes. We were close. Once."

I reached out and touched his hand. "I'm so sorry. Was there someone else?"

"No. Why would you think that? It just didn't work out. That's all."

"Sandy said . . ."

"Sandy says lots of things and most of them aren't true. Sandy knew nothing about Ellen and my relationship. Nothing. I can't talk about this." Evans arose from his chair abruptly and headed out the door. Poking around too much, Maddie. However, I had learned a few things, information that I wanted to share with Zack this evening.

I finished my tea and headed out the door. As I crossed the street, the sign in the coffeehouse changed from open to closed. A cold, sharp wind rustled leaves and blew discarded papers from the street onto the sidewalk. I picked up the papers and stuffed them in my pocket to toss in the garbage when I got home. Another stronger gust of wind made me shiver and wish I had taken my gloves with me. Winter was on its way, and I despaired at the thought of the cold and snow it would bring. The storm we'd had last weekend was simply a harbinger of what was to come. Some people liked the freezing weather and the snow, but I was not one of them. I hurried down the sidewalk toward the edge of the village, turned the corner right before the bridge that led over the creek and looked forward to the warmth of a fire and being enveloped in Zack's embrace.

The house was dark when I got home, but not empty because Spike greeted me at the door, meowing in his usual demanding way for supper. I hung my coat on the hook inside the door and went to the kitchen to fetch Spike's dry food. He gave me an angry look and added a meow signaling his annoyance that I wasn't giving him his favorite, chicken. Speaking of food, I hadn't thought about dinner for Zack and me. I opened the refrigerator door and looked in. Ah, good. Leftover chicken soup. Spike dashed over and put his front paws on the lower shelf and surveyed the choices.

"Oh, all right. I'll pick some of the chicken out of the soup."

He gave me his best friendly meow in response.

I had finished dropping some choice pieces of chicken breast into his bowl when I heard a vehicle pull up. I rushed to the door and opened it to Zack.

"Getting really chilly, isn't it?" He reached out to give me a hug and pulled us cheek to cheek.

"Your face feels frozen. Take off your coat and let's sit in front of the fire."

"I guess it's up to you to defrost me then." He gave me one of his slow, sexy smiles.

"You bad boy," I said.

"I never understood that. Why do women like bad boys?"

"You're not really a bad boy, you know."

"I know, but take your friend Jane, for example. She knows Darren is a bad boy. From what you said, she and he were an item all the way back in high school. She can't believe he's really changed, can she?"

"I guess she thinks he's exciting, a challenge. I think women are flattered when a ladies man chooses them."

"What do you think?"

"I was married to a bad boy, and I think they're a lot of unnecessary trouble."

Zack chuckled at my response.

"I'll add a few logs and start a fire if you get me a scotch." Zack placed more wood on the fire to create a blaze that made the room look cheery while I poured liquor into glasses from the captain's glass decanter which sat on the carved liquor cabinet my grandfather had brought back from China.

"I smell something yummy," said Zack leaning forward to warm his hands.

"Leftover chicken soup."

Spike jumped into Zack's lap and began cleaning himself.

"Is there any chicken left in the soup?" asked Zack, knowing Spike would have wheedled pieces out of me.

"Some." I leaned over and kissed Zack's now warmer cheek. "So what did you find out today?"

"I used the school library and read over the year books from Richard's high school years there. I couldn't find anyone named

William Werner in the graduating classes around that time. Richard said Denise's brother Manny beat up her boyfriend from high school and I just assumed it was William Werner. Manny Costa seemed to like beating up his classmates. The high school principal during those years has retired and I didn't have the opportunity to talk with him, but he still lives in the area. I thought perhaps we could pay him a visit this evening. I talked once again with Richard's neighbors to see if they remembered anything from the night of the fire. When the sheriff's officers spoke with them, no one reported seeing anyone in the area nor any cars passing by."

"So a lot of leg work for nothing new?"

"Actually there was something. One of the women living a few houses down from Richard, an elderly lady who said she takes out her hearing aids at night, thought she might have heard a car in the next block. She said she could hear it because it sounded like it had a bad muffler and made a lot of noise."

"So now we're looking for a car with a bad muffler?"

"Or a snowmobile. What did you glean from your afternoon?"

I wriggled around on the couch, eager to tell Zack what Sandy told me about Ellen and Denise's husband. And also about Matt Evans, the EMT. "But Matt told me Sandy didn't know what she was talking about."

"Well, if Ellen left Matt to take up with Denise's husband, Matt might not want to admit that."

I thought about what Zack said. "Perhaps. This is a murder investigation. Maybe you might have more leverage talking to Matt."

"Tomorrow. Right now I'm starving and could use some of that soup."

We filled our bowls and took them over to the couch loathe to give up the warmth of the fire.

"Great vegetable soup," said Zack. Spike glared at him, and Zack glared back.

Zack called the retired principal after dinner to arrange for a meeting, but the phone went to voice mail, so Zack left a message for Principal Roscoe Pantella to call back.

THE PHONE RANG JUST AS WE were about ready to go upstairs to bed.

Sheriff Burroughs was on the line. "Ellen Hawkins regained consciousness an hour or so ago."

"Were you able to speak with her?"

"Yes, I was and that's what I'm calling you about. I know it's late, but would you be willing to come to the hospital to talk with her?"

I was puzzled at Anita's request. "Why do you need me there?"

Anita ignored my question. "If you can't come, I understand, but it would help."

"I'll be there in half an hour. Zack will want to drive me. Will his presence be a problem?"

"I don't think so. We can decide when you get here."

Zack and I grabbed our coats and would have taken off then had it not been for my searching for my gloves. "I'm not freezing my hands off again." I rummaged around in the back of the down-stairs closet and found them on the floor in the back.

"This is puzzling, isn't it? Why does Anita need you at the hos-pital?" said Zack as we sped down the highway. It was late enough that there were few other cars on the road, and we pulled up in front of the hospital in less than thirty minutes.

Anita met us at the door. "I want you to hear what Ellen has to say, but I particularly want her to repeat her story to me with you in the room."

"What . . .?" I began, but Anita shook her head.

Ellen was sitting up in bed when we entered her room. When she caught sight of me, her eyes widened.

"I know you talked to Ms. Sparks about what you saw in the park that day. Would you please repeat the story you told me a few minutes ago."

Ellen's face paled and took on a yellow caste in the hospital room's light. She tried to turn away from us.

"Ellen, you need to tell us the truth," said Anita.

Ellen turned back but wouldn't meet my gaze.

"It's okay, my dear," I said.

"But I realize now that what I saw may reflect badly on your son."

I smiled and approached her bed. "Tell us."

"I know now that I was mistaken. I wanted to help Richard if I could, so I said the man holding hands with Denise Werner was her husband."

Fear worked its way up my spine. I held my breath "Then who was it?"

"It was Richard."

CHAPTER 13

"I DON'T UNDERSTAND." IT WAS MORE THAN that. Why had Ellen told me it was Mr. Werner when she now said it was Richard with Denise? "Why have you changed your story?"

"I really didn't get a good look at the man. I just kind of assumed it had to be Denise's husband, but now that I think back on it, I know it couldn't have been him. This guy was tall, like Richard. Denise's husband wasn't much taller than her."

"I don't think you know what you saw," I said, spun on my heel and stalked out of the room. Zack rushed after me.

"She's has quite the bump on the head, Maddie. It's likely she's confused about what she saw." Zack put his arm around my shoulder and pulled me to him. "Let's wait for Anita and get her take on the situation."

Anita emerged from the room a few minutes later.

"Well?" I put my hands on my hips and stared into Anita's face.

"I'm going to let her take the night and sleep on it, then interview her again in the morning. Unfortunately, she's adamant she made a mistake, and the man was Richard. She even identified the guy as wearing an oatmeal-colored sweater like the one I've seen Richard wear."

"Let's say Richard and Denise were together in the park. What motive would he have for killing her?" asked Zack.

"I don't know, but I'm certainly going to ask Richard about what Ellen saw."

Not if I get to him first, I thought. Both Zack and Anita must have read my thoughts.

"I can't stop you from talking with your son, but I don't recommend it."

"That's because you're looking at this from the perspective of a law enforcement officer, not a mother."

At first I thought Anita was going to come at me with an angry reply, but her shoulders relaxed, and she stepped back. "Point taken. Do what you need to." She turned her back on us and left.

"Was I wrong to point out the obvious to her?" I asked Zack.

"I think she already understood the difference between the perspectives."

"Right. Let's go."

"Go where?"

"Oh, Zack. Don't be ridiculous. You know where. To Richard's condo." We walked down the hall to the elevator, and I punched the button.

"We'll be getting him out of bed."

I gave Zack a sour look. "I know that. What other choice do I have?"

"You could wait to see what Ellen says when Anita talks with her tomorrow."

"No."

"Exactly what is it you're so angry about? Is it that you think Ellen is lying or is there a chance Richard was with Denise?"

"It would be unprofessional and unethical for Richard to take her on as a client if they had a romantic relationship, and he knows that."

"So you're furious at Ellen because you think she's making trouble for Richard with her revised story."

I turned to face Zack. "Yes." I then faced the elevator. "Is this thing working?" I punched the down button several times.

"You're taking it out on the elevator."

"I know." I reached out to hit the button yet again, but Zack grabbed my hand and gently raised it to his lips. Something in his touch released a torrent of feelings I was holding inside, and I turned my face into his shoulder and began sobbing. Zack offered me his handkerchief.

The elevator dinged and the doors opened to a man with a cleaning cart. The horrified look on his face said he feared my tears were the result of bad medical news. "So sorry," he said, pushing his car out of the elevator and into the hallway.

I blew my nose into the hanky and wiped my face. "Not as sorry as he's going to be if he did what she said he did." I straightened my shoulders and walked briskly down the hall.

The man with cart continued to look shaken and confused at my words.

"She'll be fine," Zack told him and ran to catch up with me.

Back in the truck, Zack started the engine but didn't put the vehicle in gear. "You're sure you want to see Richard now?"

"Absolutely. I want the truth." I settled back in my seat, arms across my chest. "Go."

When we arrived at Richard's rented condo all the lights were out. I pounded on the door. "Richard. Get up. It's your mother and I need a word."

The entryway light went on and Richard opened the door. "Do you know what time it is?"

"Yes, I do." I pushed past him into his living room. "Make some coffee. We need to talk." I took off my coat and plopped down on his couch, running my hand over the lovely buttery leather. The man had good taste in furniture. I hoped his judgement in women was as well thought out.

The door to the room next to the one Richard had exited opened and Lily stood in the doorway. She saw the tense looks on our faces and said, "I'll give you privacy," and retreated to her bedroom.

"You tell him, Zack. I don't think I can talk."

Richard raised his eyebrows in surprise. "This must be serious. I've never known you to be at a loss for words."

Zack took a seat beside me on the couch and Richard sat in the chair across from us. Zack told him that he was seen flirting and holding hands with Denise Werner. Zack kept the story intentionally vague, leaving Richard to fill in the details.

Richard's gaze shifted back and forth from Zack and me, then he bowed his head and ran his hands through his hair. "You're right. We need coffee, and maybe something stronger."

"Coffee first, then the stronger stuff," said Zack.

Richard busied himself with the coffee. I hoped he wasn't concocting a story he thought I might find palatable while he ground coffee beans, got out cups, sugar and cream.

Once we each had our cups, Richard took a sip of his coffee and slid forward in his chair. He opened his mouth to speak, but I held up my hand. "The truth," I said.

"The truth could mean my license and land me in jail."

Did I really want to hear what he had to say? I asked for the truth, but was I prepared to hear it? Richard had always been the most ethical person, Although a defense attorney, a position sometimes linked to manipulating the law without regard to guilt or innocence, I'd never known Richard to step out of line. In fact, he had the reputation for being a letter of the law attorney. Would he sacrifice that for a fling and then cross a line in defending the woman with whom he'd been involved?

"Who saw us?" asked Richard.

"That's not important right now. Tell me about you and Denise," I said.

"Denise and I have been friends for many years, but it wasn't until she and her husband separated that we moved beyond friendship into something more."

I shot him a look of disbelief.

"No, no. Don't get all upset. We talked about becoming lovers, but Denise wanted to give her marriage another chance. I had no idea anyone had seen us together. We thought we were careful, but these things have a way of getting out, don't they? When she was brought in for questioning in the murder of her husband, she asked me to defend her. At first, I thought, why not? We hadn't gone beyond friendship, so I told her I'd present myself as her attorney for the present, but that I needed to think over the situation, and we'd discuss it the next day in my office. She knew I was wrestling with the issue, and she understood my hesitance. That night, however, she came to my house. For us to meet outside the office crossed the line, so I tried to send her away, but she was scared. She told me she was being watched and she also thought she knew who was responsible for her husband's death. I told her to go home and, if she saw anyone following her or watching her house, she should call the authorities."

I thought about Ellen and wondered if she had been following Denise all along and that was how she saw Denise and Richard together. Zack and I exchanged glances. We'd need to tell Anita what Richard said about Denise being followed and about her suspicion about who killed her husband.

Richard continued his story. "I'd calmed her down and she left. I mean, I thought she'd left. It was late so I went to bed. The next morning when I left for work I saw her car still parked outside my house. When I went over to check the car, I found her, stabbed.

"I've been struggling with this since that night. If I hadn't sent her away, would she still be alive? Had I sent her to her death?"

"If someone was following her, then they could have killed her at any time. Doing it in front of your house sounds like the killer was intentionally pointing the finger at you. If you had been in your house the night the fire was set, you'd be dead also. Denise's husband, Denise and you, Richard. None of that can be coincidence. All of you were targeted, but you got lucky," Zack said.

Richard let out a deep sigh. "I still feel I shouldn't have sent Denise away that night. I saved my reputation and drove her right into the arms of a killer."

"Don't let your guilt over something you had no control over lead you into despair. You did the right thing. How could you know a killer was after her?" I reached out and patted Richard on his knee. "Now finish doing what you know is right. Call Anita and tell her you want to talk with her. Do it before she lands on your doorstep."

Richard lifted his head and met my gaze. "It's not going to change anything, Mom."

"Yes, it will. It will help lift a burden from you, then you and the rest of us can move forward to find out who is behind these crimes. Meanwhile we all need some sleep."

I hugged Richard goodbye, and Zack and I drove home to a house that had grown cold. Spike greeted us at the door.

Zack looked at the ashes in the fireplace. "I could build a fire, but I think it would be better if we just went upstairs and got into bed and let our body heat . . ."

"I'm too tired."

"No. I meant our bodies would heat up the bed and we could fall asleep."

I patted his cheek. "I know what you meant, silly. But first I've got to feed Spike."

As if he could understand me—and I was sure he could—Spike looked up at me and meowed softly.

"Bring him upstairs after he eats. He can warm our feet." Zack trudged up the stairs. There was no need to encourage Spike to join us. He gobbled down some nurdles of food and rushed to the bedroom. He was at the foot of the bed and purring by the time Zack and I got settled.

EARLY THE NEXT MORNING AS ZACK and I were having our first cup of much-needed coffee, Zack's cell rang. It was Principal Pantella.

Zack put the phone on speaker.

"I got your message. I understand there's something pertinent to a case that you think I can help with."

"I'd like to meet in person if you wouldn't mind. How about in an hour and I'll bring my assistant with me if you don't mind." Zack winked at me.

Oh, goodie.

PRINCIPAL PANTELLA LIVED IN A RETIREMENT community in Stone Side. If I didn't have my own little cottage on the stream, I would have considered this complex. It featured small duplex homes with attached garages and individual lawns in front and back, each one large enough for flower beds or a small vegetable garden. Outdoor maintenance including lawn mowing was provided in a monthly fee. For older individuals who didn't want the bother of the upkeep of a house and property, it was ideal.

When we rang the bell, a dog barked inside. Mr. Pantella opened the door holding tight the collar of a golden retriever who seemed overjoyed to meet us with much tail wagging and what looked like a giant smile on his friendly face.

"Simon, settle down. These people are here to see me, not you. I hope you don't mind dogs," said Pantella, offering his hand to Zack and then to me. "Come in, come in. Just ignore Simon. He's harmless but enthusiastic about company."

Simon's gaze locked with mine and he panted a greeting then twirled around in a circle of delight.

Zack introduced himself and then me, and a broad grin spread over Pantell's face. "Ah, yes. The lady writer and crime fighter if the rumors are correct." Pantella was a short, broad man, balding with a fringe of white hair over his ears and a full beard and mustache. If he'd been wearing a red cap on his head, I would have thought I'd walked into Santa Claus's residence at the North Pole.

He must have guessed my thoughts because he drew us into his living room and introduced his wife, shorter than him, round and red-cheeked. "Margery plays Mrs. Claus at the mall during the holidays."

"I made coffee and there's some leftover coffeecake from this weekend. Let me know if you think it's too dry." She filled our cups and placed pieces of coffeecake on individual plates.

I bit into my cake and found it moist, sweet and cinnamony. "It's delicious," I said, trying not to spit crumbs from my mouth when I spoke.

"So," said Pantella, sliding back into his leather recliner rocker, "I guess you'd like to pick my brain about the time I was principal of the high school."

"Well, not the entire time, just when a few teens that may be significant in an investigation we're conducting attended."

"Does this have anything to do with the recent murders of the Werners?" he asked.

I nodded. "The authorities think my son might have been responsible for Mrs. Werner's murder. I know better, but . . ."

"Oh, I remember Richard well, Ms. Sparks. The reason you and I have never met is because he was never in trouble unlike some other kids his age who spent time each week in my office. I knew the boy had a brilliant future ahead of him. The others, maybe not so much."

"We're interested in the Werners, especially William Werner. I was told Denise dated him in high school and then married him some years later, but there's no William Werner in the year books when she and Richard were in high school."

"No, there wouldn't be because his name wasn't Werner back then. His father died when he was young, and his mother remarried a Joseph Werner when the boy was a senior in high school. He left for college and then returned here about a decade later, but he had taken up using 'Werner' as his last name. Don't ask me why he chose to change it then."

"No wonder I couldn't find him in the year books, or any report of his being beaten up by Denise's brother Manny," said Zack.

"Try the name 'Fromish.' That was what he used in those years. You'll get an eyeful of information on young Fromish. Always in some kind of mess. I should know because his group of hooligans got in trouble daily on the school grounds and in town. He and Manny ran with the same thuggish crowd. There were even some girls who were part of the group."

"Girls? Do you remember who?" I asked.

Principal Pantella hesitated, then spoke. "I didn't mind telling you about William Werner because he's deceased, but these other folks are still around the village and, as nearly as I can tell, have kept their noses out of trouble. Besides, not all of the group engaged in serious crimes, mostly a bit of shoplifting, graffiti and getting into skirmishes."

"We'll be discreet in using this information, but it might have bearing on our investigation," said Zack.

"Right then. Well, Denise Werner, she was Denise Costa back then, was one of the young women in that group along with Ellen Thompkins now Ellen Hawkins and Sandy, uh, I don't remember her last name, but she married the local bank manager, last name of Longworth. I don't think those girls ever initiated any of the trouble, but they followed Denise's brother who seemed to serve as group leader. Manny went to prison for robbery, but he's out now, I heard. The girls, now women, seem to be leading exemplary lives. I was sorry to hear about Denise and her husband."

"Richard dated all those girls at one time or another," I said, concern in my voice.

"Yes, but he had the good sense not to be drawn into their group."

"Do you know why Manny Costa beat up William Werner?" asked Zack.

"No reason. They probably disagreed over some petty thing. The boys liked to fight, each other, or any other boy who might get in their way."

"Bad boys," said Mrs. Pantella, using the term I'd applied to Darren.

"Yes, but those boys seem to have some kind of appeal to women, don't they?"

Mrs. Pantella smiled and nodded. Her husband and Zack gave us questioning looks.

"Oh, not you two men," I added quickly. Not now anyway, I thought to myself. Do all women go through a "bad boys" stage, I wondered. Jane seemed to be repeating hers with Darren and, from the expression on Mrs. Pantella's face, she'd had a run at one in her youth.

Zack rose and held out his hand. "You've been very helpful, Mr. Pantella. And the coffeecake wasn't the least bit dry," he said to Mrs. Pantella. "Maybe you can give Maddie your recipe."

I shot Zack a warning look. I was no baker. Maybe chocolate chip cookies every decade or so.

"I'm sure Ms. Sparks is far too busy with her writing and investigations to spend much time in the kitchen. I'll just send the rest of the cake home with you." Mrs. Pantella gave me a wink. She seemed a lively and clever sort, just the kind of woman Jane and I should include in our afternoon teas.

CHAPTER 14

I SAT IN THE PASSENGER'S SEAT OF Zack's truck, the wrapped-up coffeecake in my lap, reviewing what we had learned from Principal Pantella.

"I can hear the gears turning in your head, Maddie. What are you thinking?"

"I think everyone associated with these two murders and with the fire at Richard's house have held something back when we've talked with them. Except Mr. Pantella, of course."

"Does that include Richard?" he asked.

I sighed. "Unfortunately, yes."

"So we'll start over and reinterview them."

"They're all suspects as far as I'm concerned."

Zack cleared his throat. "Does that include, uh . . ."

"No! Richard isn't a murderer, but he's not telling me the entire truth."

"So, there's Manny Costa to talk with as well as Sandy and Ellen."

I nodded. "When I think back to my days in high school, I remember a group of three girls was never stable. There was always one girl who was left out. It varied who that girl was, but I'll bet Ellen was usually the one in that position. She was younger than Sandy and Denise, shy and . . ." I didn't finish my thought.

"And?" asked Zack.

"She was most in need of some leverage to give her status in the group."

"Like what?"

"I'm not sure, but I'd like to talk with her again."

"This history is interesting, but I'm not certain how all this is relevant to our investigation. It was years ago. They were teenagers then. Now they're adults."

"I don't think age has anything to do with it, but the need to belong does. All three members of that group remained in this area along with Manny Costa who only left while in prison and William Werner returned after a ten-year absence. Until the murders the group membership remained the same."

"With addition of Sandy's and Ellen's husbands."

"And perhaps we need to consider Ellen's recent romance, Matt Evans."

Zack glanced at me. "I suppose we should include Darren. You're certain he's in some kind of relationship with Sandy because of what you saw in the farm market the other day."

As much as I disliked the man, I couldn't see how Darren could be involved, and Sandy's husband along with Ellen's relationships also were recent. How could these men be involved?

Zack must have read my thoughts, as usual. "Let's leave everyone associated with Sandy, Ellen and Denise in the mix. If you're right about the dynamics in the group of the three women continuing to the present, I don't think we should eliminate the men who were involved or are still involved with them." Zack shot me a puzzled look. "But I'm not certain what those dynamics are.""

"That's what we need to find out. Richard is a useful resource for their teen years." My thoughts remained on Darren. What should I tell Jane? That the man she was gaga over was one of our murder suspects?

"You don't tell Jane anything, Maddie."

He did it again. Read my mind.

I playfully gave him a punch in the shoulder, tilting the package of cake on my lap precariously to one side.

"Hey. Careful. If you dump it on the floor, what will I have with my tea this afternoon?"

"Stale cookies from my pantry?"

"No sense in breaking the routine."

I could have punched him again, but decided he was right. I cooked most of our evening meals, but the stale cookie routine was getting stale, uh, old. Maybe I should try my hand at baking Mrs. Pantella's coffeecake. How hard could it be? I'd call her and invite her to have tea with Jane and me one day this week and ask her for her recipe.

"Let's stop at Richard's office and update him on what we found out from Mr. Pantella."

"All of which he already knows from experience," I said, once more cradling the coffeecake safely in my lap.

"True, but your take on the group of young women then and now is something I'll bet Richard never considered."

ZACK WAS WRONG. WHEN WE GOT to Richard's office and sat down with him, Franklin and Lily to tell them what we'd discovered, Richard looked pensive for a few moments after he listened to Principal Pantella's stories of Richard's teenage years and my assessment of the group now grown older. Not only did Richard add to what we had discovered from Pantella, but he also seemed to understand how the group functioned.

"Huh. The good old days. Mom's right. Ellen tried so hard to be part of the group, but so did Denise. The leader was Sandy. She was popular and with all that long blonde hair and her deep blue eyes she was the dating target for every male in the school."

"Including you, Richard, "I added.

"Yep, but I was a fast learner."

"Fill in the blanks for us," said Zack.

Richard leaned back in his office chair and put his arms behind his head, intertwining his fingers. "In a way it was an unusual group, made up of both girls and boys. The members allowed Ellen to tag along. She was three years younger than the rest of them."

"She had a crush on you," I said.

"Did she? I didn't know that."

"She told me the other day in the coffeeshop."

"I guess I never noticed. I rather liked Denise and tried to keep her away from the shenanigans including some illegal stuff like drag racing and shop lifting. She dated some guy called Frobish. I wonder what happened to him?"

"He disappeared from here for about ten years then returned as William Werner. The principal filled me in when I couldn't find William Werner in the yearbooks. She didn't tell you that?"

"No. Why would she?" Richard looked uncomfortable, rocked his chair forward and dropped his gaze.

"She had plenty of opportunity when the two of you began seeing each other while she and her husband were separated."

"We didn't talk about her marriage before someone killed her husband and we had no time after he was found dead."

"Not even while you two were strolling in the park, laughing and hugging?" I snapped at him.

"What are you talking about, Mom?"

"You know. Someone saw you in the state park, taking a friendly hike and you confirmed the two of you were seeing each other."

"But not in the park. Denise and I never did that. We met several times, yes, but at restaurants north of here. She didn't want anyone to see us together because she and her husband were in divorce proceedings, and she was worried his lawyer would make more of our relationship than simply friendship. Then she decided we should go no further in our relationship because she wanted to repair her marriage."

Zack and I looked at one another.

"Someone saw the two of you together in the state park right before her husband was killed," Zack said.

"The last time I saw Denise before the authorities took her in for questioning and the night she came to my house was weeks prior to those events. Who told you we were at the state park?"

"Ellen told the sheriff that and a good thing, too, because you finally admitted the two of you were having a relationship. Otherwise we wouldn't have known, and the authorities might have found out from Ellen. The DA would have had a grand time with that information."

Franklin, silent throughout this discussion, leaned forward and gazed at Richard with a piercing stare. "You've told the sheriff about your meetings with Denise prior to her husband's murder, haven't you?"

"Not yet." Richard's usual confident manner had vanished, and he looked world weary. "I haven't had the time."

"I suggest we do that now. Meantime, Zack and Maddie should follow up with Ellen."

"She's lying," said Richard. "I don't understand why she would do that."

"I need to know when and where you and Denise met. Give that information to Zack and Maddie to check. I told you, Richard, this is a story we need to get ahead of."

"There's something odd about Ellen's story. She told Jane and then me that she saw Denise at the park with her husband, and then when the sheriff questioned her after the car accident, she said Densie was with Richard. I think we need to find out what the sheriff knows about the accident. Initially it looked as if someone accidently ran her off the road. Maybe the sheriff has information about who it was or at least about the kind of car or if anyone saw the accident and can provide more details. Maybe it was intentional." I worried that someone ran Ellen off the road to prevent her from talking to the sheriff. Did Ellen tell someone she was on her way to the sheriff to speak about what she saw? It could have been a warning to keep her mouth shut or to change her story. Lily took all this in without saying a word. I wondered what her take on Richard's high school history and his more recent contact with Denise was. She kept glancing at me as we sat in Richard's office, and I was certain she had something to tell me.

I was about to draw her to one side for a private conversation when my cellphone twittered at me. I held up my finger to signal her to wait while I took the incoming call.

"Ms. Sparks? Hi. It's Ellen."

"Ellen. How are you?"

"I'm fine, just fine." She didn't sound fine to me. Her voice was breathy and so low I could barely hear her."

"Can you speak up, dear?"

"I need to explain to you. I'm leaving the hospital. Are you home? Can I come by?"

"Well, I'm on my way home now. I'll be there is a few minutes."

"See you then." She disconnected.

I turned to Zack. "That was Ellen. She wants to meet me at home in a few minutes. I'm surprised the hospital is releasing her so soon. She sounded panicky."

"Let's hurry then." Zack grabbed my arm, and we headed out of Richard's office.

"Oh. Hold on. I think Lily wants to speak to me." I turned back to Lily, but she wasn't there.

"I think I heard Richard call her back into his office," Zack said.

I shrugged my shoulders. "I think she had something she wanted to say to me. Oh, well. I'll contact her later."

It took less than fifteen minutes for us to drive from Richard's office to my house.

I hopped out of the truck and dashed for the door. "I'll put on the pot for tea." I tossed my coat on the sofa and headed into the kitchen to fill the kettle with water. "Oh, no!"

"What happened?" Zack asked.

"The coffeecake. I left it in the truck."

"Never mind. I'm starving. I'll make tuna salad."

While Zack busied himself putting together the tuna for

sandwiches, Spike, hearing the siren tuna call, bounced down the stairs to sit in front of his bowl.

"Don't forget to leave the mayo off Spike's portion." I poured the hot water into the pot to let the tea steep and sat on the couch to wait for Ellen. A half hour later she still hadn't arrived.

"She should be here by now. I assume she either called a taxi to pick her up or a friend is giving her a ride. Her car isn't drivable, and I wouldn't think she'd be up to arranging for a rental."

"I'm surprised the hospital released her. She looked in pretty bad shape when we saw her. She'd been unconscious for hours, so she must have had a concussion from the accident." Zack looked longingly at the plate of sandwiches he'd made.

"Go ahead and eat one. I can't have you drooling all over them."

"That's only fair. I already gave Spike his share of tuna." Zack bit into a sandwich and poured himself a cup of tea.

I went to my front window and looked out, then sat back on the couch and stared at the clock on the wall. "Unless . . ."

"Unless what?" asked Zack.

"Maybe she just left the hospital. Maybe they didn't release her. I can call but I don't think they'll tell me if she's still a patient there. I'm not a relative."

"The sheriff would know," aid Zack. "I'll call her."

Zack and I heard the ring as if it was nearby.

"What the . . .?" I ran to the front door and swung it open. Anita stood on my doorstep.

She looked a combination of annoyed, concerned and frazzled. "May I come in?"

"Sure. Did Richard get in touch with you?" I asked, gesturing her into the room.

"He called me not long ago and admitted he and Denise had been seeing each other before her husband's death. I've asked him and his lawyer to come to my office this afternoon. His story confirms what Ellen told me."

"It confirms one of her stories," I said.

"Yes and that concerns me, so I went to the hospital to talk with her again."

"But she wasn't there," Zack said.

"No, but how do you know that? I'm looking for her."

"C'mon in and we'll talk. Have you had lunch yet? I can give you tea and a sandwich. Zack makes a mean white albacore tuna sandwich. It's Spike approved."

Anita paused for a second, undecided, then her shoulders slumped, and she sighed. "I could use the energy." She tossed her hat on the table next to the door.

"Here. Take a seat." I pointed to the overstuffed chair near the couch. "You look as if you need a break. I'll bring you a sandwich and some tea."

Anita dropped into a chair. "You wouldn't know where she might be, would you?"

Zack and I exchanged knowing looks.

"I don't know where she might be, but I'm not going to lie to you. She called me from the hospital not an hour ago and asked to meet me here at the house. She should be here by now, but she hasn't shown up. We were surprised the hospital released her so soon."

"They didn't. She left on her own, sneaked out. I have no idea who might have given her a ride or where she's gone. I wonder what she wanted to meet with you about."

"I'm not certain but I suspect it had to be about her story. Which one of them was true? She certainly did not see Richard with Denise in the park although he admitted to us that he and Denise met several times. He and Franklin will fill you in when you see them at your office."

"I'm pleased he's finally being truthful about his relationship with Denise, but I'm puzzled at Ellen's change in her story about Denise and the man in the park. And I'm worried especially now that she's disappeared. Ellen's car crash might not have been an accident. It appears that someone crossed the center lane from the other direction and headed straight toward her. The driver of a car some distance behind her said the car in her lane swerved at the last minute and Ellen veered off the road and into the ditch to avoid it. The driver of the car who saw the accident said it looked as if the car was playing 'chicken' with her."

"And the car didn't stop. Did the driver behind Ellen get a look at the driver or the make of the car or a plate number?" Zack asked.

Anita shook her head, took a bite of her sandwich, chewed and then said, "Nope. The guy who saw what happened was too rattled to give us anything except to say the car was white or some light color. Not much help. These hit and runs are difficult especially since the car crossing the center lane didn't contact Ellen's car so there would be no damage to it. We can only hope that the individual rethinks their actions and decides to turn themselves in."

"That's not likely if the driver meant to run Ellen off the road," said Zack.

Anita finished her sandwich and took a final sip of her tea. "Well, thanks for the pick-me-up. I needed it." She grabbed her hat and started to leave but hesitated before she opened the door. "Say, what is it with that female looks-like-a-fed in Richard's office. And she's packing, too."

"Richard doesn't want whoever torched his house to make another attempt on his life. Actually, his lawyer, Zack and I encouraged him to hire someone for protection."

"So she's with him twenty-four seven?"

"Yes. She's got a permit to carry and she's ex law enforcement," Zack said.

"She's a good-looking woman," Anita said, her voice tinged with what I thought was jealousy. "Name?"

"Lily Brandeis." I opened the door for Anita.

My cell chirped. I checked the caller ID. "Oops. Got to take this."

My caller was Jane, and I was relieved to use her call as an excuse to get out of answering any more questions about Lily. I waved goodbye to Anita as she got into her car, then cheerfully answered, "Hi, Jane. What's new?"

"Oh, you'll never guess. I'm so happy. I know I'm being impulsive, but Darren asked me to marry him, and I said yes."

Oh yet another ick for Jane's soon-to-be, and this was a double ick.

CHAPTER 15

Jane continued to chat on about her impending marriage. My shock at her announcement interfered with my hearing all her details, told in an excited voice, of course. I managed a reply, but I doubted my less than sincere congratulations penetrated her joy. Of course she was happy, I told myself. For once, I controlled my mouth and simply murmured uhms and yeses as she enthusiastically continued to share her good news.

"And, of course, Maddie, I'll want you to be my matron of honor, and do you think Zack would give me away?"

I wanted to tell her Zack would be happier giving the bridegroom away to anyone who would have him. "I'll ask him. He's here now." I held my hand over the phone and told Zack what was happening. He raised both eyebrows in surprise.

"So what did he say?" asked Jane.

"He's more than happy to do it. And when is the ceremony?"

"Oh, soon. Maybe next week or the week after. There's so much to do and I want your help, Maddie. What do you think about having the wedding at the coffee shop in the room adjacent to the main room? Oh, I'm all in a flutter. You're the first person I've told. Gotta run now, but we'll get together soon to talk about the details. And shopping for a dress, of course. You'll help me pick out something. Bye."

Before I could say goodbye, she disconnected.

I plopped onto the couch. "What is she thinking?"

Zack shook his head. "Obviously, she's like a teenager. Her hormones are doing the thinking for her."

"And at our age there are darn few of those, so any thought has to be coming in drips and drabbles."

My cell rang again. And again it was Jane.

"I just got the best idea. How about we make it a double ceremony with you and Zack?"

I gasped.

"What did you say?"

"I'm without words."

"I knew you'd like it. Talk to you soon. Bye."

I turned off my phone. I didn't want to talk to Jane again. I needed time to process everything, especially her last suggestion.

"Jane has totally lost her senses. She suggested we make it a double ceremony, the four of us."

I expected Zack's response to a frown, but instead his face lit up. "What do you think, Maddie?"

"I think you and Jane should have adjoining rooms in a mental hospital."

"That's no way to respond to a marriage proposal."

"You didn't propose."

"Well, then. How about it? Will you marry me?"

"No. Not now. And especially not in a ceremony where the other man is a bum marrying my best friend. That's just bad karma."

He looked disappointed. "So, you will marry me sometime is what you're saying?"

Oh, dear. The man was serious, and I didn't want to hurt his feelings, but I'd never considered getting married again, not after the disastrous marriage with my ex-husband Dan. I loved Zack more than I'd ever loved anyone, but I needed time. Unfortunately, we had so little of that at our ages. Should I say yes?

"We've only known each other for less than six months."

"Jane's only known Darren less than six days and she knows how she feels."

"I know how I feel, too, Zack. That's not the issue here. I just never thought I'd marry again especially at my age."

"Don't you see, Maddie? Our meeting each other is the beginning of a new life for both of us. I've become a private investigator and you're writing a whole new series of romance novels. Let's throw marriage into the mix."

I looked at him aghast. "I'm not really the romantic type, but I don't think 'throwing marriage into the mix' is a good springboard for a relationship."

The excited look on his face faded. "Bad choice of words, I guess."

I decided to change the subject. "Let's focus on Richard's dilemma. We have plenty of time to think about the other." Maybe saying "the other" to refer to our relationship was as bad as what Zack had said. Zack gave me a sharp look. "I mean, we'll talk more about us and our future when we don't have other things interfering. We should dedicate time to our relationship, not wedge it into other considerations. Or what Jane and Darren are doing. I think a wedding needs more time to plan than the week or two Jane wants to dedicate to it."

My words seems to mollify Zack. He grabbed me around the waist, picked me up and swung me in a circle. "You're right, as usual. We can discuss all of this in a week or so."

I was thinking we could put off any discussion of marriage for longer than that, maybe months or years, but I didn't share my thoughts with him. I mentally patted myself on the back for curbing my tongue again. I was getting better at this, I thought.

"Back to Ellen. Was her car crash an accident or was it to kill her or warn her off before she could tell the authorities something important to Richard's case? What could she know?" I asked.

"She seemed to want to talk to you, Maddie. But again, as with her appointment with the sheriff, she failed to show up. Did she rethink the meeting, or did someone waylay her so she couldn't meet with you?

"I'll give her a call at home."

There was no answer, so Zack and I decided to drive to her house. We'd been there before, but the visit was short, only to ask her about what she saw at the state park. She lived in a neighborhood south and west of town, not so far from Leon's parents' home. Like their place, Ellen's house was off the main highway, on a county road that climbed a ridge and led into a development of relatively new homes. Ellen and her husband had bought a modest house when they first married. It was a three-bedroom raised ranch, but a fire several years after they moved there burned it to the ground. They had neglected to have the creosote cleaned from the chimney. They thought they caught the blaze early and called the fire department who came and extinguished it. However the fire reignited early in the morning and Ellen and her husband fled from the house with nothing, no clothes, furniture or even pictures. They felt lucky to be alive. Lawsuits, insurance claims and other issues made the rebuilding of the structure slow, but after three years, the new house was finished. This time it was not so modest. The house should have marked a restart for the young couple, but it did not. Just one year after moving in, they divorced. Ellen got the house, and her husband left the area.

This time when we pulled up to the house, I took a good look at it.

"I hadn't noticed before, but it's huge, isn't it, like a mega mansion. Maybe Ellen and her husband hoped to fill it with children and then they divorced. I can't believe she's living here alone. I'd sell the place, wouldn't you?" I unbuckled my seat belt and got out of the truck. I passed the attached three-car garage and peaked in through the window. Two bays were empty, but the third held a car and what a car it was. Of course, Ellen's vehicle had been totaled in the crash, so I didn't expect it to be here. But wow! I motioned Zack over. "Take a look at this."

He peered in also. "That's a new Mercedes. Where did Ellen get the money for that?"

"It's a convertible, so she wouldn't be likely to drive it much in the winter."

Zack and I continued down the walk to the front portico, and I rang the bell. It sounded hollowly through the house. We waited and I punched it again. "I don't think anyone is home."

"Let's go," said Zack.

"No. Let's snoop." I started around the side of the house peering in through the windows.

Zack followed. "We're trespassing. We have no right to be here."

"Yes we do. We're checking on a sick friend who may be too ill to summon help." I continued to the back patio and looked through the glassed-in hot tub area. "No one's here. Unless . . ."

"What?"

"I'd love to get in there to see the hot tub. The cover's on so it's impossible to determine if there might be . . ." I didn't finish my thought but bent over searching for a rock.

"You mean like a body in there?" asked Zack in a skeptical voice.

"Why am I not surprised to find the two of you here?"

I jumped at the voice and turned to find Anita behind us.

"What are you doing here?" I asked.

"I'm the sheriff, remember, so I have the right to look for a person of interest in these murder investigations. I assume the two of you are just snooping. Again. As usual?"

I put one hand on my hip and hid the other with the rock in it behind me and pierced her with a stern stare. "We were checking to make certain Ellen made it home from the hospital okay."

"We were snooping, like you said," Zack admitted.

"She could be drowned in that hot tub," I said.

"So you thought you'd break the glass with that rock you're hiding behind your back," said Anita.

I gave her a weak smile and nodded.

"I can appreciate your concern, Maddie, but that's my job, not yours. Her keys were in the items she forgot at the hospital." Anita held up a key ring and jangled it.

"If that's her only key, she couldn't have gotten in," I said.

"I'm certain there's another key hidden someplace. I doubted Ellen came back here when she skipped out of the hospital, but I needed to have a look." Anita used the key in the lock on the patio door. "You stay out here. I'll take a look around and be right back."

I ignored Anita and followed her into the house. Zack followed me.

We watched Anita enter the glassed-in hot tub enclosure and lift the lid on the hot tub. I held my breath. Anita caught my eye and shook her head, then dropped the lid.

"Thank goodness." I grabbed Zack's hand in relief.

"Stay here," Anita said.

When she started upstairs, I grabbed Zack's arm. "C'mon."

"Anita said to stay here."

"I know, but she's only one person. She could use the help."

Zack shook his head and followed me into the house. We retraced Anita's walk-through.

"Did you see her look in the bathroom off the hot tub area?" I asked Zack.

I opened the door to the bathroom located to the right of the hot tub and stuck my head in. Two towels lay on the bathroom floor. I bent over and picked one up. Still damp. Someone had been here recently.

"You two don't follow directions well, do you? I thought I told the two of you to stay put." Anita leaned against the doorway to the room.

"Gah!" I jumped at the sound of her voice. "You've got to stop sneaking up on people."

"And you've got to stop poking around where you shouldn't," she replied. "And, yes. I saw the wet towels."

"I can't believe Ellen left the hospital to come here for a soak in her hot tub, then left," I said.

"Two towels. If she did come here, someone was with her." Anita looked around the small bathroom and opened the medicine cabinet. "Nothing of interest here. Hmmmm."

All three of us gazed at the two wet towels on the floor.

"Someone has been using the hot tub. Two towels. Not Goldilocks and one of the bears and probably not Ellen. I'll be right back." Zack left the bathroom and in a few minutes returned with something in his hand. "You were right, Anita. There was a house key under one of those fake rocks out front. Why do people think anyone would mistake that plastic for a real stone?"

"When Ellen called me, she sounded frightened, and she said she wanted to explain something to me. I think she's hiding out from whoever tried to run her off the road. She knows something about the fire and the murders."

"You're convinced Richard was never in the park with Denise, right?" Anita asked.

"He and Franklin talked to you today. You know Richard saw her and a relationship was developing, but they never met in the park. That story was a lie. Denise told Richard she and her husband were trying to repair their relationship."

Anita gazed out over the back yard of the house into the woods beyond. "I believe Richard. What I can't figure out is why Ellen told two different stories and if she didn't see Richard and Denise together, then who did she see and why is that so important for Ellen to hide?"

"It could be her original story was correct. Denise and her husband were in the park, and they were no longer getting a divorce. It makes sense. When he was killed, he was in the yard raking leaves, not what one would expect of an angry husband," I said.

"None of this makes sense," said Anita, "but it's my job to make it make sense."

"Doesn't Sandy live in this same development?" I asked.

"Do you think she knows what's going on with Ellen?" asked Anita.

"They were close friends in high school and Richard says they remained close. It's worth talking to her."

"I will." Anita hesitated. "I'll follow you to your car out front."

"Can we come along to Sandy's, assuming that's where you're going now?" I asked in my best I'm trying to be helpful manner.

I thought she was going to say no, but she rolled her eyes and said, "You might as well. You'll just pester the woman after I've been there with the same questions I'm going to ask. C'mon then."

"We'll follow you. We don't know Sandy's address," Zack said.

We got lucky. Sandy answered the door, toweling her hair dry. "I just got out of the shower after my run. I was about to have coffee. Join me?"

All three of us shook our heads.

"I have a few questions about Ellen," said Anita.

"Sure. C'mon in and take a seat." Sandy was trying to be friendly, but her expression held a note of reserve.

"You and Ellen have always been close, so we thought you might know where she is."

Sandy looked surprised. "I thought she was still in the hospital. Has she been released?"

"No, but she's gone. Signed herself out. We were just at her house but didn't find anyone at home. I have her key, so I went in to take a look around. It appears someone was there and used her hot tub recently."

Sandy's surprised look changed to one of concern and then her gaze shifted around the room as if she was nervous.

"Is there something wrong?" asked Anita.

"I'm worried about her, that's all."

"She didn't call you to ask for a ride, did she?" asked Anita.

"No. I just told you. I'm back from my daily run."

"Did you check your voice mail?" I asked. "Maybe she left a message."

"Look. We are friends, but we're not really that close. Not now, anyway."

"Why is that?" I asked.

Sandy stopped drying her hair and slung the towel onto the living room couch. "As I told you the other day in the coffeehouse. Ellen dumped poor Matt to start an affair with Denise's husband."

"We have reason to believe that Denise and her husband were getting back together. That would have ended Ellen's relationship with him. How hurt or angry would that have made her, do you think?" asked Anita.

"I'm sure I don't know anything about that." Sandy moved toward the door, signaling that she wanted us gone.

"Would Matt know anything about this?" I asked.

"Ask him. Now, if you don't mind, my husband will be home soon. And I need to get dinner started."

As we walked back to our cars, I turned to look at the house. "Nice home, spacious, well-furnished, but nothing to compare to Ellen's place."

"So?" said Anita.

"Just an observation. Are you on your way to talk with Matt now?"

"I guess I should be. If I don't go now, you'll beat me to it."

"So you're saying we can't come with you?"

"Right." Anita opened the door to get into her car.

"We could follow you, you know," I yelled at her before she could close the door.

"Isn't it past time for your afternoon tea?" She gave me a smug smile and drove off.

"Do you think I annoyed her? I asked Zack.

"Let's give it a rest and do what she said." He hustled me into the truck. "Teatime."

"I fancy a hot chocolate. Let's stop at the coffeehouse."

"Someone there you want to interrogate?" asked Zack with a smile on his face.

"I understand Sandy's husband likes to stop by after he leaves the bank and goes home." I returned Zack's smile and cocked my eyebrow.

CHAPTER 16

I N THE AFTERNOONS, THE COFFEEHOUSE WAS often crowded and that was the case today. I noticed there were no tables free as Zack and I plowed through the crowd to the counter. While he placed our orders, I perused the crowd of people seated as well as those standing throughout the room. I didn't spot Jonathan Longworth, but I did see Matt Evans standing toward the back of the room by himself. He looked worn down as if he'd had an arduous day.

I caught Zack's attention and nodded my head toward Matt to signal Zack where I was heading.

"You look purely tuckered out," I said as I approached Matt. "Busy day at work?" Matt worked as a mechanic in a garage outside town. His work as an EMT was volunteer work.

"Thanks for asking, Mrs. Sharps. I spent most of the afternoon on a transmission."

"Is this your first break then?"

"No. My boss gave me an hour for a late lunch, but I had errands to run so I never got a chance to eat the lunch I packed." He held up a partially eaten sandwich. "You'll excuse me for chowing down, won't you?"

"Of course. What errands could be more important than eating your lunch?"

About to take another bite of his food, Matt paused and looked worried at my question. "I, uh, had some personal business to address."

I was about to ask him if it involved picking up a friend who was leaving the hospital, but a tap on my shoulder drew my attention away.

"Here's your drink, Maddie." Zack held out the hot chocolate I had him order for me.

When I turned back to continue my conversation with Matt, he excused himself saying he had seen someone he needed to talk with.

"Shoot," I said to Zack, "I was just getting to the good part."

"From the look on poor Matt's face, it looked as if you were about to launch an inquisition."

I nodded and lifted the cup to my lips to take a sip. The hot chocolate was hot, hot, hot, and the melting marshmallows stuck to my upper lip burning it. "Oh, that hurts."

Zack reached over and wiped away the sticky white mess with his fingers. I lifted my gaze to his, about to thank him when I caught sight of someone entering the door, someone I was keen to speak with—Jonathan Longworth. I shoved my cup at Zack. "Hold this for me, will you? I need a minute." In the time it took to hand my cup to Zack and head across the room to buttonhole Jonathan, he caught my eye and turned back toward the entrance. Had it not been for a couple entering after him who blocked his exit, He would have been out the door, and I would have been out of luck.

"Jonathan," I said, "we were just at your house talking with Sandy. Ellen is missing. We thought perhaps Sandy knew where she was. You haven't run into her, have you? We're worried about her since she signed herself out of the hospital."

"Why would I have seen her?"

"No, reason. I thought perhaps she might have stopped by to do some banking business."

"I haven't seen her." He looked offended at my questioning of him. "Now, if you'll excuse me, I need to talk to someone." He started across the room and was lost in the crowd of people. I was too short to spot him even though I stood on my tiptoes.

Everyone seemed to have someone other than me they needed to talk to. I continued to scan the crowd to see who else was here.

Zack joined me and handed my drink back to me. "It should be cooler by now."

"Later," I said, hurrying across the room to waylay two men I spotted entering the side room. By the time I got in there, Jonathan Longworth and Darren, Jane's intended, were having words, angry words, but when they saw me, they stopped talking. "Trouble, gentlemen?"

"Ah, there she is. My favorite lady private detective. So did Jane ask you if you and Zack would be joining us in our nuptials? Oh, I see you haven't gotten yourself anything to drink yet. Let me buy you a coffee." Darren was cheery and his face wreathed in smiles. He took my arm and led me over to the couch. "Wait here, my dear, and I'll be right back with your drink. What will it be, coffee or tea? How silly of me. It has to be tea, doesn't it." Off he went, a goofy smile on his face.

Darren's exuberant chatter distracted me, and when I tried to let him know I already had a drink, Jonathan slid past me and almost ran out of the door to the street. Well, this was frustrating. Cornering people in their homes or at the coffee shop was a strategy getting me, rather us, nowhere.

Zack came into the room. "I think this hot chocolate is cold by now. What are you up to, Maddie?"

"No one wants to talk to me."

"I wonder why."

"Don't be snide. Let's go."

"But . . ."

"Darren's coming back in a minute, and I definitely don't want to talk to him."

"Why not? I just chatted a moment with Matt. Did you know that he and Darren work at the same garage?"

"Do they? How interesting."

We waited for Darren to return with my tea, but after several minutes, I sent Zack to find him.

"He's gone," Zack said on his return.

"And my hot chocolate is too cold to drink. I give up. Everyone is avoiding me. Let's go home and I'll put a pot on."

We stepped outside to gently falling snow. Zack took my arm, and we headed down the steps and outside to the truck which Zack had parked across the street. Down the main street almost to the village limits stood an old building. It had been a storage barn on a nearby farm, but the farmer sold it, and it was moved to its present location and now operated as a bar. I'd never been inside, and I suspect most women entered it only when they were looking for wandering husbands. It wasn't the kind of place one went to have a cocktail. I don't even know if they knew how to make anything vaguely resembling a cocktail. From what I had heard, it was mostly draft or bottle beer and a chaser of whiskey.

As we were about to get into Zack's truck, I spied the old beater car Darren had bought while his motorcycle was in winter storage in Jane's garage. If Darren had left the coffeehouse, why was his car still parked half a block away?

"Instead of going home, let's have a drink."

"What?" Zack said in surprise. "We'd have to drive to Stone Side and I'm uncertain what the weather is going to do."

"We can get a drink here. At the Drop Dead Inn."

Zack looked confused for a moment, then said, "You mean the Drop In, don't you? And why would you want to go in that place?"

"I've never been inside. It might be interesting."

Zack skewered me with one of his penetrating looks. "What's up, Maddie?"

"Darren offered to buy me a drink but never got around to it. I thought I'd take him up on his offer. I'll bet he's in the Drop In right now. Let's go."

Zack shook his head and sighed, then started the truck and made a U-turn to head toward the bar. "I'm going to regret this, I know," he muttered under his breath.

We drove the block and a half to the bar, parked and headed in. When we opened the door, the patrons, all men, seated on mismatched stools at the bar, turned to look at us. All conversation stopped. Sure enough, Darren was one of them.

"I thought I'd take you up on your offer of a drink." I walked over to him, unwound my scarf from my neck and pulled off my gloves.

"Sure," Darren said in an uncertain voice. "What will it be? And don't get too fancy. This is a good old boys place, you know. No cosmos or slow gin fizzes or frozen daiquiris here."

The guy seated on the stool next to Darren vacated the seat and offered it to me. Darren signaled Zack to take his stool.

"I'll stand," said Zack.

I took one look at the stool and wondered if I wanted to sit. The vinyl cover on it was cracked and the stuffing that had padded it was half gone. And the stool was a bit high for me, but with Zack's help I mounted the thing and settled in.

"So?" said Darren.

"I'll have a shot of whiskey."

"Call?" said the bartender, a woman with brassy blonde hair and a black knit top cut low enough to reveal substantial cleavage.

"Oh, hi, Evelyn. I didn't know you worked here."

Evelyn was a member of the historical society and had been a volunteer at the library.

"I just finished the last book in your series, Maddie. When's the next coming out?"

"I've got a new series I'm working on. Romance."

Evelyn smiled. "We can all use a bit of that." She reached for a bottle of Jameson, but I shook my head.

"The bar stuff will do."

Heads turned toward me in looks of astonishment. Evelyn poured my shot, I picked it up and downed it in one gulp. Man that seared on the way down, but I didn't flinch.

Zack was the only fella in the bar who wasn't surprised. Well, maybe a little surprised, but he covered it well.

Evelyn didn't bat an eye. "Another?" she asked, the bottle poised over my shot glass.

"Sure."

All eyes in the bar focused on me. The silence was so overwhelming you could hear a mouse burp. She poured my shot, I lifted it to my lips and gulped it down. My body felt this one more strongly than the first, but I'd be durned if I'd let the boys in the bar think I was a wimp. I held the shiver that ran up and down my spine in, smiled and made an "ah" sound of satisfaction.

The patrons turned their attention back to their conversations, tall tales and laughter.

"How about you?" Evelyn asked of Zack.

"I'll have a draft."

"Now," I shifted my focus to Darren whose mouth had dropped open watching me swig two shots of rot gut whiskey, "let's talk commitment. Because that's what marriage is all about. If you give my friend Jane one bit of heartache, I'll make certain you pay for it."

"How?" His look was challenging.

"With your past, there's bound to be something the police haven't heard about that they'd like to know. I'll ferret it out, believe me."

His look softened. "I'm crazy about Jane. I really am. Marrying her is the best thing I will do in my miserable life. And I'll be good to her."

"Lily says you have a habit of not treating women well. Since she was your parole officer at one time, she would know. Does Jane know about Lily and your past?"

"I confessed to Jane everything that could stand between us."

"You better have."

I continued to glare at Darren, then decided I'd get nothing more out of him. I could have asked him about Sandy, but I decided to keep that quiver in my bow until the time came when I could use it most effectively.

"Let's go, Zack."

Zack swallowed the last of his beer and we left.

"The snow has let up." Zack looked up, the stars just beginning to show in the darkening sky. "There's the big dipper. Do you see it?" He pointed up.

"I don't think I want to see it."

"Why not?"

"Because if I look up, I'm going to fall over. Get me home. Two shots of bar whiskey have troubled both my sense of balance and my empty stomach."

"You're not going to throw up, are you.?

"Well, not here. The guys in the bar will see me. I have a hard-won reputation to uphold. But get me home. Quick!"

"You should have something in your stomach," said Zack when we got home.

"No food. I want to go upstairs to bed." I started up the first step and realized I needed help. I reached back and Zack grabbed my hand, half carried me upstairs and helped me into bed. I didn't remember falling asleep, but I must have slept until morning when Zack came into the bedroom and asked me if I wanted coffee.

"How about a gallon of water first?"

"That was some stunt you pulled at the bar, but it earned you the respect of the guys there including Darren."

"Well, I figured I had to do something to get him to take me seriously before I lectured him about Jane."

"You got the message across." Zack chuckled. "So, what's on your sleuthing agenda for today?"

I groaned. "I don't think I can get out of bed. I'll take a down day."

But my desire to rest for the day was interrupted by a phone call from Jane.

"Zack says you don't feel tip top today, and I heard you were in the Drop In last night drinking."

"I was not drinking per se. I had a couple of drinks. Zack and I left the bar before five pm."

Jane chuckled. "I know. Darren filled me in. He said you followed him into the bar to congratulate him. Which brings me to what I called you about. Now that you and Darren seem to have made peace over the wedding, I thought I'd catch you up on our plans. The ceremony will be next Monday, so I only have a few days to find a dress. Can we go to Albany to the mall? I know you hate to drive in the winter, but I thought perhaps you could ask Zack to drive us if you don't want to drive, but there's only flurries in the forecast today."

"Today? You want to go today?"

"Sure. Don't tell me you're hung over. You said you only had two drinks. Besides, I don't have much time before the ceremony."

"Why don't we drive to Stone Side? There's a mall there with some stores that might carry a dress you'd like."

There was silence on the other end, followed by the sound of a hmmpff. Finally, Jane said, "Fine, but if I don't find anything I like then you'll drive me to Albany, right?"

I agreed, thinking I'd do my best to make her think a feed sack looked exactly right if it would spare me the long drive to Albany.

"I'll jump in the shower and grab something to eat. See you in half an hour."

Zack stood at the end of the bed holding a cup of coffee. "Hold out your hand." He dumped two aspirins into it. "I'll make breakfast."

WHEN I PULLED UP TO JANE'S house, she rushed out the door and bounced into the passenger's seat.

"I am so excited I can hardly think straight. I never thought this day would come, did you?"

"Fasten your seat belt."

"How are you feeling? You sounded dreadful on the phone. I can't believe you went to the Drop In Inn to drink."

"I didn't. I only went there to talk to Darren. I tried to speak with him at the coffee shop, but he left. I think he was avoiding me."

Jane shook her finger at me. "No one can get away from Maddie, can they?" She stopped vibrating with happiness and settled into the seat. "Why do you have Zack's truck?"

"I can shift it into four-wheel drive in case the roads get bad. He insisted I take it. He's stuck with my car and the tires are old."

"I know how you feel about driving in the winter, but I'm sure we won't run into any snow. You're just such a sweetie for doing this." Jane leaned over and gave me a peck on the cheek.

It was difficult to remain in a down mood given Jane's exuberance over her upcoming wedding.

"This will be fun," I said and immediately felt better. My best friend was happy. Why shouldn't I be? Darren said he had shared his life with her. If she had any reservations, she wouldn't be marrying him, but in the recesses of my mind, there remained a couple of neurons of doubt.

There were only two stores carrying dresses for mature women in the small mall in Stone Side. Jane tried on several dresses in the first one but rejected all of them.

"Too lacy. Too dark. Too see through. Too small. Too old-looking." She tossed each dress out of the changing room. "There's nothing here for me."

"Let's try the outlet store."

We selected two dresses in the outlet.

In the changing room, neither suited Jane. "No. No. No. I like it, but it's too small. No. No. No." Jane sounded on the verge of tears.

"Okay. We'll have to go to Albany," I said.

When we walked out of the mall, snow had begun to fall, but, as Jane had said, the weather forecast had predicted only flurries. We headed out of town and onto the interstate, but as we drove north, the snow didn't decrease. Instead, the wind began to whip it around creating white out conditions in a few areas.

I gripped the wheel and leaned forward. My cell rang. "Would you get that, Jane. I need to concentrate on keeping us on the road."

"It's Zack. What's up? You sound upset. Oh, I see. I'll tell her." Jane ended the call. "Zack says there's been a change in the forecast. Now they're predicting almost a foot of snow, more heading north. He said not to head for Albany."

"To be honest, Jane, I'm not sure where we're heading. I can't see the road." I gently braked to make certain the truck didn't go into a spin, but suddenly there was a loud whump and the truck shuddered and veered to the right side of the road. Only there was no road. The pavement had disappeared, and we were headed downhill. A momentary break in the snow gave me a moment to see I was driving into the ditch straight toward a drop-off into a half-frozen bog.

CHAPTER 17

I STOMPED ON THE BRAKE, BUT THE truck kept rolling and rolling and rolling into the icy water. I heard Jane scream. "Brake, brake, brake!"

"I am. I am."

Suddenly just as the front of the truck entered the bog, it hit something under the ice and came to a shuddering stop. I pulled on the emergency brake to make certain it wouldn't go farther.

Jane and I stared across the snowy expanse, dead trees poking out of the water. We breathed a collective sigh of relief.

I felt jittery from the rush of adrenalin when I thought we were about to go underwater, but other than that, nothing really hurt and there was no blood. "Are you alright, Jane" I asked.

"I think so, except for my ankle."

I looked over at her foot. "Pull up your pants leg." Oh, boy. It was beginning to swell.

"Do you think it's broken?" she asked.

"I don't know, but you need medical attention. I'll see if I can get a signal from here." I held up my phone, but there were no bars. "I'm going to get out and climb up to the road. You stay put. Don't try to put any weight on that ankle."

I climbed out of the truck and began a slippery climb up to

the highway. Gusts of wind blowing snow in my face made the ascent even more difficult. Finally at the top, I took my phone out and held it up again. One bar. It would have to do. I punched in the connection to Zack, but the call went to voice mail. When I tried 9-1-1, nothing happened. The single bar had disappeared. I walked back and forth trying to get a signal, but none appeared. Suddenly out of the snowy blur I could see dim lights. As they drew nearer I realized they were on the other side of the interstate, that lane being another climb down. I struggled across my side of the highway, slipping and sliding on the slick pavement, then down the snowy median separating the lanes. The wind continued to blow the blanket of white obscuring my vision. How was I to flag down the vehicle? I unwound my scarf from my neck and stepped onto the highway, waving the scarf around. The vehicle bore down on me. A snowplow! And it wasn't slowing. Its lights blinded me. At the last minute, I jumped off the road into the median. The plow roared past, shoving snow and slush onto me as I tumbled to my knees.

I spit snow out of my mouth and stood up watching the red lights of the plow fade into the distance. The nearest exit was at least two miles back the way we had come. I decided I had to walk back there. If I remembered correctly, there was a gas station at the exit. I couldn't risk my energy climbing back up the hill to the other side of the highway and then down to the truck to let Jane know what I was doing. Trudging back up the embankment from the truck after I talked to Jane and then down the highway through the blinding snow for two miles was more than I could accomplish. I had to trust Jane would remain in the truck until help came. I began my slow slog for the exit.

After I had walked for what felt like an hour, a large road sign loomed in front of me. I could barely read it through the swirling snow. It read "Exit__" the number was obscured by impacted snow on the sign, but I could read the mileage to the exit, "2 miles." I leaned against the signpost, too weary to go on. Vehicle lights coming over the knoll I had just walked down shone through the snow. Another plow. I remained where I was, not chancing another encounter with the plow, but I half-heartedly pulled my scarf off and waved it. The plow went past me with inches between the sign and the plow's giant blade. Several feet down the road, the plow stopped.

The driver jumped from the cab and walked toward me. "I thought that signpost looked odd. What are you doing out here in this weather?"

I explained my situation. "Can you give me a ride to the exit?" I struggled to speak because of my exhaustion and the wind which blew my words away.

He helped me to the plow and into the cab. "I'll call to let the state police know about your truck and then call an ambulance."

"Can we go back to the truck? I'm sure my friend is worried."

He took the exit ahead and we turned around. By now it was difficult to tell where the truck had gone off the road, but when I mentioned the bog, the driver remembered the mile marker. He pulled off the road when we reached the marker. Flashing lights appeared behind us.

"There's your ambulance and the troopers."

"Thanks so much. You're a life-saver." He had rescued both Jane and me. I stumbled down the hill to the truck. Jane was tucked away in the corner of her seat and her eyes were closed.

"Jane. Jane. Are you alive?"

"Of course, I'm alive. What took you so long?"

I wanted to snap at her for being so insensitive, but she was probably in pain.

"The ambulance just pulled up. They should be down to transfer you to a stretcher."

"Tell them to bring me a flask of brandy. I'm freezing to death here."

"Jane, they're not Saint Bernards, and this isn't a mountain rescue. Here they are." I moved out of the EMTs way to let them get to Jane. They carried her up the hill and loaded the stretcher into the ambulance.

"Can I ride with her to the hospital?"

One of the EMTs helped me into the ambulance. "C'mon. You look as if you're half frozen. We don't want hypothermia to set in. We'll have the doctor at the emergency room have a look at you, too."

I was grateful for the blanket they wrapped around me and for the warmth of the ambulance. I held Jane's hand until we pulled into the emergency entrance. Inside, we were separated, but I had the cubicle next to hers.

"You have your phone, Maddie?" she said loud enough I could hear her.

"Yes. What do you need?"

"I need Darren, that's what I need." She sounded scared and as if she might break down in tears soon.

"I don't know his number."

"Oh, no," she wailed.

"Shush. I think I know someone who can reach him."

I connected to Richard's cell and explained what had happened.

"Are you okay, Mom?"

"Just a little cold. The doctor is looking at Jane's ankle right now. She wants to talk with Darren. I'm sure Lily has his number. Could you ask her for it?"

"Better yet, I'll have her call him. We'll be at the hospital in a matter of minutes."

"No, no. I'm fine. I'll contact Zack and have him give me a ride home. I'm sure they won't keep me overnight. It's just a bit of a chill."

"I'll be there. Don't leave." Richard ended the call before I could insist again he not come.

My cell rang. I answered it without looking at the caller ID certain it had to be Zack, but it was Geoffrey.

"I heard you and Jane were headed to Albany to shop and I'm calling to let you know the roads are bad. Stay home."

"Uhm, I already know how bad they are. I ran Zack's truck into a ditch. Jane's in the hospital with what may be a broken ankle. I'm with her. They're going to make certain I don't have hypothermia. I had to walk to get help, but . . ."

Geoffrey cut me off before I could tell him I was fine. "Abigail and I will be right there. Don't move." He disconnected.

I punched in Zack's number. He'd be furious at me if he had to learn what happened through someone else, but when he answered I found he was also enroute to the hospital.

"Maddie! I was worried sick. When I heard the change in the forecast, I tried to contact you, but got no answer, so I contacted the state police at the barracks in Stone Side. They told me both you and Jane were transported by ambulance to the hospital."

I had held it together during the accident, my frozen walk in the snow and the trip to the hospital. Suddenly I felt overwhelmed when I heard Zack's voice, and I broke down. "I wrecked your truck," I sobbed, tears running down my cheeks, "and I need a tissue because there's snot gushing out of my nose."

"I'm pulling into the hospital now. Don't worry about the truck. I've already arranged to have it pulled out of the ditch. If it won't start or it's not drivable, it will be towed."

"Okay," I whimpered, but what about my tissue?" I wiped my nose on my coat sleeve.

"I'll stop by the gift shop and buy a box."

"No! Come get me. I'll use toilet paper from the bathroom down the hall." I jumped off the bed and pulled back the privacy curtain between Jane and me.

"Ah, Ms. Sparks. I'm finished here and was about to come see you," said the doctor who looked young enough to be my grandson, but then all medical personnel nowadays looked as if they were barely out of high school. Or was I just getting older?

"I'm just fine," I repeated for what I hoped was the last time today. "How's my friend?" I asked.

"I'm sending her up to X-Ray. It's likely a broken ankle."

"Will she be able to walk on it?"

"It depends on the kind of break. It it's a simple fracture, we can put a soft caste on it, and she'll have to use a cane to help her get around."

"It better be a simple fracture," Jane said, "because I've got a wedding to attend in a few days."

"You can have someone assist you to your seat and then sit back and watch the bride walk down the aisle." The doctor patted her arm.

"I am the bride."

"We can postpone the ceremony." I smiled encouragingly at her.

"I'm not postponing. Let's giddy-up to X-ray and see what's going on. I need to get out of here. I've got wedding plans to attend to." Jane's determined look faded and she slumped back on the hospital bed. "I've got no dress."

Zack entered the room in time to catch Jane begin a loud wail. "She's seriously hurt, doctor?" He rushed over to me and wrapped his arms around me. "Not another concussion. Are you admitting her?

"Not me, Zack. Jane. She may have a broken ankle, but that's not the real problem."

"Damaged spleen? Ribcage crushed? Dislocated shoulder?"

"Nope," I said.

Jane left off her wailing. "Much, much worse. Maddie is threatening to call off the wedding."

"I am not."

Jane's shoulders slumped in defeat. "We might as well forget the wedding. I have nothing to wear and no time to prepare for it."

Two attendants entered, one pushing a gurney.

"Let's get you off to X-Ray and see what damage there is," said the doctor.

They transferred Jane to the gurney. As they pushed her out of the cubicle, I told her, "I'll be out of here in a few minutes. I'll use one of my dresses and alter it for you. And Zack will call the coffeehouse to make arrangements to use the extra room there.

We'll invite all your friends. Don't worry. By the time the hospital releases you, everything will be set for your big day." I gave her a cheery wave as she was wheeled down the hall.

Zack looked skeptical. "One of your dresses, Maddie? Jane is quite a bit larger than you."

"Never mind. Just get me out of here. We have a lot of work to do."

The results of the X-ray indicated Jane had a broken ankle, but it was a simple break which the doctor told her would heal in a walking caste and they would release her the next day. Darren finally showed up at the hospital. Jane was so thrilled to see him that no one had the heart to ask him where he had been. The emergency room doctor gave me a quick look over and said I could go home.

The snow had slowed down by the time Zack and I left the hospital.

"You really need to replace these tires. I'm not even certain they're legal now, but regardless, there's no tread left to grip in the snow. The garage called and said my truck wasn't drivable. The undercarriage hit a submerged tree in the bog. It will take some time to repair it. They have to order parts."

"Sorry."

"It's okay. I'm just relieved you and Jane weren't hurt more seriously." He hugged me to him. "I know you don't approve of Jane's and Darren's wedding, but you're being generous about it by making certain Jane has the wedding she wants. You're a good friend, Maddie. I know she appreciates it."

I smiled up at him. "I just hope I don't regret doing this, but I mostly hope Jane doesn't regret marrying this guy."

Back at the house, Spike greeted me at the door with an accusing look on his face and an indignant meow.

"Would you feed him? I need to go upstairs to see if I can find my old sewing machine and look through the dresses in my closet."

As if he understood what I said, Spike wound his body around Zack's legs in anticipation of food and pointedly ignored me.

Upstairs I rummaged through the closet in the second bedroom and found the sewing machine on the floor in the back. How long had it been since I used it, and would it still work? And did I remember how to wind a bobbin? Where was that sewing kit with all my threads? I got down on my hands and knees to explore the back of the closet and pulled out one of Spike's favorite stuffed mouse catnip toys. I wondered where that had gone. Ah, there was the sewing kit in the far corner of the closet.

I sorted through the hangers in my bedroom closet, removed one and slipped off the garment bag to reveal a floor length dress I had worn to a New Year's Eve celebration the last year my ex-husband Dan and I were together. The dress was strapless, blue satin with silver thread running through it. In some ways I hated to do it, but I took the dress from the hanger and began to remove the back zipper and the side seams. I'd insert a corset closure in the back, shorten it to tea length and use the fabric I removed from the skirt bottom to make sleeves. There was sufficient seam allowance for me to let it out a good two to three inches on each side. With the corset closing, I could adjust it around Jane. I carried the dress downstairs and asked Zack to get the machine for me.

"Set it on the kitchen table."

"Aren't you hungry?" he asked. "It's almost midnight."

"I think there's a frozen pizza."

Zack heated up the pizza while I continued to disassemble the dress and turn it into a wedding gown. Half an hour later, Zack shoved a slice of pizza under my nose. I had the dress in pieces and was ready to put it back together in an entirely different form.

"I'll take a short break and eat a slice, but I want to finish this tonight if I can." I took my slice to the sofa to rest my back. Bending over the table to play seamstress made my spine complain. I ate half the slice and returned to my task. I found a length of Gros grain ribbon in my sewing box that I could use for the corset lacing. The only thing I had left to do was to construct the sleeves from the extra material. I looked at the clock. It was three in the morning and Zack had muttered something about being tired several hours ago. I found him asleep on the sofa with Spike on his chest.

EARLY THE NEXT DAY, SUNDAY, I finished Jane's dress and called the coffeehouse when it opened to see if they would allow us to use the room off the main area for a small wedding ceremony. They eagerly accommodated the request and offered an urn of coffee for the celebration. Next on my list of things to do was telephoning the bakery at one of the supermarkets in Stone Side to order a sheet cake with the appropriate congratulatory writing on it. I knew we couldn't afford flowers from a flower shop, so I planned to grab flowers from the market also and rearrange them into pots which could be placed around the room, taking a few of them for a bouquet for Jane and, if Darren managed to find a suit jacket to wear, a boutonniere for him, his best man (which one of his biker buddies would that be?) and Zack who would walk Jane down the aisle. I gave Zack the task of reaching Darren to let him know what was expected of him—a clean shirt, jacket, maybe a tie, and the name of his best man. Zack would also drive Darren and Jane to the courthouse to get a marriage license the day before the wedding. Breathless from all this last-minute planning, I called the bride that evening to make certain the hospital had released her and told her about her wedding day.

"Oh, Maddie, you're the best."

"Are you too tired for me to bring over the dress?"

"You got a dress for me? Where? How?"

"It's a surprise."

"Bring it over." Jane held the receiver away from her and yelled to Darren. "It's on!" He said something that sounded less than excited, but Jane, bubbling over with happiness, said. "He's so happy."

Maybe he was. Maybe not, but he'd asked her, and she had said yes, so by golly there was going to be a wedding.

Sheriff Burroughs stopped by that evening after dinner. "I thought you might want to know that a hiker spotted an abandoned snowmobile near one of the state trails, up north of here. I checked the registration, which was not up-to-date, but I traced it to an Eli Masters." She stood just inside the door, holding her hat in her hand.

"We just finished dinner and were about to have a cup of coffee, decaf. Join us." Zack gestured Anita in, and she took a seat in the living area. I brought a tray of cups and the pot in and poured for us.

"Why is this of interest to us" I asked, settling back into the couch next to Zack.

"You remember that piece of fiberglass discovered on Richard's property? We thought someone had driven a snowmobile there, a feasible way for an arsonist to get to the property and away without anyone noticing. Well, the piece we found fits the abandoned snowmobile."

"Why would Masters have a reason to set Richard's house on fire?" asked Zack.

"I talked to him right before I stopped here. He insisted his snowmobile was in his shed, that he hadn't yet taken it out to use it, hence the expired registration. He took me to the barn to look at it. Guess what?"

"The snowmobile was missing." Zack replied.

"Mr. Masters hadn't checked on it since he parked it there last winter. Someone stole it."

"That doesn't give us the identity of the person who took it and burned Richard's place, unless Mr. Masters is lying." I set my mug back on the coffee table with a disgruntled sigh.

"Oh, but it might. We hauled the snowmobile in and are checking for prints."

"Wouldn't the thief have worn gloves?' asked Zack.

"Maybe, but we're going to go over it carefully in case whoever took it was careless and removed their gloves at some point."

"A promising idea, but only if the fingerprints are in the system. It's a long shot." Zack frowned.

Anita grinned. "All we need is a little luck. Maybe the person has a record of theft."

CHAPTER 18

JANE LOVED THE DRESS I MADE for her and when I told her what Zack and I had done for the ceremony, she was grateful and so excited. "It's perfect, simply perfect. Oh, Maddie. You're such a good friend. You took care of everything. C'mere, you." She reached out and hugged me as if she was never going to let go.

"You'd do the same for me."

"I wish I didn't have to use this cane. It cramps my style. No dancing at the after-ceremony party, I guess."

What party, I wondered. "We thought we'd keep it simple. Coffee and cake."

She looked a bit disappointed. "Maybe we can celebrate in a month or so when we get back from our honeymoon."

"I guess you're keeping where you're going a secret, huh?"

"Well, it's a secret Darren's keeping from me, too. I have no idea where we're going."

Now that worried me, but I reassured myself it couldn't be too bad. It was winter and his bike was in storage. No roaring off with Jane on the back of the bike, I assured myself.

"I'm sure wherever he's taking you will be wonderful." Or so I hoped.

"Get a good night's sleep tonight," I told her. "I'll help you into your dress and then Zack will drive us to the coffeehouse. I've called everyone I thought you'd like to know about the wedding." I handed her a list. "If you think of anyone else, let me know. Darren needs to contact those he wants there. I don't know his friends."

"He can make his calls tonight and tomorrow morning."

"The owners of the coffee house are putting up a notice of the ceremony for anyone who wants to attend. It will be in the window tomorrow morning."

"There's just so little time to get this together."

"You aren't having second thoughts, are you?"

Jane wrinkled her face in a look of horror. "Absolutely not!"

"Okay then." I hugged her and left, wondering if I should have asked Darren if he was having second thoughts. He was awfully quiet tonight.

THE NEXT MORNING I AWOKE TO the warmth of the sun shining into my face through my window. Zack's side of the bed was empty, and I heard him downstairs in the kitchen. I bounded out of bed, ran to the window and greeted the sunshine by twirling around in absolute joy.

"I just read the weather for today," Zack called up the stairway. "It's going to be around fifty degrees. A heat wave for this time of year. And no snow predicted. We couldn't ask for a better day for a wedding."

"You haven't gone to buy the champagne yet, have you?"

"I just got back from the liquor store."

After the ceremony and the cake and coffee, we planned to ask a few of our family and close friends of Jane's and Darren's back here for a champagne toast to their happiness. Any reservations I had entertained about Jane's choice of a husband left me, replaced by genuine happiness at Jane having found her soul mate—at least she thought so, so who was I to argue?

What to wear, what to wear. I perused the choices in my closet and decided upon the dress I had worn on Zack's and my first date.

It's swirly skirt showed off my legs and the V-neck gave just a hint of a bustline not too diminished by age. I showered, dressed and did my make-up—just a touch of blush, mascara and lip tint, nothing extreme. When I came into the kitchen, Zack gave me a look of admiration.

"You look good enough to . . ." he began.

". . . make breakfast for?"

"No. This." He took me in his arms and kissed me, leaving me breathless.

"Not before I've had my coffee." I felt warmth work its way up my cheeks. I could have been the blushing bride.

I sat at the kitchen table and drank my coffee. "I've got to get over to the coffeehouse to set things up. I'd walk, but I can't carry the room decorations, flowers and the cake."

"I'll help you load everything into the car and carry it in. We can both set up."

"The ceremony will be at three, but I'll have to help Jane get dressed and I'd appreciate you being there to check that Darren looks presentable. He might just decide to wear his biker leathers."

Zack chuckled. "You can't predict, can you? You are such a good friend to do all this for Jane."

"That's what she told me, but I'm still wondering if I'm making a mistake."

"If you didn't plan this for Jane, she and Darren would simply run off and elope."

We ate a light breakfast of toast and orange juice and set off for the coffeehouse around eleven. Tab and Jon, the owners, waved to us as we came in. They were busy with orders, but when they caught up, Jon came into the side room to offer his help.

"I think we're fine. We're keeping it simple."

"Who's officiating?" asked Jon.

I almost dropped the container of flowers I was holding. "Who's officiating?"

He nodded.

Oh, no. In my frenzy getting Jane's dress ready, ordering the cake and buying the flowers and decorations, I had entirely forgotten about who would perform the ceremony. Zack and I exchanged shocked glances.

"We don't have anyone. I forgot that part. Jane is going to kill me. I've failed." I sunk down onto the couch and put my face in my hands.

"No problem," said Jon. "I can do it. I have a license. I've done lots of these ceremonies."

"Are you sure?"

"I can show you my credentials if you're concerned."

"Not necessary. If you say you can do it, then I'm fine with that."

"Problem solved." Zack held his hand out to me to help me off the sofa. "Let's finish these decorations and grab some lunch at home."

My knees were still weak from the shock of discovering I hadn't arranged for someone to officiate at the ceremony. I let out a long breath of relief, took Zack's hand and resumed the room preparations. Well, what could go wrong, went wrong and was righted. Everything was now running smoothly. We'd cruise through the rest of the day with no hiccups and Jane and Darren would be off on a honeymoon trip for a few days, destination unknown. They were keeping it a secret I suspected because Darren knew his riding buddies would likely want to pull some stunt if the fellas knew where they were going. I could only imagine what a bunch of bikers had in mind for a newlywed joke. No, I couldn't imagine, and didn't want to. Smooth sailing for the happy couple.

ZACK AND I DROVE TO JANE'S an hour before the ceremony. I helped Jane into her dress and tightened the corset.

"Not too tight. I want to be able to breathe and eat cake." Jane balanced herself with her cane and looked at herself in the mirror. "Oh, it's perfect. Thank you, Maddie. What would I have done without you?"

She and I went downstairs where Zack waited for us in the living room.

"Where's Darren?" Jane asked.

"He stepped out back to make a call, something about his best man."

I turned to Jane. "Who did he pick for his best man?"

"I don't know. He's keeping it a secret."

"That's odd." Why would anyone keep the identity of the groomsman a secret?

Zack and I exchanged worried looks.

"You don't suppose he's skipped out on the wedding?" I whispered to Zack who shrugged.

The back door to the kitchen opened and Darren appeared. "A bit of a glitch in the plans."

I stepped over to Darren and stood toe to toe with him, trying to control my anger. "What do you mean?"

"I planned to have one of my biker pals stand up for me, but I forgot that all of them took a vacation trip to the Florida Keys, loaded their bikes into a U-Haul and are speeding down US 1 to Key West as we speak." Darren gulped and gave me a weak smile.

"Just when did you think to ask one of them to be in the wedding?"

He swallowed again. "This morning. How was I to know they wouldn't be around? It's not riding weather, so I thought they'd be available. I forgot about the trip. I should be with them, but I decided to stay here with Jane." He reached out and put his arm around Jane and squeezed her to him. "Huh, honey?"

Jane's happy face quickly disappeared, and tears filled her round, blue eyes.

"But, don't worry. I've got a plan. I just now called one of the guys who works at the shop with me. He's downtown at the Drop In. He said he'd be glad to do it. He'll just pop down the street and meet us at the coffeehouse." Darren planted a kiss on Jane's cheek. "It's all fixed."

"What is he wearing?" I asked.

"Probably what he usually wears. Tee-shirt and jeans."

"Do you have another jacket, shirt and spare tie?"

"Are you kidding? This is it for my wardrobe." He gestured at the slightly rumpled jacket, off-white shirt and garish plaid tie he was wearing.

"Zack, we need to stop by the house and pick up a jacket, shirt and tie of yours. What size is this guy?"

Darren shrugged. "About my height, I guess."

The four of us got into my car, Zack driving back to my place. He ran into the house and grabbed a change of clothing for Darren's pal. Zack was much taller than Darren, but so what if the sleeves were a little long on the guy. When we pulled up to the coffee-house, we could see it was already crowded with people Jane and I knew. Abigail, Geoffrey, Sara and Leon, her fiancée, were there.

"Is Richard coming?" I asked Geoffrey.

"Yup. He said he'd be here a little late with his bodyguard."

At least Darren would have one person he knew well at his wedding. Lily.

Everyone cheered as we entered the coffeehouse.

"Where's your pal?" I asked Darren who looked around the crowd anxiously.

"Here he comes."

A man with a bald head wearing a jeans jacket ran up the steps to the coffee house. He was a bit taller than Darren, so that was good.

"Quick, take him to the restroom and get him changed into Zack's clothes." I handed Darren the hanger of clothing and shoved him toward the back of the room. His friend followed, the two of them slapping each other on the back and laughing. People crowded around Jane, hugging and kissing her. Jon, our officiant, had changed into a dark blue suit with white shirt and teal tie. He looked very dapper. I introduced him to Jane.

"Where's the groom?" he asked.

"Right here." Darren and his friend, now dressed in one of Zack grey jackets came from behind us. "This is one of my buddies, Hal. Happy Hal, we call him at the shop. He's going to be my best man."

My gaze ran over the man. He did, indeed look happy, but I wondered if that was due to his nature or to the smell of whiskey emanating from him. As for his appearance, Darren had forgotten to tell me the man had a huge beer gut. Neither the shirt nor the jacket fit around his belly. The shirt pulled taut at the buttons, leaving gaps and exposing skin. He had left the tie untied.

"Give me that." I tied his tie and pulled it over the gaps in the shirt. "Try not to breathe too deeply." I tried to button the jacket, but it wouldn't stretch around his bulging middle. Oh, well. It would have to do. Darren moved Happy Hal to his side where Jane couldn't see the guy's appearance. From my perspective Hal looked as good as Darren, maybe even better..

I rummaged in my purse and pulled out a handful of breath mints which I slipped to Hal. "You'll need these."

He looked offended. "I don't do drugs."

"They're mints."

He gave me one of his happy smiles and gulped the entire handful.

Leon, Sara's fiancée, had volunteered to play his guitar. He stepped into the side room and began to strum a soft tune. The crowd quieted and Jon announced the ceremony was about to begin. People crowded into the room and soon filled all the chairs there, leaving many standing in the back and in the doorway. Darren and Happy Hal took their places in front of Jon, and I walked in after them, carrying a small bouquet of white daisies. Then as Leonard played the traditional wedding march, Zack escorted Jane in. She carried a single white rose and was beaming with joy as she took Darren's hand. Jane, saying she was an old-fashioned gal, had opted for the timeless wedding vows, pledging troths until death parted them. I glanced around the room. Zack and I had done a spectacular job, simple, but elegant. The early winter sun shone through the side window and bathed Jane and Darren in its golden light. Every face in the room reflected the smiles on the wedding couple's face. Jon lifted his gaze from the pair, saying the usual words about anyone speaking against the marriage. As expected, there was silence. Jon nodded to continue with the ceremony when, from the back of the room, a lone voice was heard.

"He's already married."

All heads turned to see who had spoken. Female. Dressed in a blue pants suit. Dark Hair with a streak of white. Shoulder holster half hidden by the jacket. It was Lily.

"He's married to me," she said.

"We're divorced," said Darren. "We have been for years."

"Not true. You never signed the papers."

Jane wobbled a bit on her cane and looked at Darren, her lips trembling "Is this true?"

"I'm sure I signed them No, wait a minute, I remember now. I meant to sign them. In fact, I was at some bar at a bikers' rally. Lot of drinking and women. I could have forgotten. They're probably in my leather jacket or on my bike. I can go home and check if you'd like." Darren turned to leave.

"Stay right there. You're not going anywhere. You're under arrest on suspicion of arson and attempted murder." Sheriff Burroughs pushed her way past the people standing in the back of the room. She removed her handcuffs from her belt, approached Darren and fastened the cuffs on him.

"No, no! Don't take him away." The cry came from a blonde woman who threaded her way through the crowd. "Daddy! Daddy!"

I turned at the sound of the scream.

Sandy Longworth? What was happening here? Her husband grabbed her arm and pulled her toward him and away from Darren.

"Don't worry, honey," Darren said as he passed Sandy. "I'll take care of everything."

Jane started to slump forward, but Zack put his arm around her waist. "I think she's fainting."

"No. I'll be fine. Just let me get my feet under me."

"We'll take you back to Maddie's place." Zack started to walk her out of the room into the main area of the coffeehouse. Darren followed. Sandy clutched at him when he passed.

"Watch the cake," I warned as they threatened to topple the table on which Zack and I had set it.

"Let me." Jane freed herself from Zack and, balancing her hip on the table, reached out with both hands, lifted the cake and smashed it into Darren's face.

She then took her cane in hand and reached again for Zack's arm. "Let's go drink champagne. I hope you bought a lot because I need it." Zack cocked one eyebrow in amusement and ushered her toward the door.

Meantime, the crowd of people who had been silent through the episode, began talking again, some expressing shock, others cheering Jane. Head held high, Jane exited the coffeehouse like a queen.

CHAPTER 19

I RUSHED TO CATCH UP WITH ZACK and Jane, and realizing that I still carried my bouquet, I shrugged, stopped in front of the door and tossed it over my shoulder. First there was a gasp from the crowd, then laughter followed by clapping. I turned to see what was happening. Happy Hal had caught the bouquet.

He stood transfixed, staring at the flowers in his hand, then broke into a wide grin. "Does this mean I'm next?"

"Give me that." I yanked the bouquet from him. "I'll hold these while you get out of those clothes. And be quick about it." I leaned out the door and shouted to Zack. "Take Jane to our place. I'll grab a ride with someone."

Well, I might as well do something useful while waiting. I glanced around the room looking for Sandy who appeared to be arguing with her husband.

I planted myself in front of her. "Your husband didn't know Darren was your father?"

She shook her head.

"I'm surprised too. I'll bet everyone here is. We all thought we knew your parents. I saw you and Darren at the market several days ago and I thought you were a thing, you know, dating."

"I was adopted."

"Really, when did you find that out?"

"I've known for years. My parents never hid it from me. I didn't know who my father was until a few months ago, however."

"And did you know the identity of your biological mother?"

"You know, you are the nosiest women, Maddie Sparks."

Yes, but asking questions sometimes leads to discovering valuable information despite how intrusive that might seem.

Sandra seemed to reconsider talking to me for a moment, but then probably decided I'd just keep probing.

"All right then. My mother died giving birth to me. She was a classmate of Darren's. I don't know what their relationship was like, but she did put his name as my father on the birth certificate. He knew about me, but wasn't in a position to parent me, so . . ."

"So you were put up for adoption."

She nodded. "My adoptive parents felt there was no reason to advertise the names of my parents, especially given the circumstances of my conception. You know how people around here talk. Why ruin the reputation of a young woman who made a mistake?"

I nodded. "I'll bet your adoptive parents never wanted to make public who your father was given his reputation as a teen who always was in trouble and then went to prison for robbery when he was a young man. So how did you find out Darren was your father?"

"The woman who is your son's bodyguard told me."

"Why?"

"I guess she thought I should know when Darren came back into town. I think he wanted me to know, so she told me."

Sandy's husband hadn't said a word during our conversation, but the irritated look on his face told me he had a number of things to say and none of them positive.

"Sandy told me a few days ago. The timing couldn't have been worse what with the bank closing and my position there in limbo. She apparently thinks it's cool to have a dad who's an ex-con and a biker."

"And you don't?"

"No. I told her to stay away from him."

"Perhaps she was simply happy to know who her biological father was, a missing piece in her life after she lost her mother as an infant."

"I can't understand why. She had parents. They were pillars of this community, but no. She wants the world to know how badass her dad is. I know she can't help who her parents were, but why announce it to the world? It could impact my position with the bank."

I got the picture loud and clear. He was worried about his career and cared little about his wife's feelings.

"Did you know Darren was married to Lily?" I asked Sandy.

"No."

"I wonder why she waited until now to announce it. She knew he and Jane were in a relationship."

"I don't know. Look, this has been a terrible day for me. I'd like to go home." She looked up at her husband with a pleading gaze.

"Fine. We need to talk anyway." He grabbed her arm and steered her out of the coffeehouse.

Someone tapped me on my shoulder: Lily.

"You really made a mess of things. My friend Jane's day, her life has been ruined by your ill-timed announcement." I was furious with her and turned to Richard who stood behind her. "Fire her and hire someone else. I don't want to see her face around here."

"Let me remind you, Ms. Sparks. I'm not the one at fault here. Darren never signed those divorce papers."

"Was it really necessary to make today all about you?"

"Look, I asked Darren to sign those papers a year ago. He said he would. Then he shows up back in town, says he'll sign them, but doesn't. I warned him I would make trouble for him, if he didn't do it, but he kept putting me off. I knew he was getting serious with your friend, but I had no idea he was going to marry her. I only learned that when your son told me we were going to a wedding today. I had no choice but call him out."

"You chose to ruin Jane's happiness."

"She wouldn't have been happy with him."

"That wasn't your decision to make."

"As long as Darren and I are married, it is."

Richard stepped in between Lily and me. "Let's leave this for now. I'm sure Jane wants you with her, Mom. Lily and I will talk." Richard walked her out, leaving me still fuming in the coffeehouse.

Someone tapped me on my shoulder again. I whirled around.. "What now?"

Jon handed me a cup. "I'm sure you can use a cup of tea. Come sit down for a moment, then I'll have someone drive you home."

"You're so kind." I took the cup and sank into a chair. "Was this the worst ceremony you ever presided over?"

"No way. I've had lots worse. I'll tell you about them sometime."

"Just tell me one story now. I can use it."

"I'll make it brief because I know you want to be with your friend." Jon took the chair across the table from me.

"Several years ago, I was performing a ceremony out on Long Island. It was held in a small chapel, a very lovely nondenominational stained-glass window at the front. Both the bride and groom appeared to be very much in love. No one objected when I asked, well, you know, like today. I asked the bride if she would take the groom to be hers and she said, 'I do.' When I turned to the groom and asked him the same question, the doors of the chapel were flung open and a woman wielding a shotgun appeared. 'If I can't have him, then neither can you.' She aimed the weapon at the groom, pulled the trigger and he fell to the floor. He looked up at me with absolute horror on his face but crooked his finger at me. I bent down and heard him say, 'I do, too.' Hearing his reply, the armed woman shouted, 'No you don't,' and fired again. This time the shot went high and hit the stained-glass window behind us."

"Was he dead?"

"No, but he was severely wounded. He recovered, but they had to postpone their honeymoon for over a month. The woman who shot him was arrested and is still in prison. That was one jealous woman. Sadly, the marriage didn't last."

"Not an auspicious beginning. Well, I guess we should be glad Lily didn't shoot Darren."

"Really?"

"She's Richard's bodyguard and always armed."

"I guess we got off easy then."

"I don't think she cared that Darren was marrying someone else. She just wanted those papers signed. And I don't think there was any money in her becoming his widow. The man works in a garage parttime and is living in Jane's house."

"You're not happy about him as Jane's spouse, but you went to all this trouble." He swept his hand around the room.

"I did it for Jane."

My cell rang. It was Zack calling.

"Jane's had half a bottle of champagne and now she wants to go to the county jail to see Darren. She says she's thought it over and forgives him."

"Well, if he was the one who set the fire at Richard's house, I certainly don't forgive him. And I'm not eager to see the man either."

"You talk to her."

Jane's voice filled with sobs and what might have been too much champagne came over the connection. "I need to talk to him. I need to talk to you. I need a ride to the county jail."

"I don't think that's wise."

"Maybe not," she said, sobbing, "But if you won't take me there, then I'll call a taxi. You're my friend. I thought you wanted what was best for me."

"I do, and seeing Darren is not it."

"I want to see him! Now!"

I held the phone away from my ear. "Don't yell. Everyone can hear you."

Jane could be stubborn as a cat on a leash. No amount of urging, pulling, pushing or petting would move either Jane or the cat.

"Okay. Come by the coffeehouse and pick me up."

"How about me?" Happy Hal asked.

"If you want to go visit Darren, use your own car."

"I'm too drunk to drive. Had too many beers and chasers at the Drop In."

"Do you mind if Happy Hal comes along?" I asked Jane.

"Fine, but only if we stop at my place and I run in to find the divorce papers, Darren could sign them and then we could finish the ceremony. Bring the guy who performed ceremony. Jon isn't it?"

"Are you out of your mind?" I yelled into the phone.

"Maddie, I know Darren. He's a bad one, but he's no killer. Besides, I already promised to take him as my husband through thick and thin and even if he's somehow railroaded back into prison if it comes to that. Until death does us part. And neither of us is dead."

I gave up trying to talk sense into Jane over the phone. Maybe I would be more persuasive in person. "We'll talk on the way to the county jail. Stop by and pick Happy and me up."

"Jon, too?"

"He's working. Besides, not only do the papers have to be signed, but they also have to be recorded. You can't get married until that's done."

"Okay."

"You still want Happy to come along?"

"I really don't care. Ask him how he feels about Darren and me."

I dutifully turned to Happy. "She wants to know how you feel about the two of them."

Happy shrugged. "I never met the bride before today, but if Darren likes her, then so do I."

I relayed the information to Jane.

"See you in a few minutes. Should I bring the champagne?"

"No!"

Zack pulled up in front of the coffeehouse with Jane in the passenger's seat, so I had to get in the back with Happy Hal. The drinks he had earlier at the Drop In had obviously gotten to him. He fell asleep on my shoulder. I tried to nudge him off, but he only snuggled closer.

"What if the evidence against Darren makes a compelling case for his being the one who set fire to Richard's house? What then? Can you forgive that?" I asked Jane.

"Why would he do that? He had no reason to want Richard dead."

"But . . ." I began.

Jane cut me off. "I don't want to talk about it anymore." She faced forward and crossed her arms over her chest.

Zack looked at me in the rearview mirror, shook his head and mouthed, "Leave it for now."

He was right. My trying to mount a case against Darren was only making her more stubborn. I could only hope that Sheriff Burroughs had sufficient evidence to establish Darren's involvement in the arson.

When Zack pulled up in front of the county jail, Jane immediately jumped out of the car and hobbled her way with her cane to the front door. Sheriff Burroughs stood in the entranceway and seemed to be expecting us.

"Can I see him?" asked Jane.

"I don't understand why you would want to, but I'll take you back to the interview room where we're questioning him when we're through. Wait here until then." She gestured to several chairs.

"I'll stand," Jane announced in a determined voice.

"Can I have a word?" Zack said to the sheriff.

"If you want to know why we arrested him, it was easy making the decision. Do you remember that snowmobile we found abandoned? As I told you, it had been stolen and we tracked down the owner through the expired registration. The broken snowmobile parts we found in Richard's yard matched exactly the parts missing from the stolen snowmobile. We checked it for prints, and guess what? The prints were in the system, and they belong to Darren. Case closed." Burroughs looked pleased with herself.

"But I don't understand Darren's motive," I said.

"That's my line," said Jane, overhearing the sheriff's explanation.

"We'll get it out of him soon."

"So Darren was driving the snowmobile, probably stole it too, but is there anything else that ties him to the fire?" asked Zack.

"A container of gasoline on the back of it?" smiled Burroughs.

"And his fingerprints on the container?" asked Zack.

"Well, no, but . . ."

"That's enough for me," said Jane pushing her way in front of the sheriff.

"Darren, honey, I found your divorce papers." Jane made her way down the hall waving the papers in her hand.

"I'll stop her." I rushed after her and blocked her from the interview room door.

"Get out of my way, Maddie."

I grabbed the papers out of her hand. "These can wait."

"But if he signs them now, I can take them to the courthouse next door and file them."

Sheriff Burroughs stepped in front of Jane. "I can't let you in until we're finished. If you don't step aside, I'll charge you with interference with an ongoing case."

"I've never done jail time." Jane looked eager to remedy that. "Would you put me in a cell next to Darren's?"

Sheriff Burroughs shook her head.

"Fine. I'll wait. Take all the time you want. I'll be here." Jane walked back down the hall toward the entrance and the chairs we had been offered, then started a conversation with Happy Hal.

"What do the two of them have to talk about?" asked Zack.

"Darren." I said.

At least a half hour passed before the sheriff emerged from the interview room, leading Darren toward us. "We need to process him and put him in a cell. Come back tomorrow and you can talk to him."

Jane appeared about to argue with the sheriff, but Anita raised her hand. "Don't, or I won't allow you in tomorrow. If you want to help him, get him a good lawyer." She and a deputy walked Darren through a door toward the cells. Darren turned and blew kisses at Jane which she returned.

"I might have some information for you, Sheriff Burroughs," said Jane.

"Not now."

The door closed behind Sheriff Burroughs, Darren and the officer.

"What information?" I asked. "You're not going to alibi Darren, are you?"

"No. That would be a lie. But just now Happy Hal . . .," Jane looked around for him, but he had disappeared, "said he and Darren were at his place the night of the big snowstorm, the night Richard's place was set ablaze. He said Darren got a call from someone about a snowmobile that needed work. It was kind of late, but Darren said the person needed it to bring supplies to a friend of theirs in an off-road location, so Hal loaned him his car and off he went. When he returned a few hours later, Hal said he seemed upset but wouldn't tell Hal why."

"Hal needs to tell the sheriff about this," said Zack. "Where did he go?"

"I tried to encourage him to speak with the sheriff, but he said he was getting uncomfortable just being here. I don't think he likes the authorities much," said Jane.

"Like many of Darren's buddies, Hal probably has a record. Makes him twitchy when he gets around uniforms," said Zack.

"I didn't know Darren had a cellphone," I said.

"He doesn't," said Jane.

"Then how did he get that call? On Hal's cell? I doubt it. If we can find the cell he received it on, we could trace the call back to the person who made it."

"Trace what call?" asked Anita as she walked back through the door.

We explained what Hal had told Jane.

"I'd like to talk to Hal. Where did he go?" she asked.

"He's in the wind." Jane pounded her cane on the floor. "Some pal he is."

CHAPTER 20

Sheriff Burroughs finally convinced Jane she couldn't visit Darren, and Jane reluctantly agreed to leave and return tomorrow. We walked her out to my car.

"Do you want to go home or come back to my place? I don't think you should be alone. I've got a chicken casserole I can defrost for dinner."

"Your place. I think there's at least two more bottles of champagne left."

"Let's take it slow on the liquor. I'll make us a nice cup of tea."

"I'm tired of tea, unless you put a shot of something in it." Jane yawned.

"I think the adrenalin rush and the champagne are taking their toll. Maybe you should have a lie down before dinner," I suggested as we pulled up to my house.

Jane stumbled a bit as she stepped onto my front porch. "You're right, but how can I get up your stairs? The three steps here are effort enough."

"I'll settle you on the couch. Zack and I will be real quiet in the kitchen."

Five minutes later, Jane was curled on my sofa, emitting soft puffing snores.

Zack and I quietly pulled out chairs at the kitchen table.

"What do you make of all that happened today?" asked Zack.

"I wish I knew."

We both sat, elbows on the table staring into space.

"We're forgetting something." I said.

"What?"

"Ellen. Where is she? And who is she with if anyone?"

I grabbed my phone and punched in a connection. "No answer at the landline at her house." I disconnected and tried another contact. "Sandy? Sorry to bother you. I know this must have been quite a day for you, but have you heard from Ellen, or do you have any idea where she might be?

"We don't much stay in touch anymore."

"And why is that? I thought the two of you were good friends. You came to visit her when she was in the hospital, didn't you? Did she say anything about who she thought might have run her off the road?"

"No. I don't think she remembers much about the accident. Short-term memory loss, I guess. Have you tried her house?"

"No answer. Do you have her cell number?"

"Yes. Just a minute while I check my list of contacts. Ah, here it is." She read me the number.

"Thanks, and could you give me the names of any of her friends?"

"I really don't know who she's hanging out with now." She didn't sound as if she cared much either. "I'm making dinner. I've got to run." She disconnected.

"Sandy wasn't eager to talk. I'm going to call Richard. He might know who Ellen's friends are."

"Then can we eat?" said Zack. "I'm starved."

"Pop the casserole in the microwave while I call Richard."

I looked over to determine if Jane was still sleeping. She was in the same position as before although her snores had quieted.

Zack put the casserole into the microwave, hit the timer and then opened the refrigerator. "I'll also throw together a salad."

Richard answered immediately. "I was wondering when you would call."

"You could always call me, you know."

"I suppose you'd like a recommendation from me on a good defense lawyer."

"What? Oh, sure. A lawyer for Darren, but I'm not certain what he can afford."

Jane had awakened and heard what I said. "I'll pay for the lawyer. Get the best."

I turned to her. "The best defense lawyer was the one whose house Darren burned to the ground."

She shot me an angry look, got up from the couch and hobbled over, then grabbed the phone from my hand. "Okay, Richard. We know you're the best. Who's second best in this county then?" Jane listened for a few minutes, then asked for a pen and paper to take down the names Richard suggested. "Thanks, Richard. I'll turn you over to your mother. She has something else to ask you."

"Ellen is still missing, and we think it's important that we track her down. I know she's keeping something about her accident to herself, but what? Can you give me the names of her friends?"

"I think Sandy would be the best source for that information."

"She told me she and Ellen were no longer close, not that I believed her, but for some reason she seems to want to distant herself from Ellen."

"Well, Ellen was seeing Matt Evans. But that ended. Of course, she was still friends with Denise, but that's no help." Richard was silent for several minutes, the said, "You might try Denise's brother, Manny Costa. It's a long shot, but they were close in high school. Maybe they are still in touch."

"Are you convinced that Darren was the person who set fire to your house?"

Richard hesitated. "Fingerprints on the snowmobile say yes."

"Hal told Jane that Darren got a call from someone that night asking him to repair a snowmobile that wouldn't start. If that's true, maybe that person is involved."

"That could be. Did Hal talk to the sheriff?"

"Nope. Hal split and, like Ellen, his whereabouts are unknown."

"I'm sure Anita will follow up on Hal."

"So will Zack and I. Tomorrow. Talk to you soon."

"Do you want to contact any of the lawyers Richard recommended before we eat or leave it until tomorrow?" I asked Jane.

"Tomorrow I'll see Darren and run the names by him, I don't recognize any of them, but he might. It has to be his choice," Jane said.

And your money, I thought.

Zack helped Jane to the table.

"What possible motive would Darren have for burning down Richard's house?" asked Jane, her tone accusatory.

"I don't know, but perhaps the sheriff has gotten some information out of him." I passed Jane the rolls.

"The two of you are acting as if he's guilty."

I gave Zack an uncomfortable look.

"I can't eat." Jane tossed her fork down. "I need to go home. Can you call me a taxi?"

"Don't be silly. Zack will drive you and see that you're all settled comfortably. Where are you going to sleep at home? You can't manage your stairs."

"I've got a recliner that I slept in last night. It's wonderfully comfortable."

I didn't argue with her. When Jane set her mind to do something, there was no way to convince her otherwise. I packed up some rolls and a serving of the casserole to send home with her.

THE NEXT MORNING AFTER BREAKFAST, I drove Zack to the automobile garage where his truck had been towed for repair. The owner had called last night to tell Zack it was ready for pickup. We had agreed that Zack would take the truck to Manny Costa's to find out if he knew where Ellen might be. If anyone could get information out of Costa, it was Zack. I drove my car to Jane's to give her a ride to the county jail to see Darren.

Anita greeted us before we went in to talk with Darren.

"I think he's keeping something from us. I'm sure there's someone else involved in this snowmobile theft and its use as transportation to Richard's house. Maybe you can convince him that telling us everything will help his case."

"Did you find Hal?" I asked.

"We checked his place but there was no one there. He's hiding out somewhere."

"More likely he's drinking somewhere. Try the Drop In," I suggested.

Anita showed us into the visitors' area where Darren awaited us. He and Jane fell into each other's arms, Jane showering him with kisses.

"The sheriff says you're holding back something. You didn't just go out and steal that snowmobile, ride to Richard's house and burn it down. I talked to Hal yesterday and he said you got a phone call from someone who you said wanted you to repair a snowmobile that night. Tell them who that was."

Darren shook his head. "I never got a call. You met Hal. You know how much he drinks. He's mistaken. How would I get a call anyway? I've got no cellphone. You know that, Jane."

"I wondered about Hal's story when he told me about the call."

"Listen, Babe. I'm gonna confess. I did it. I set the fire."

Jane stepped away from Darren and peered into his eyes. "I don't believe you. I know you've done some terrible things in your life, but you're being charged with attempted murder. And you had no reason to burn down Richard's house. Why would you do that?'

"I had my reasons."

"I'm not going to let you plead guilty. I don't want to be a bride who can only see her husband in a jail cell. Richard was nice enough to give me a list of great defense attorneys." Jane reached in her purse and pulled out the list. "Here. Take a look, choose one and make the call."

"No." Darren reached out his hand and gently touched Jane's face. "I'm no good for you. Don't visit me again." He got up and signaled to the guard that he was ready to leave.

"Darren." Jane tried to go after him, but the door closed, and Darren was gone.

"C'mon, Jane. There's nothing more we can do here. Let him think on this for a while and maybe he'll change his mind."

Jane raised her tear-filled eyes to mine. "He sounded certain, more certain than I've heard him sound. What is he hiding?"

Anita stood just outside the visitors' room. "Any luck?"

"Can I hire a lawyer for him?" Jane asked.

"Not if he doesn't want one," replied Anita. "Did he talk about the phone call he supposedly got that night?"

"No. He said Hal was drunk and made up the story, probably to try to help Darren."

"I don't know, Jane. If Hal wanted to help Darren, why didn't he give him an alibi for that night? Why make up a story about a phone call?"

"When I locate Hal, I'll find out the truth," said Anita. "After he sobers up."

"Where were Darren's fingerprints located on the snowmobile?" I asked.

"Nowhere but on the engine and the ignition switch."

"Meaning he did do repair work on it and started it, gloves off, but with gloves on when he drove it, if he drove it."

"Maddie, you're reaching. You think Darren repaired the machine, started it and someone else drove it to Richard's?"

"It's possible, especially since Darren has no known motive for trying to kill Richard."

"We'll find the motive," said Anita.

"Find a motive or find the person who did it."

Anita gave me a hard look. "I'll find Happy Hal and see what he says. Even if there was a phone call doesn't mean Darren isn't responsible for the fire."

Jane limped her way to the exit and pushed through the door without another word to Anita. I knew she was mad and distraught, but there was little I could do to help her except be supportive of her feelings. Besides, I, too, was having my doubts about Darren's guilt. I was certain he repaired the machine, but I couldn't believe he was capable of trying to kill Richard. Who would he want to protect? Jane, yes, but she clearly wasn't guilty. Who else? One of the guys he worked with? A member of his biker group? Lily? His daughter, Sandy? When I reviewed those names, I came up with the same issues. None of them had reason to want Richard dead. Only Manny Costa had believed Richard killed his sister, Denise. I'd have to wait to see what Zack discovered when he questioned Manny. He was my primary suspect, but was he? Manny had his own snow machine. Why would he call Darren to repair one he had stolen? My thoughts circled back to Ellen. Missing now, perhaps hiding out. She dropped her boyfriend to take up with her friend's husband, Werner. She seemed to believe he decided not to divorce Denise. Aha! Now I got it. Ellen killed Werner—a case of, if I can't have you, no one will—made it look as if Denise did it, then followed Denise to Richard's house where she killed her making it look as if Richard was responsible. Ellen would have been afraid Denise told Richard she suspected Ellen killed Werner. It all fit so well. There was one problem, however—the snowmobile. Why would Darren cover for Ellen? My head hurt thinking of all these possibilities, all of which were flawed. I rushed out the door to follow Jane to the car.

"Come in for a cup of tea." At her house, Jane maneuvered herself out of the car without my help.

"You're moving much better," I said.

"For all the good it does me or Darren." She tossed her coat on a chair and went to the kitchen to put on the kettle. I took a seat on her sofa. Something poked me in the back, and I worked to retrieve it from where it had lodged between the end of the couch and a cushion.

"What's this?" I held up the object. "I didn't know you bought a cellphone."

Jane stuck her head out of the kitchen. "What? That's not mine. You know I have no use for those things, just bother you with unwanted calls. Other than you, who do I know to call?"

I tapped the screen. It wasn't locked, so I scrolled through the list of calls received.

"Help me with the tea, would you?" Jane called from the kitchen.

I carried the tea tray into the living room and poured us each a cup. I settled back into the couch and continued to examine the calls received.

"A lot of calls here, but the numbers are all blocked. Whose phone is this?" I asked.

"I have no idea." Jane fussed with her cane.

"Yes, you do. It's Darren's, isn't it?"

"Oh, I don't know, Maddie. Maybe."

"He probably wasn't lying when he said he got a call the night of the fire. Anita needs to see this."

"No!" Jane lunged forward and grabbed the phone from my hand. "If it belongs to Darren, then we have no right to give it to Anita."

"But she might be able to determine the identity of those blocked numbers. It could help Darren's case."

"Are you sure?"

"Well, it proves Hal wasn't lying about the phone call. Darren is protecting someone, and Anita might be able to find out who it is."

For the first time in two days Jane looked hopeful. "Call Anita then."

I connected to Anita's cell. I told her what we'd found.

"I'm going to tell Darren about the phone and hope he will allow us to search through the calls. Better yet, maybe he'll tell us who the call was from. I'll call you back after I've talked with him."

Jane and I sipped our tea in silence, both of us anxious to hear back from Anita.

After half an hour, my cell chirped with the return call from Anita.

"Darren says he knows nothing about a phone. He said it's not his. He did say he found a cell phone at Jane's, but thought it was hers or that someone left it there. I need to stop by and pick up that phone. You're at Jane's? I'll be there in fifteen minutes. I know you've both handled the phone, but could you leave it be for now? I'd like to get any prints I can from it and find out from the provider to whom its belongs."

I told Jane what Anita said.

"How silly of me to believe it belongs to Darren. He doesn't have the money for cell phone service."

"It could be a onetime use phone, the kind you can buy in a drugstore or a convenience store like the one here in town."

"We'll see." Jane sat back in her chair with a stubborn look on her face.

Anita arrived minutes later, put on gloves and carefully dropped the phone in an evidence bag.

"I'll need both of your fingerprints, so can you drop by the office later?"

"I'll drive Jane. We'll follow you back there."

"Good. I know this is difficult for you, Jane, but this could mean a break in the arson case and maybe in the murders."

WE FOLLOWED THE SHERIFF INTO THE county department and the officer there fingerprinted us.

Sheriff Burroughs entered the fingerprinting area a few minutes after we finished.

"Darren told the officer in charge of the cells that he wanted to talk with me. I assume you'll want to see him while you're here, so come on back with me."

Darren sat in the same room we had used to meet with him earlier. This time the look on his face had changed. He appeared calmer and when he spoke, his tone was firm. "The sheriff told me you found my phone at the house and that she would get a search warrant to go through it. Eventually she'll find who called me. I want to come clean and tell you who it was because I don't want to spend my life in prison when I could be happily married to the gal I love."

"Oh, Darren, honey, I knew you couldn't be responsible for trying to kill Richard." Jane blew a kiss to him.

"So who called you?" Anita asked. "And no lying to get yourself off the hook."

"It was Manny Costa."

Ah, that made sense. Manny believed Richard killed his sister, but why would Darren try to cover for him?

"Let's have the whole story," said Anita.

"When I did time, Manny was in also. Because we were from the same town, we got to talking and struck up a friendship of sorts. One day another inmate and I got into a fight. He started it. What I didn't realize is that he had fashioned a shank out of a spoon and pulled it out to use on me. Manny stepped in and took it away from him. He saved my life. I owed him. When he called me that night and told me he had a snowmobile that needed repair right then to take supplies to a friend who lived back in the woods, I never questioned his story. He picked me up and we went to his house. I repaired the machine, and he gave me a few bucks for my work, then dropped me back off at Hal's. When I discovered you had tied the snowmobile to the fire, I realized what Manny had done. I wanted to cover for him, but I wanted a life with Jane more."

"We'll go pick him up. His story and yours better jibe or you're both in trouble." Anita ushered us toward the door.

"But . . ." Jane began.

"You can talk with your boyfriend later, when we've sorted through all his lies." Anita sounded aggravated. I didn't blame her.

CHAPTER 21

"WELL, THAT'S THAT." JANE WALKED OUT of the county jail with a bounce in her hobble.

"You're forgetting one thing." I said, opening the passenger's door for her.

"What?"

"Actually two things. Werner's murder and Denise's. I doubt Manny killed his own sister or her husband."

"You think the sheriff might accuse him of murder?"

"I wouldn't think so. I'm sure she'll check his alibi, but what motive could he have?"

Jane gave a sigh of relief as she settled into her seat, and I drove out of the parking lot and headed toward our village.

"My house or yours?" I asked.

"Mine. I'm exhausted. I need a long nap in my lounger."

"With the way you're progressing on that ankle, you'll soon be able to get up your stairs to the bedroom."

Jane smiled. "Or perhaps some man will be there to help me. When do you think he'll be released?"

"In a few days, I'd guess."

"Days! What reason do they have for keeping him?"

"You forget he withheld evidence in an arson and attempted

murder case."

"Piff. He was only trying to protect himself and a friend."

When it came to Darren, I'd never be able to make Jane see his flaws. "Here we are. I'll help you into the house. Are you sure you want to be home by yourself?"

"Absolutely. Darren might call, you know."

I made Jane a pot of tea and a few sandwiches and told her I'd stop by later with dinner. I was eager to get home to see what Zack had learned from Manny. Maybe he'd pressured Manny into telling him his role in the fire at Richard's.

"No such luck," Zack told me when I got home. "Manny denied everything. Had I known about Darren's confession to getting that call from Manny, I might have had some leverage, but I guess it's now up to the sheriff. Knowing Darren gave him up, Manny may insist that Darren is solely responsible for the fire, saying that Darren repaired the snowmobile then rode off on it."

"The sheriff will pick up Manny and bring him in for questioning. We might learn more after her interrogation especially when Manny discovers Darren put him in the picture. Jane has her hopes pinned on Manny admitting he burned Richard's house."

"She's probably correct. That may solve the arson case, but it does nothing to shine light on who murdered the Werners." Zack plopped on the couch. "Let's go out for dinner and give these cases a rest."

"That sounds lovely, but I promised I'd bring Jane something for her dinner tonight."

"We'll pick up something from the restaurant for her. C'mon, Maddie. We deserve a breather." Zack put his arm around me and gave me a squeeze followed by a kiss on the lips.

"Hmm." I turned and melted against him.

"Or, we could stay in and eat peanut butter and jelly sandwiches upstairs in bed."

I gave him a playful shove. "Don't be silly. We can do both, eat out and come home to dessert in bed."

He gave me a wink. "I like your thinking."

WE CHOSE A RESTAURANT OUTSIDE THE village on the river our creek emptied into. The views were better than the food, but tonight we didn't care. Taking in the broad expanse of water with the sunset throwing shadows through the pine trees on the far bank compensated for the so-so offerings. We had finished a meal of steak and were examining the dessert menu when Matt Evans came into the restaurant alone. He stopped at the hostess station and talked with the woman there. She smiled and nodded, then headed to the kitchen. Matt looked around the restaurant and I caught his eye. He smiled, somewhat nervously I thought, and mouthed hello.

"I'll be back in a minute." I left Zack and walked over to Matt. "I haven't seen you in a while."

"I've been working a lot," he said.

"No time for cooking then?"

"Take out." He chuckled. "But the food here is a lot better than what I make for myself at home."

The hostess returned carrying two take out bags. "That comes to thirty-four seventeen. Cash or credit?"

Matt took out his wallet and extracted his credit card, glancing at me and clearing his throat.

"You must really be hungry," I said, nodding at the bags.

"Leftovers. For tomorrow. Well, nice to see you, Ms. Sparks." Matt glanced over at Zack and nodded a greeting.

I scampered back to the table. "Quick. Pay the bill."

"But what about dessert? And something for Jane?"

"Forget it. I want to follow Matt. That's a lot of food for one person even if he is an active guy. It's enough dinner for two people. I think the other one might be Ellen."

Zack rushed to the counter where he paid the bill, and we were out the door in time to see two taillights leaving the parking lot. We jumped into the truck and sped after the vehicle assuming it had to be Matt.

"Do you know where he lives?" asked Zack.

"I think he has an apartment in the village next to the old firehouse."

"Well, he's not heading back to the village. He turned north at the intersection ahead. He's heading toward the lake. Once he turns off on one of those roads leading up the hill, we'll lose him if we don't catch up." Zack punched the accelerator, and we caught up with the vehicle. "Unfortunately he's sure to see that we're following him."

"Keep after him. He has to stop somewhere. His food is getting cold."

We continued to follow the car and, instead of turning toward the lake, it took a left down a short road that ended at a county road familiar to us.

"I know where he's going. He's heading toward the neighborhood where Ellen's house is located. I was right. She must have returned home at some point and is holing up there, keeping out of sight."

Sure enough, Matt pulled into Ellen's drive, jumped out of the car and headed toward the front door. No lights were on in the house. "She's really lying low," I said.

Zack slowed the truck enough as we cruised by the house where we observed Matt using a key to enter the front door. Soon, lights came on and we could see Matt moving around in the living room.

"Stop the truck and wait here. I want to see what Matt's up to." I ran across the front lawn and rang the doorbell. After a minute. Matt opened the door.

"It's you. I thought someone was following me."

Zack appeared behind me. "We'd like to come in and talk with Ellen if we could."

Matt laughed. "She's not here. I'm looking after her house while she's away for a few days."

"I thought you were bringing her food while she kept out of sight."

"You might have noticed I didn't bring the food in, so, no, I'm not doing that. I have a key, so it's perfectly legal that I be here."

Matt held up a house key. "I check the house each evening after work."

"And do you and someone else take a soak in the hot tub?"

"What are you talking about?"

"When we were here the other day looking for Ellen, there were damp towels on the floor of the hot tub bathroom."

Matt turned and walked down the hall toward the back of the house. We followed him to the hot tub. He opened the door to the bathroom, and we all looked in. There were no towels there.

"Just as I found it last evening when I checked." At this point, Matt appeared unhappy with our presence and my questions. He scowled. "Why did you follow me here?"

"We were concerned when we didn't hear from Ellen after she left the hospital. She called Maddie to say she would drop by, but she never showed."

"I picked her up from the hospital and brought her home to pack some clothes and other items. She wants to be alone, and frankly, I think she's scared of something, but she wouldn't tell me what was going on. I haven't heard from her since she left."

Zack reached in his wallet and extracted his business card. "Call me if you hear from Ellen. Maybe I can help."

Zack took my hand and led me to the front door. We walked to where Zack had parked the truck on the road and got in but didn't drive off until we saw Matt exit from the house and back his car out of the drive.

"That's still a lot of food for one person." I buckled my seat belt. "Do you believe what he told us?"

"I think he's telling what he knows, but that may not be the entire story. We now know of two women who have acted frightened of something—Denise Werner who told Richard she thought someone was following her and Ellen, whose behavior after her accident was erratic and who Matt said was scared. Anyway, we're not going to get away with following him again. He's on to us, so if he intended to bring the food to someone, he'll never lead us to them. Besides, he's taking the road back to the village. I think he's headed home."

"Someone will go hungry tonight," I said. Oh, oh. That reminded me of my promise to Jane. "Let's get home. I've got to whip up something for Jane's dinner."

I pulled some spaghetti sauce out of the fridge to heat up and put on a pot of water to boil pasta, while Zack threw together a salad. When everything was ready, I put it into a plastic container along with a few cookies from the pantry.

"She can pop this into the microwave to heat it up. Here, you take this over to her. Apologize for being so late." I handed the food to Zack.

"Me? Why me? Why don't you come along?"

"Jane is likely to question me about what we were doing, and I don't feel like explaining to her about following Matt. With what happened at the wedding and Darren's arrest, she's looking for something to occupy her mind and you know what that means when Jane gets restless."

Zack nodded. Jane liked to be included in our sleuthing activities, but past adventures resulting in near arrest by authorities and damaged property, all part of Jane helping play detective, made me want to keep Jane in the dark about following Matt tonight. She'd delight at the event, but she'd insist on riding shotgun the next time and demand I promise she be part of the team. The image of Jane waving her crutch at a suspect and the ensuing chaos was more than I wanted to deal with.

Zack was of the same mind as me when it came to deputizing Jane. "I'll tell her the restaurant was crowded and slow service delayed us."

As soon as Zack left, I called Richard.

"Hi, honey. I have a question for you. I know Ellen, Denise and Sandy were popular girls in high school, but were they also tomboys?"

"Tomboys? What do you mean?"

"Did they like to do what the boys did, go hunting, skiing, snowmobiling, fishing, stuff like that?"

Richard laughed. "You should know how teens around here are, or should I say were when I was in school. Everyone raised in the country hunted, fished, camped, snowmobiled, skied. It was part of growing up in a small, rural community. Those gals were into everything the boys did, even drag racing. What's up with the questions?"

"Nothing. Just thinking. Talk to you soon." I disconnected and poured myself a shot of brandy which I took to the couch. If Denise knew how to handle a shotgun and owned her own, the weapon that killed her husband, then Ellen or Sandy could have done that also. Denise said someone was following her. Who was it? I was inclined to believe it was Manny, making certain she was safe. Maybe he had reason to believe whoever killed her husband also wanted to harm Denise. Ellen was rumored to have had a thing going with Denise's husband. Maybe he told her it was over, that he was going back to his wife, so she killed him and Denise. I thought back on our inspection of Ellen's house. Her kitchen had all the high-end equipment one would expect—chef grade stove, stainless steel appliances, marble countertops . . . And on the countertop sat a knife block with expensive knives similar to the ones Richard had in his kitchen. One of those knives killed Denise Werner, but, with the fire destroying everything in the house, there was no way to determine if that knife came from Richard's kitchen. I couldn't remember if there was a knife missing from the block in Ellen's kitchen. Our walk through had been too quick to notice details. I needed to get back into that house to take a closer look.

My phone rang and it was Zack calling. "I dropped off the food to Jane and I was fortunate enough to dodge any of her questions because I got a call from the sheriff's office. Anita picked up Manny and she asked if I was interested in observing her questioning him. I'm heading there now. I'll keep you posted."

As soon as he ended the call, the phone rang again. Unfortunately, we weren't off the hook. It was Jane. Before she could say anything, and even though I knew better—hadn't I just had a talk with myself about her earlier tonight—I said, "I could use your help, Jane."

"Help?"

"Yes, on a case. I'll pick you up in a few minutes." I knew I would regret asking Jane to accompany me, but this was the perfect time for me to take another look around Ellen's house without Zack knowing what I was up to. Although I knew where the key to her place was hidden, I didn't have permission to enter the premises. Being the stickler for compliance with the law that he was, Zack wouldn't have wanted me in the house. Perhaps more importantly, I told myself, taking Jane along on this ride would prevent her from cross-examining me about why her food arrived so late. I didn't want her to ask questions for which I hadn't yet answers. Including her in a little snooping seemed easier . . . or so I thought.

I pulled up in front of Jane's house ten minutes later. She was waiting on her doorstep and worked her way down the steps carefully using her cane for balance.

"Maybe this isn't such a good idea. Your walking is still dependent upon support." I opened the car door for her, and she slid in.

"Don't be silly. I'm fine. I could throw away this cane right now if I wanted to. I use it only for a sense of security." She tossed the cane in the back seat and buckled her seat belt. "Let's hit it."

She wiggled around in the seat to get comfortable, then turned to me. "So what's the plan? Where are we going?"

"I'll tell you but no more questions. Your role is to be lookout in case someone disturbs us."

"I can do that. I've done it before you know."

"Yes, I know, but this time you follow orders, no driving away and no property destruction." On an earlier occasion when I asked Jane to stay in the car as lookout, we almost landed in jail.

When we pulled up to Ellen's house, I parked on the street behind other cars and intended to leave Jane in the car as lookout, but I worried that she might not remain there. I decided to keep her close to me. "Both of us will go in, but you remain at the door and keep watch in case someone comes by. Grab your cane and let's make this quick."

"I told you I don't need it."

"Take it just in case."

"No."

"Yes."

Jane limped past me and waited at the front door. "See. I'm good."

I took the key from under the fake stone and let us in. "No lights. I'll use the flashlight on my phone. Follow me."

The open concept of the living and kitchen area made it easy to find my way to the counter where I shined my phone light onto the knife block there. Sure enough, one of the knives was missing and I was certain it matched the one used to stab Denise Werner. Oh my. I couldn't believe Ellen was the culprit, but here was the proof. I snapped several pictures, hoping photos of the missing knife would propel Anita to obtain a search warrant so the missing knife could be used as legal evidence.

"Okay. I've found what I was looking for." I turned around expecting to find Jane at the door, but she was gone. "Jane, where are you?"

"I'm in here. Did you know Ellen has a hot tub inside in a room by itself? Fancy."

"How did you find your way in here?" I asked.

Jane held up a miniature flashlight. "I take it with me when you and I do snooping so I'll have a light if I need it." Jane lifted the cover of the hot tub and steam billowed out. "Hey, my glasses are steaming over. I can't see a thing." She spun around and tried to retreat, but she miss-stepped and started to fall backwards. I rushed to catch her and the two of us went down together. As we fell her flashlight dropped out of her hand into the hot tub. "Aaargh. I lost my light."

At that moment, a car's lights shone out front and stopped in front of the house.

"Someone's coming. We need to get out of here." I grabbed at Jane, but she had bent over the hot tub trying to retrieve her flashlight. She reached her hand down into the steamy waters, but she was too short to grab the light and the steam too heavy for her to see where it was. She stood on tiptoe and leaned farther in.

"No, no, no. Don't . . .," but my warning was worthless. Jane fell headfirst into the water. I lunged for her, my hands grabbing at her coat, but the weight of her now-wet clothes pulled me in after her.

"Sheriff's office. Who's there? Come out with your hands raised."

Our wet clothes weighed us down and I knew we'd never get out without help. "Don't shoot. We're just taking a soak."

Sheriff Burroughs entered the room, gun drawn.

"Just a nice hot soak on a frosty night. See, I've got a key." I held up the key I'd extracted from under the stone out front.

"You. I should have known." She holstered her weapon and hands on her hips said, "Do you always hot tub fully clothed?"

"We were in a hurry to get in," I said.

CHAPTER 22

"I SHOULD ARREST YOU," SAID ANITA, HELPING to pull us out of the water.

I ignored her and shed my sopping wet coat. "I thought you were at the office interrogating Manny Costa and that Zack was observing."

"I sent Zack home. Manny's not talking and now Darren isn't either." Anita took out her phone and made a call. "I'm not going to explain over the phone, but you need to get to Ellen's house and bring a change of clothes and some blankets for two snoopy gals who should be in jail. Do it now."

I went into the adjoining bathroom and tossed my remaining clothes into the tub there, grabbed a bath towel and headed toward the kitchen.

"Whoa. Where are you going?" asked Anita.

"You're going to love this. I hit the light switch and pointed to the knife block on the counter. "What do you see?"

Anita followed me and leaned over the counter to take a closer look. "A missing knife."

"Uh, huh."

"Maddie, I could hug you."

"Did you have to call Zack?" I asked.

"How else did you think you were getting home, riding in the car in the cold with wet clothes?"

"Or naked," said Jane who stepped into the kitchen toweling herself dry with another of Ellen's towels.

"That's more than I need to see." Anita turned her back.

"Wrap it around you, for heaven's sake," I said.

"Won't fit. I'm too chubby."

I pushed Jane back into the bath off the hot tub room. "Stay in there until Zack comes."

"You two came here tonight because you thought Ellen stabbed Denise."

"Of course. I noticed the knife block when we were here the other day, but I didn't get a good look at it. I suspected there was a knife missing and now we have proof."

"But we don't have Ellen."

"No, but I have a hunch where she might be."

I told Anita about following Matt Evans here earlier tonight. "I'm sure he knew we were following him, so he came here with the excuse he was checking the house for Ellen who he said had gone away for a few days."

"So?"

"I'll bet Ellen is at Matt's place. We could go there now and find her."

"There will be no 'we' doing anything of the sort. I need to see if the knife that stabbed Denise matches this set."

"Don't you need a search warrant?"

"I entered the premises because a neighbor called reporting some lights in the house and when I arrived I found the door unlocked. I don't need a search warrant when I'm checking on a break and enter."

"This was more like a visit and snoop, and we had a key, remember?"

There was a knock at the door.

"Come in and get these wet ladies out of here." Anita opened the door to Zack who entered carrying a large shopping bag and a sour look on his face.

"You think you're unhappy, Zack. How do you think I feel? I told Maddie I should arrest the two of them."

"Go ahead," said Zack.

My mouth dropped open. "How can you say that? We're partners in this case."

"You explain it to her, Sheriff." He dropped the bag on the floor. "I'll see you at home, Maddie, whenever you get there. Please drop off Jane before you come home. I don't want a witness to the scolding I'm going to give you." Zack spun on his heel and left.

"Oh, good. He'll be there waiting for me." I pawed through the bag to find sweatpants and shirt, socks, a pair of my old snow boots and my barn coat. There were several blankets for Jane since my clothes wouldn't fit her. I looked around as I hopped on one foot to put on my sock. Where was Jane?

"Jane?" I called.

"Here," was her reply. Anita and I headed back to the hot tub where Jane had completely removed the cover and had found the controls. She sat in the bubbling water, steam circling her head and dampening her curls. "I should get one of these. This is making my ankle feel much better."

"Out." I gestured with my hand and held out a beach towel and two blankets brought by Zack. "We're going home."

"Five minutes more."

I tossed the towel and blankets on the floor. "I'll take our wet clothes and meet you in the car. There's a pair of old garden boots here, too."

"She's no fun," I heard Jane say to Anita. "Help me out, would you?"

I grabbed our wet clothes and put them in a large plastic trash bag Zack had also provided. The man thought of everything. Wrapped in the beach towel and blankets and wearing the boots, Jane, guided by Anita, shuffled her way to the car.

"I can't get the seat belt around me."

"Oh, let me." I grabbed the buckle and pulled it across her, tugging it tight to buckle it.

"Now I can't breathe."

"Take shallow breaths." I punched the accelerator. "I want to get out of here before Anita changes her mind and off we go to jail."

"You're mad at me," said Jane.

"It was my fault."

"I know."

"Don't push it."

We drove in silence until I pulled up in front of Jane's house.

"I mean it," she said as I grabbed her cane from the back seat and helped her up the walk and into the house.

"What are you talking about?'

"I'm going to have one of those hot tubs installed on my back porch. Then Darren and I can have a soak every night before bed. And of course, you can come over to use it sometimes, too. You and Zack, I mean."

I ignored her comments. "I'll go upstairs and get your nightgown and robe and get you settled in."

"And make me some tea, too, would you" Jane called as I went upstairs to grab her clothing.

By the time I came back downstairs, Jane had opened her laptop and was scrolling through the internet.

"Here." I handed the clothes to her. "What are you doing?"

"I'm sure they sell hot tubs on the internet." She looked up at me, her blue eyes twinkling. "Or do you think I should buy one in a store around here?"

I bit my tongue to prevent saying anything I would regret later. "I'll make your tea."

"Make a cup for yourself, too."

I heated the water, plopped a teabag into the pot and took the pot and a cup into her.

"I can't stay. I've got a mad man at home. I need to explain things to him." I would explain, but I doubted he would be interested. It would take a lot of saying I'm sorry and I won't do it again, which we both knew was a lie, before he would forgive me.

"Uh, huh." Jane waved as I left. "I'll let you know what I find," she called after me.

"I'll take your wet clothes home and put them in my dryer."

"Uh, huh."

When I pulled up in front of my house, I let the car idle for a few minutes while I decided what story I wanted to tell Zack about why Jane and I were found in Ellen's house, but no matter how hard I tried to make my usually creative brain work—I mean, I authored novels, didn't I? I should be able to produce some kind of story—but only the truth about what I was doing at Ellen's came to mind. The truth, it was. It would have to do. I squared my shoulders and took a deep breath then jumped when a rap on the driver's side window startled me.

"Coming in or are you thinking of running away?" Zack wasn't smiling, but the grim face he had left Ellen's place with had softened just a little.

"Here." I handed him the garbage bag with our wet clothes in it.

"I made hot chocolate," he said when we got inside.

"I think I could use something stronger."

Zack added a shot of brandy to each cup of hot chocolate, then lit a fire in the fireplace. We sat together on the couch and gazed into the flames.

"I guess I should explain," I began.

"I think I can figure out everything except why you were there. You took Jane with you to snoop into Ellen's house. Did you find what you were looking for?"

"I found what wasn't there, a knife missing from the knife block. Anita thinks it might be the knife used to stab Denise Werner."

"That seems pretty straight forward although you know what you did is not exactly legal."

"I don't think it's as straight forward as you might think." I hesitated. "I like Matt, and I like Ellen."

"Yes, but . . ."

"Do you really think Ellen had a thing with Denise's husband and loved him so much that when she found he and Denise weren't getting divorced that she killed both of them. I mean, stabbing Denise. That's so up close and hateful. Ellen doesn't seem like the type."

"I can tell you from years' experience that there is no 'type' when it comes to murder."

"Maybe not, but love is another thing all together."

"Denise Werner's husband could have been Ellen's 'bad boy.' From what you've said, it appears that even the most intelligent women have one in their lives. You did."

"No, no. Ellen had already done that with her husband. She was over that phase."

"But she did have an affair with William Werner."

"We only have Sandy's word for that."

"And there are rumors around town." said Zack.

"Rumors aren't always true. I need to think on this for a while." I smiled. "Now about tonight. "Don't you want to know how we got so wet?"

"No. I do not. I want to go to bed. I'm exhausted just imagining what you and Jane have been up to."

"I should put our clothes in the dryer. My wool coat is at the cleaners and my parka is soaking wet. I have nothing to wear outside."

"Leave it until tomorrow. You can dry the clothes then. It might be a good idea if you stayed put for a while anyway."

"You don't trust me, "I said with a pout.

"No. I do not."

"Where's Spike?" I looked around the room realizing that he hadn't greeted me at the door.

"I think he's hiding in the spare room under the bed. I yelled at him for scratching the arms of the couch and he ran up the stairs. We've got to get around to clipping his claws. See what he's done." Zack pointed to the loose threads at the end of the couch.

"I'll do it tomorrow while I'm stuck here. What will you be doing while I'm housebound?"

"I'll be meeting with the sheriff to see if the murder weapon matches the knife you found and learn if there's any progress with Darren and Manny Costa. I should be back by noon especially if that snowstorm comes in as predicted."

I could hear Spike hollering as we mounted the stairs. "Get him out of the spare bedroom. There's no way we can sleep with that racket."

Zack returned with Spike at his heels. "He hates me now."

"Only until you feed him." I patted the bed and Spike jumped up, circled several times, then curled up at my hip and began purring.

"Tomorrow it's pedicure time," I warned. Spike's ears pricked up and he let out a growl as if he could understand what was ahead for him.

ZACK LEFT THE NEXT MORNING TO talk with Anita. The weather forecast on our local television station indicated snow arriving around noon with over two feet predicted.

Jane called midmorning.

"I miss Darren. I called the sheriff, and she wouldn't tell me when he would be released." Jane sounded sad and tired.

"How's the ankle?" I asked.

"It still hurts especially when I try to get up the stairs or stand too long in the kitchen preparing my meals. I guess I could just eat sandwiches for the next few days, assuming I have enough bread in the house to get me through this storm coming in. I hope the power doesn't go off. I'd be alone in the dark." She sighed. If Jane was trying to make me feel sorry for her, she had succeeded.

"Look. There's no need for you to be there on your own. Pack a few clothes, grab another winter coat and I'll be over to pick you up. You can stay with us until the storm is over. Zack's at the sheriff's office right now and should be back before noon with news about Darren."

"Thanks, Maddie."

When I started to grab my coat I realized I had forgotten to put our wet clothes in the dryer, so I called the cleaners to check on the wool coat I'd dropped off several days ago. It wasn't ready yet for pickup. I'd have to make do with wearing a couple of heavy sweaters, but I wasn't worried because it was only a short ride to Jane's, and I could turn up the heat in the car. When I opened the front door, I was hit with blowing snow. The forecasters were off. It was only nine in the morning and the storm was in full fury. I could barely see my car parked in the drive. I wrapped my wool scarf around my face and made a run for the car, got in and started it, then turned the heat on full blast. My tires spun as I backed out of the drive. Why hadn't I bought new ones? I drove slowly through the streets which were now snow covered. The plows wouldn't be out for a few hours, and I slipped and slid on the icy pavement.

I left the car running when I pulled up to Jane's house and rushed in.

"What are you wearing?" I asked. She looked like a bear with mange.

"It's all I have. This was my father's muskrat coat. He trapped them himself and had a tailor make the coat. It was in the back closet. I think it's somewhat moth-eaten, but it will be fine for the short ride to your place." Jane handed me her overnight bag.

"Grab your cane," I said.

"It won't be of any use in the snow."

"You'll be in the house. I'm not parking you outside, you know."

Jane pulled her coat tight around her and we held onto each other as we trudged through the gathering snow and wind blasts to the car. The trip back was slower than the one to Jane's because of the deeper snow. I pulled into my drive, grabbed Jane's bag and cane from the back seat and helped her to my door. Huddled on my front porch was a shivering figure.

"Ellen! What are you doing here?"

CHAPTER 23

I WAS SOMEWHAT NERVOUS INVITING ELLEN INTO my house. Despite the possibility she might be a killer, I could hardly let her freeze on my doorstep.

"I'll make tea," I said.

"Maddie," Jane said to me in a low voice, "aren't we convinced Ellen killed two people and burned your son's house down? Why are you playing hostess?"

"I'm calling Zack right now," I whispered back. "Hang up your coat and sit down. You too, Ellen."

"Don't call Zack." Ellen took off her coat and hat and followed me to the stove.

"Is that a threat?"

Elie looked surprised. "No, of course not. I just want to talk to you first before Zack or the authorities are called in. Matt told me last night about you and Zack following him from the restaurant. I've been staying with him, hiding out, but I can't have him involved any longer."

I turned to stare her in the eyes. Ellen still looked like a sweet young woman, her face unblemished and innocent. Did that artless façade hide a killer? I had carefully followed the trail of breadcrumbs leading to Ellen as the murderer, but I still held doubt she was responsible for two deaths and a fire. The tracks were too strategically laid as if someone was leading us to a reasonable conclusion, but perhaps not the right one.

"Did you have a relationship with Willliam Werner?"

"No, never. Who said that?"

"Matt believed you did. In fact, he thinks you broke it off with him because of your feelings for Denises' husband. Didn't you tell him that?"

She shook her head.

"No. I just wasn't ready for a serious relationship and Matt was."

"Did the two of you talk about your relationship?"

"I wanted to explain to him, but he said he didn't want to hear it, so we never talked, but when I needed a friend, I knew Matt would come through for me."

"Not Sandy?"

"No." When Ellen said this her eyes filled with fear. "I don't trust Sandy. Not anymore. We were once best friends, but now . . . I think she was the one who ran me off the road."

Was Ellen lying to me?

"That's why I decided I had to speak to you. I've always admired you, Ms. Sparks. You're not only clever with your writing, but I know you've solved two murders. Will you help me?" She reached out and grabbed my hands, the look on her face earnest and true.

"I think you should be talking to the sheriff."

"Not yet."

"Why the delay?"

"Because of this. I found it under the door this morning after Matt left for work." She reached into her pocket and handed me a folded piece of paper. I opened it up and read the message on it:

If you want to see Matt alive, go to Ms. Sharps' house and wait. You will be contacted. Don't let anyone else know.

"Someone thinks you and I know too much." I handed the note back to her.

"What do we do?" she asked.

My phone rang. It was Zack.

"How are you doing, Maddie? Is everything okay?"

"Yes, fine. Jane is here with me." I glanced at Ellen.

"I thought you'd like to know the whole story with Darren and Manny and the snowmobile. Manny did call Darren to repair a snowmobile for a friend who lived off road. Manny picked him up from Hal's and drove him back to his house where Darren worked on the snowmobile. Darren figured it was stolen, but since the two were old prison buddies, he felt he owed Manny to keep his mouth shut. He fixed the machine, the two of them had a few beers and Manny drove him back to Hal's. Sometime later that night someone stole the snowmobile Manny had stolen. Ironic, huh?"

"Does Manny have any idea who took it?"

"He says no, and I believe him."

"So do I."

"It was the Werners' murderer and the arsonist. Everything points to Ellen." Zack spoke with certainty.

I glanced at Ellen. "Uh, can I call you back?"

"Sure. But there's something else. The roads are terrible. If you don't mind, I'll wait until the plows come through."

"Be safe, "I said.

"Of course. I love you, Maddie."

"And I love you."

Before I could disconnect, the front door swung open and someone in a snowmobile suit and helmet stood in the doorway.

"Hey, you're letting in all the snow," Jane said. "Quick, get in here before we all turn to icicles."

I laid my phone on the kitchen counter, wondering who would be out in this weather. What worried me more was what the person was carrying—a shotgun, a weapon that at this range no one argued with.

The individual strode into my living room, slammed the door and stamped their boots on the rug.

"Who's that?" said Zack through the phone. I hoped the snowmobiler didn't hear Zack, but the individual did and gestured toward the phone and then made a cutting motion across the throat. I disconnected. Spike, in his usual nosey manner, had been sitting near his food bowl in the kitchen. When Jane had hung her ratty coat on the hook by the door, Spike's ears pricked up. He began a slink across the living room floor, but when the snowmobiler barged in through the door, the noise and the angry words upset him, and he bolted under the couch and peered out at us.

"You really didn't think you could outwit me, did you, Ms. Sparks? I've been one step ahead of you since I shot William Werner, that worthless, spineless bum." The snowmobile figure removed the snowmobile helmet so we could all see her face.

"Sandy," I said.

She smiled, not a friendly smile, but one that invited fear.

"Clever Maddie Sparks and her brilliant son, Richard." Sarcasm seemed to drip from her voice.

"You killed Willliam Werner because he rejected you and decided to go back to his wife, Denise."

"I almost ended my marriage because of him. I was angry and hurt."

"It seems to me that the same thing happened years ago with Richard after you turned him down for a prom date, then later you made a play for him, but he wasn't interested. Richard saw something in you that he didn't like. I guess you still can't handle rejection, can you?"

Sandy gave a snort of derision. "Richard's lucky he's still alive when he should have burned to death in the fire."

I was beginning to put the pieces together. "You've been a busy girl, haven't you? You followed Denise to Richard's house, ran Ellen off the road, even used Ellen's hot tub when she was gone. Someone was with you. Another man in your life? You stole that snowmobile from Manny's house. How did you know about it?"

"I overheard Manny tell one of his buddies about it at the coffeehouse. The guy needed a cheap snowmobile and Manny said he knew just the one, that it needed some work, but he also knew someone who could repair it."

"Was Darren in on any of this?" I asked.

"Not unless I can find some way to weave him into my plan."

"But he's your father."

"So what? He didn't want me either, did he? Not until recently anyway." Sandy continued to stand with the shotgun pointed at us. "It's more crowded in here than I thought it would be. I figured on Ellen and you, Ms. Sparks, but not your friend here." She swiveled the weapon in Jane's direction. "Dad seems to like you, but that can't be helped. You know too much."

Ellen stepped toward Sandy. "That's my shotgun."

"Yes, it is, and it will be responsible for killing Ms. Sparks and her friend, fired by you, my dear friend. I mean, you were my dear friend until I also figured you killed the Werners and set Richard's house on fire. I followed you here, knowing that you intended to kill Ms. Sparks, but got here too late. You had killed both of them and tried to turn the gun on me, but you failed, you poor dear."

All the pieces finally fell into place. "You tried to set up Denise as her husband's killer, but she saw you."

"Well, she saw someone. I couldn't take the chance that she recognized me, so she had to go also. I was forced to adjust my plan somewhat. I worried that Denise told Richard she saw me, so I asked myself, who can I put in the framework for her husband's murder? Richard would do, but if Denise blabbed to him about me, then he was a liability, but one I wasn't unhappy to take the blame for Denise's murder. See how quickly I pivoted in my plans?"

"But you failed. You set fire to his house, but Richard wasn't home." I said.

"Luck was with me. If Denise had told Richard she could identify the person shooting her husband, he would have revealed that right off to the sheriff. That didn't happen, did it? He knows as little as anyone about the murders."

"If I were the killer, I wouldn't want to trust to luck," I observed.

Sandy looked somewhat flummoxed by my words. She ran her hand nervously through her hair and tossed her helmet onto the chair near the door. The helmet hit Jane's fur coat, knocking it to the floor in a plop. Startled by the coat falling onto the floor, Spike prepared to attack, eyes round with intent. He charged across the floor to bounce on the wet, mangy animal he saw there and jumped on it, then realizing it wasn't what he thought it to be, he tried to run off, but his long claws caught in the coat's fur, and he could not free himself. He tried to charge toward the stairs, but the coat, now firmly attached to him by his long claws, made him tumble and he and the coat flopped around in all directions sliding and jerking across the floor right onto Sandy's feet.

"Get that thing away from me!" she shouted.

Jane grabbed her cane, stood and tried to untangle the coat, cat and Sandy's feet, but instead the cane caught in the coat's lining. Jane went down onto the coat, cane swinging, and it caught Sandy's ankles, and brought her to the floor also. The shotgun fell from her hands as the mass of women, coat and cat continued to struggle to free themselves from one another. I lunged for the shotgun, grabbed it and pointed it at Sandy who was somewhere in the furry and feline people pile.

"Get up, Sandy, and put your hands in the air."

"Are you kidding? I don't even know where my hands are," came the muddled reply. "Ugh. I think I've got fur in my mouth."

I heard coughing and spitting as well as growling and hissing.

Jane managed to free her cane and used it to get to her feet, but cat and murderer were still inextricably tangled in the coat.

"Here, hold this." I handed the gun to Jane. "And don't fire unless you have a clear shot at her, not the cat."

I bent over and shoved the flailing Sandy to one side along with part of the coat while I grabbed Spike's paws and was able to extract his claws or most of them from the coat. He snatched the remaining one free. "So sorry, big guy. Are you hurt?"

"Is *he* hurt? What about me?" yelled Sandy.

"You're lucky you're wearing that snowmobile suit, or he would have scratched the heck out of you."

She raised her hand to her cheeks. It came back with blood. "My face, my face."

"He was only trying to protect his prey from your taking it for yourself." Spike rubbed against my ankles and meowed, then sunk his teeth into the coat and dragged it toward the stairs. "Don't lug that thing upstairs. I don't want to find it in my bed tonight."

Sandy continued to lie on the carpet, hands over her face sobbing, a woman utterly defeated.

Ellen took pity on her, and helped her to her feet, leading her to the couch.

"Where's Matt?" I asked Sandy. "Where did you take him?"

"Wouldn't you like to know?" She bit back, then once again dissolved into tears.

"I'm so sorry for everything," Sandy said through her tears, "but I had no choice, you know. William said he loved me, that he was going to leave Denise. He lied to me."

"I warned you he was a liar. I warned Denise, too. You weren't the first woman he led on and then dumped." Ellen held Sandy, rocking her as she continued sobbing.

I watched the two longtime friends and wondered how Ellen found it in her heart to forgive her friend for setting her up as a murderer.

Jane expressed my thoughts as she held the shotgun steady on Sandy. "Maybe you can excuse her, but she killed two people and came here to kill us."

Ellen nodded. "I know, I know, but look at her. She's clearly messed up by what she did and sorry for it."

"Sorry isn't enough. She'll have to pay for her crimes." I bent down and stared Sandy in the face. "Where is Matt? Tell us and we'll let the sheriff know you cooperated."

She shook her head and leaned into Ellen. "Help me."

I punched Zack's contact into my phone.

"Zack, are you still in Anita's office? Can I talk to her?" I told Anita what had happened with Sandy.

"I'll be there as soon as I can. I think the plows are coming through right now."

"She's no threat to us now. We can hold her here until you come." I disconnected.

Sandy stopped crying for a moment and looked up at me. "Am I going to be arrested?"

"Yes. The sheriff should be here shortly.."

"He was a bad man," she said.

"Yes, but his wife was your friend, your closest friend and you killed her." I said.

"He was a bad man," she repeated, then laughed. "I think that's why I loved him."

I rolled my eyes at her remark. Another woman taken in by a "bad boy," but this time it led to murder.

Without warning Sandy pushed Ellen away, and in one sudden move jumped up, toppled Jane to one side and ran to the door. "I won't go to prison." She opened the door and fled into the blizzard. Before we could follow her, I heard the snowmobile start and drive off. I ran to the open door, but when I tried to look out, the swirling snow swallowed the snowmobile's tail lights and they grew dim, then faded altogether in the blowing snow.

"Are you two hurt?" I asked, helping Jane up from the floor.

"I'm fine, just a little shook up." Ellen picked up Jane's cane from the floor and handed it to her. The fur coat remained where Spike had dragged it. I heard growling coming from under the couch where Spike had taken refuge.

"What do we do now?" asked Jane.

"I'm going to call Sheriff Burroughs and tell her Sandy's on the snowmobile. I think she headed north. If she stays on the road, the sheriff might encounter her on the way from the office."

"I'll keep an eye out, but I doubt she would stay on the main road. She probably took to the woods," Anita replied when I connected with her. "Stay put and lock your doors. She may circle back. The plows just came through on their first run. Zack is on his way to you."

"Okay." My gaze took in the frightened looks from Jane and Ellen. "Don't worry. Sandy won't return here."

"What about Matt? We need to find her, or we will never know what she did with Matt."

"All we can do for now is wait. Both the sheriff and Zack should be here soon. Until then, I'll make tea."

Jane settled herself once more on the couch. "Oh, don't be silly, Maddie. We need something stronger than tea. Brandy? Or bourbon. Brandy and bourbon?" She gestured with her cane at my carved liquor cabinet.

The wind continued to howl and a peek through the windows revealed curtains of snow falling and swirling. The storm appeared to be gathering in intensity, and I worried about Zack on the snowy roads. Over an hour later and on our second snifters of brandy, someone pounded on my front door. "Maddie, it's me."

"Zack's here." I ran to the door and threw it open.

Zack stomped in and slammed the door behind him.

"You're safe." He threw his arms around me and eyed the shotgun which I had placed on the floor near the door.

""You're safe, too. I was worried about you."

He laughed. "You were worried about *me*? I wasn't the one at the wrong end of a shot gun." He continued to hold my hands, and his look turned serious. "There's been an accident."

Ellen got up from her chair. "It's Sandy, isn't it?"

"Yes. I was following the sheriff here when a snowmobile shot out of the woods in front of her car. Anita slammed on her brakes, but she hit the snowmobile broadside. I stopped and ran to assist

Anita. The rider had no helmet on. I don't think the person could see much of anything in the whirling snow and had no idea that the road was in front of her or that there were cars on it. We called an ambulance. Anita insisted I come here to see how you were, but she stayed. Sandy was still breathing when I left, but her injuries are extensive."

"I want to go to the hospital to see her." Ellen said.

"We need her to tell us what she did with Matt. If she dies, we may never find him." I added.

"We'll all go," said Jane.

"No. You stay here and comfort Spike. He's been traumatized by what happened to him."

"But . . ." Jane got off the couch, but the combination of her injured ankle and two brandies made her unsteady, "Uh, maybe I should stay here. I mean, poor Spike. He needs some TLC."

"Food will help," I said. "And, Jane?"

"Yes?"

"No more brandy."

CHAPTER 24

THE HOSPITAL HAD RUSHED SANDY INTO surgery and told us it would be hours before there would be any word on her condition.

"I recommend you all go home and come back tomorrow. We'll call if there's any change." The nurse gave us a sympathetic smile.

"I'm leaving an officer outside the room," said Anita.

"I hardly think she's a flight risk," said the nurse.

"Protocol," said Anita.

"I'm staying." Ellen planted herself firmly on the waiting room couch, her intention not to move clear in the set of her chin..

"Has anyone called Sandy's husband?" I asked.

"I called but got no answer. He may be out of town on business," said Anita. "I left a message for him to call me. Let's go, folks. There's nothing you can do here." She made a shooing motion.

By the time we left the hospital, the snow had lessened, and the roads had been plowed several times. I filled Zack in on what had happened with Sandy at my house.

He looked over at me, his expression a mix of relief and worry.

"I'm fine. In retrospect, I'm glad I didn't clip Spike's claws. Getting entangled in that coat was part of why Sandy fell to the floor. Of course, Jane's cane was some help."

"I wish I had been there to see that." Zack chuckled.

"Tomorrow Spike is getting a pedicure. Don't tell him."

The worry lines deepened on Zack's face. "I suppose you'll want me to help."

"Thanks for offering." I knew Zack was wondering where his leather gloves were. "In the garage. I'll get them out for you tomorrow." I was almost as good at reading his mind as he was mine. We held hands all the way home.

When I opened my front door, we found Jane asleep on the couch with the old fur coat over her and Spike curled on top of it.

"I guess Spike has a new friend," I said.

"I thought Spike and Jane were well acquainted."

"No. I meant that ugly coat."

Spike looked up at us and blinked, then stood up, circled around and dropped back down on Jane.

"She looks comfortable enough there. I'm not going to wake her. Let's go to bed."

At six the next morning, the phone rang. It was Ellen calling from the hospital. "Sandy's awake."

"How is she doing?" I asked.

"Not well, but she's holding on. She wants to see her father. The hospital called Anita to let her know and told her it might help Sandy's recovery if she could see Darren. Her husband's here, but she said she didn't want to see him. Anita is bringing Darren to the hospital because she thinks Sandy might talk with him and tell him where Matt is. I think she's right. It's our only hope of finding Matt."

"Zack and I will be right there."

Jane was wide awake, though moving slowly. "I ache in every bone in my body."

"I'm going to make a pot of coffee and then Zack and I are off to the hospital." I told Jane about Sandy's request to see Darren.

"Then I'm coming, too. I need to see him."

Zack and I exchanged glances.

"Maddie, I have a right to see the man I love."

How could I argue with that?

Fueled by coffee and bagels I'd toasted, we left for the hospital. Other than the snow-covered fields and trees and the snowbanks alongside the road, there was no sign of the storm from yesterday. The world looked like a white fairy land, sun sparkling off the snow.

"You know what," said Zack. "Thanksgiving is soon."

"Is it? I'd completely forgotten, I'm not prepared for the holiday."

"I am," said Jane. "I bought a turkey several weeks ago when the market had a sale. I'll defrost it. There's enough to feed your family, Darren and me. A real old-fashioned holiday."

I wondered if it would be as happy an event as Jane believed it would be, but I appreciated her positive outlook.

We sat in the hospital's waiting area for the sheriff and Darren to arrive. When Darren walked through the door, Jane tossed her cane aside and almost sprinted across the room to throw herself in his arms. The two embraced for what seemed like several minutes. Jane was reluctant to let him go, but Anita untangled him from her.

"I need Darren to talk to his daughter, Jane. She has to tell us where Matt is."

Jane nodded and stepped away.

Anita took Darren off to see Sandy while Jane, Zack and I remained in the waiting room.

"You never fully believed Ellen was responsible for the Werners' murders and the arson, did you, Maddie? Why not?" Zack said.

"It felt to me as if all of us were being deliberately led to Ellen as the suspect, so contrived. Besides, I always liked Ellen."

"Likeability isn't necessarily a trait killers don't have, you know."

"Yes, but Richard liked her also and he spends his career defending both the guilty and the not guilty. I remembered how Sandy dumped Richard for the football player, then tried to get him back. When he wasn't interested, Sandy didn't take his dismissal well. She made quite a scene and spread lies about him."

"That's slim evidence." Zack replied.

"I know, but I considered the dynamics of the threesome from what Richard told me. Ellen was younger by several years than Denise and Sandy. According to Richard, she followed their lead. Of course I came to this understanding late, too late to help Matt. Where would Sandy stash him?"

"If she hasn't already killed him," said Jane.

I sank back into the uncomfortable waiting room chair and sighed. After a few more minutes, Anita came down the hall, looking very glum.

"She wouldn't talk about Matt. She acted as if she didn't understand what we were asking her. I let Darren remain in the room with her."

Darren followed Anita out of the room a few minutes later.

"What did she say?" asked Anita.

Darren shook his head. "She's tired. The doctor said she'll recover from her injuries, but it will take a while. She also knows she'll be facing prison time, but I promised I'd be with her every step of the way. Her whole life has been nothing but a series of rejections. I was the first. I didn't want a child, so, with her mother dead, I willingly signed adoption papers for her and sent her off to a home where she received little love. I have a lot to make up to her." He sat down beside Jane and continued talking.

"Jane, I love you madly, but I hope you'll understand that I need to devote my time to my daughter." Darren kissed Jane's cheek.

"I need some air." Jane got up from her chair and hobbled down the hallway toward the exit. I followed her.

"Bad boy turned good," said Jane, leaning on her cane and looking out into the night.

I hugged her and we stood there together watching the moon rise over the hilltops.

What a schemer Sandy was, a manipulator of people's insecurities, probably because she had so many of her own. She certainly must have had a plan for getting rid of Matt after she took care of Ellen. Not before? She didn't have time to do that, did she? She probably grabbed Matt on his way to work with some kind of story about Ellen. What would she tell him that might make him believe Ellen was in danger? Or perhaps that was all wrong.

I gave Jane another hug, then ran back inside.

"Ellen! Matt left before you did this morning. What did you talk about before he left?"

"Uhm. He told me to stay put until he got back which he assumed would be late because of snow emergencies. I told him I was worried about the house because I had turned down the heat and I was concerned the pipes to the hot tub might freeze. They sometimes did in the winter if a frigid wind was blowing strong enough out of the north. There's a heater in the hot tub room that should be turned on to prevent that, but I hadn't thought of it until this morning. He told me not to worry, that he would take care of it."

"Of course. Matt would have gone to your house before he checked in at work. Sandy followed him just as she had followed you to his place. And she confronted him there. Where better to stash Matt until she could return and make it look as if his murder was also your doing."

"I still don't understand why Sandy would want to hurt Matt," said Ellen.

"You suspected Sandy, didn't you? You thought she was the one who ran you off the road. Sandy was all about tying up loose ends. She had to get rid of Denise because she thought Denise saw her kill William. Then Sandy worried Denise talked to Richard about what she saw. So Richard had to die in a fire. That was unsuccessful and she couldn't get to him after he hired Lily as his bodyguard. She wanted to point suspicion away from her, so you were her fall guy."

"Running me off the road wouldn't make the authorities suspicious of me."

"No, but you might have been killed, then she would have found a way to set you up for the murders and the arson or, if you were only injured in the accident, then you would be vulnerable to any plans she might have to kill you. But you got scared so you went into hiding after the hospital released you."

"I'm sure you're right about all this, but that still doesn't tell us where Matt is," said Zack.

"At Ellen's house, of course. After she finished with Jane and me at my place, making it look as if Ellen killed us, she planned to take Ellen back to her own house, stage the murder of Matt with Ellen as the killer, and then make it look as if Ellen took her own life in a moment of despair and guilt."

"I don't understand why Sandy would kill Maddie," said Ellen.

Zack laughed. "From what I know, Sandy didn't like Maddie much, but she did respect her abilities. Afterall, Maddie had solved two murders in this village and Sandy knew Maddie would certainly solve this one. She couldn't just set up Ellen as the killer, Sandy had to get rid of snoopy and clever Maddie. What better way than to bring them together in Maddie's house? Two for one."

"Three," Jane added.

"But what about you, my dear?" I asked. "You were my partner in solving those murders."

"No," Zack said, "if you had a partner, it was Spike. I was incidental."

"You're never incidental where I'm concerned." I gave Zack a sideways hug.

Anita had stepped away to make a call. "I have an officer in the field only minutes away from Ellen's house. I just called him to check the place." Her cell rang. She smiled. "That was good news. He found Matt tied up in the hot tub room, but Matt is fine. Worried about Ellen."

"He's been a good friend to you." I smiled meaningfully at Ellen.

She returned my smile and blushed a little.

Jane put her arm around me. "Don't forget the role I played in chasing off Sandy."

"You, your ratty old coat and a cane you should use more often."

"Don't scold me," said Jane.

"I'm not. You and your accoutrements were important."

"What will happen to Darren?" asked Jane. "He wasn't involved in any of this."

"Darren says Manny didn't tell him the snowmobile was stolen, but then they're both ex-cons and they like to stick together especially since they knew each other in prison. I think Manny might stick to his story. He broke the terms of his parole of course, so he'll be back inside for a time. I can't see anything I can charge Darren with other than to caution him about doing favors for the wrong people. From what I heard him tell Sandy, I think he has the chance to become a better man. I also believe you had something to do with that, Jane."

"I do, too, Jane. I'm sorry you didn't have the wedding you wanted," I said.

"I've still got the dress. I'll wait."

We dropped Jane off at her house.

I helped her in and settled her on the couch. "Should I make you a pot of tea?"

She shook her head. She looked so sad that despite wanting some time with Zack alone, I said, "You could come home with us for a while."

"No. I think I want to be alone."

I patted her arm. "Are you sure? You've been through a lot these past few days."

"So have you. Go on with you. Zack needs you." She gave me a weak smile.

"I'll call you later."

"Worried about Jane?" said Zack as I buckled myself in.

"Yes."

"Me, too."

"Oh," I leaned over and kissed his cheek. That's so sweet of you. I thought Jane wasn't one of your favorite people."

"Well, she can be a pain sometimes, but you like her, and I admire her grit."

I leaned my head back onto the headrest and sighed,

Zack glanced at me. "That's a big sigh. Want to share your thoughts with me?"

"I was thinking over the last two weeks, about friendship. Sometimes it feels so fragile and it can be. There's no manual on how to friend, but I've learned that sometimes a friend has to hold back on being honest. Not that honesty isn't part of being friends. Take Jane and me, for example. I've practically bitten my tongue raw keeping my thoughts about Darren to myself, but there's the matter of respect and trust. If I truly love and respect Jane, then I have to trust her decisions, not that I shouldn't nudge her at times."

Zack nodded. "I've been so proud of you, Maddie. I know how you felt about Darren, but you let Jane have her way. Mostly, anyway."

"Jane knew I had misgivings, but she didn't try to change my mind about him. She accepted our differences." I hesitated. "Do you think he's changed?"

Zack shook his head. "We'll see."

I thought about Denise, Ellen and Sandy. "Some friends betray you. Especially when their needs for love and acceptance are overwhelming and unmet by family."

"I wonder if the damage can be healed," said Zack.

I knew he was thinking about Sandy. "I think that may depend upon Darren."

At home, I asked Zack if he thought Richard had been informed about Sandy.

"I'll call him." Zack connected with Richard and the two of them talked for several minutes.

"Let me talk to him." I took the phone. "I guess you can let Lily go now."

"I've gotten used to having her around. She's had an interesting life. I'm thinking of getting a motorcycle this spring and riding with her and her pals."

"You'll do no such thing."

"Mom, I'm a grown man. Hey, listen. I've got to go. I've got work to do." He disconnected. I considered calling him back, but because I knew he didn't want to discuss the motorcycle thing, he'd probably not answer the call.

"Guess what? Richard is going to join a motorcycle gang." I handed Zack's phone back to him.

"I can't believe that, Maddie."

"I don't want to." I sighed.

CHAPTER 25

THE NEXT MORNING I REALIZED I was itching to get back to editing my manuscript, but before I did that, I had to catch up with my other family members. I particularly wanted to find out how the wedding plans were advancing for Sara and Leon. I gave Sara a call.

"Mr. Powles was lukewarm at first, but he seems to have changed his mind. Do you know anything about that?" Sara sounded her usual cheery self.

"Me? I'm certainly not a person who interferes with others' lives. Besides why would he listen to me?" I crossed my fingers behind my back as I spoke. His wife, Kate, and I had discussed the wedding, and she had reassured me that her husband would come around . . . with a bit of prodding on her part.

"Someone must have had a word or two with him."

"Probably his wife."

"By the way, Dad says he hasn't heard from you in days. Is there anything we should know?'

"We wrapped up the Werner's murder case and the fire at Richard's. Sandy was responsible for both and for some other things, too. I'll fill you in later with the details."

There was a moment's hesitation from Sara. "I assume there's an exciting story behind all this."

"No. Just the usual boring work in any case."

"I can't believe that."

I chuckled. "I'll call your Mom and Dad. Talk to you later."

Instead of calling, I decided I needed a walk. The temperature outside was above freezing and the sidewalks had been cleared of all but a few patches of slush. I stopped by the diner in town, grabbed the last of their Danish and then walked up the street to Abigail and Geoffrey's office.

Abigail jumped up from her desk, ran over and hugged me. "We heard about your run in with Sandy from the mail carrier who was just in here. I was about to give you a call. Are you all right?"

"It's like the post office is FBI headquarters. The personnel there and the carriers know everything happening in town almost before it's over. I'm sure the story he told you is much exaggerated."

Geoffrey emerged from his office and eyed the Danish. "Is this by way of an apology for not keeping us in touch with what's going on in your life?"

"No, dear. It's a treat to have with your morning coffee break. I'll join you."

Geoffrey leaned over and gave me a kiss.

Abigail poured us coffee and we sat around their small conference table to enjoy the pastries.

"Here's something you may not know since the postal carrier hasn't been to your place yet this morning," said Abigail, wiping a few crumbs from her lips. "Sandy Longworth's husband has been let go from the bank."

"Well, we all know this branch of the bank is closing."

"It's not that. He won't be moving on with the bank to another branch because he has been discovered playing loose with banking funds. I don't know the full story, but the rumor is he's resigned and put their house up for sale."

"Without her husband, Sandy will need her father by her side more than ever," I said.

"So Jane isn't marrying Darren then" asked Geoffrey.

"No. Darren is determined to help his daughter through her recovery and then the legal proceedings that follow."

"I never thought the man had it in him to think of anyone else first," said Geoffrey.

"I guess Jane saw something in him that others didn't although the emergence of his better self meant Jane is heartbroken."

We sat in silence for a while. I knew people weren't always the way they portrayed themselves to others. Sometimes that meant they were not as good as we thought them to be, but it also could mean they only needed the opportunity to let out a better person.

"Got to run," I said.

I strolled back home thinking of all that had happened over the past few weeks. This investigation had been difficult and chaotic, twists and turns, murder, arson, and the splintering of old friendships. I hoped we were back to normal although I wasn't sure what that was.

I was surprised to see Lily's car out front when I arrived back home, but I was more surprised that Jane was with her. Zack had gone over his notes from the case while I was on my walk and was taking a coffee break.

"Look who's here," he said as he took my coat from me.

"I see. What's going on, ladies?"

"Lily stopped by my place to see how I was doing and we got talking. We decided to go out to lunch, but I asked her to drop by here first. I really need my winter coat. I can't wear this old fur coat."

"Oh, right. I almost forgot about your coat. I dried it and it looks like new. I'll get it from the laundry room."

Jane followed me. "You know I didn't think I'd like her, but Lily is quite nice. It's a great comfort to me to have someone who understands how I feel about Darren. She gets that I'm aware of his shortcomings but that I love him anyway."

"How nice the two of you are there for each other." I was happy for Jane although I didn't quite get the emerging friendship between them. They seemed so different from one another.

"You want to come to lunch with us?" asked Jane, removing the bedraggled fur coat and slipping into her winter coat.

"No, I think I'll stay here with Zack. Here, let me take that. It's in such bad shape we ought to toss it into the trash." I walked out of the laundry room with the fur coat over my arm. "Zack and I need to take on the onerous job of clipping Spike's claws. This coat is a testament to what those claws can do." I tossed the coat onto the couch. Spike jumped from the floor onto the couch and began making a nest for himself on the coat, purring in delight.

"I guess Spike has made friends with the fur, so I'll give it to him," said Jane, who sat on the couch and lifted the coat and cat into her lap. "Get the nail clippers. Maybe I can clip his claws."

"I wouldn't do that, Jane. He'll attack with a furry. It's the one thing he hates to have done."

"Let me try, anyway."

I got the clippers out of the kitchen drawer and held them up for Spike to see to prepare him for what Jane intended to do. He looked up at the clippers in my hand and growled. "See?"

Jane reached for them, gave Spike a smooch on his head and began clipping. Spike continued to purr and squirm happily in the fur.

"All done." Jane placed the fur and cat back on the sofa. "Well, I guess we should get going. You're sure you don't want to go to lunch with us, Maddie?'

I was so surprised by the claw clipping success it took me a few moments before I could answer Jane's question. "Uh, no. You two have fun."

Lily and Jane waved goodbye, chattering as they left.

"Wasn't that interesting," said Zack.

"Bonding over their affection for one man."

"You think Lily still likes Darren?"

"I do. She's an interesting woman, tough, realistic but with a generous heart. She understands Jane's attraction to Darren but isn't interested in revisiting their relationship. She seems happy Jane loves him and still wants to marry him."

"Speaking of marriage . . ."

"Were we?"

"Well, don't you think we should be?"

"Is that the best you can do, Zack Montgomery?"

"You want a proper proposal, do you?"

"Yes. I do."

"I think I'm too old and creaky to get down on one knee."

"Do it anyway. I'll help you up if you need me to."

Zack knelt with a small grunt and a bit of a grimace on his face. "Maddie Sparks, will you marry me?"

I took his hand and pulled him to his feet. "Yes."

He took me in his arms, and we kissed, then stood looking at each other.

"Now what?" he asked.

"I'll make tea."

Cows, Lesley learned growing up on a farm, have a twisted sense of humor. They chased her when she herded them in for milking, and one ate the lovely red mitten her grandmother knitted for her. Determining that agriculture wasn't a good career choice, instead she uses her country roots and her training as a psychologist to concoct stories designed to make people laugh in the face of murder. Unusual protagonists appear in many of Lesley's works including Desdemona the crime fighting potbellied pig, a hobo turned county sheriff and Lesley's zany back-home-on-the-farm relatives (*The Killer Wore Cranberry*, all six anthologies).She is the author of several cozy mystery series (*The Eve Appel Mysteries, Laura Murphy Mysteries, The Big Lake Murder Mysteries* and her newest from Camel Press, *Maddie Sparks Mysteries*, featuring a senior sleuth and her rescue cat). Her cozy mysteries have won several Readers' Favorite Awards and a short story Sleuthfest Award. Find out more at www.lesleyadiehl.com.

www.ingramcontent.com/pod-product-compliance
Lightning Source LLC
Chambersburg PA
CBHW011513100726
47899CB00010BD/3354